Miss Kopp Investigates

MISS KOPP INVESTIGATES

AMY STEWART

THORNDIKE PRESS
A part of Gale, a Cengage Company

Copyright © 2021 by the Stewart-Brown Trust.
A Kopp Sisters Novel.
Thorndike Press, a part of Gale, a Cengage Company.

ALL RIGHTS RESERVED
Thorndike Press® Large Print Mystery.
The text of this Large Print edition is unabridged.
Other aspects of the book may vary from the original edition.
Set in 16 pt. Plantin.

LIBRARY OF CONGRESS CIP DATA ON FILE.
CATALOGUING IN PUBLICATION FOR THIS BOOK
IS AVAILABLE FROM THE LIBRARY OF CONGRESS.

ISBN-13: 978-1-4328-9638-6 (hardcover alk. paper)

Published in 2022 by arrangement with HarperCollins Publishers LLC.

Printed in Mexico
Print Number: 01   Print Year: 2022

To Elizabeth Anderson

1

That Fleurette emerged from her first assignment unscathed, her dignity intact, her virtue unassailed, and her pride in place was, she felt, a triumph, and a sign of further good fortune to come. Having carried out the job in secrecy, with her sisters knowing nothing of her whereabouts, her success tasted all the sweeter.

She emerged from the blazing lights of the hotel lobby into the blue and frigid night, an absolute dream of a coat swishing luxuriously around her legs as she walked, a fur collar tucked under her chin. What a picture she must've made. She felt the eyes of strangers on her, but she didn't dare return the glance. Her instructions were to get out quickly, without attracting attention or raising suspicion. Still, she couldn't help but thrill over the notion that someone was watching her rapturously, wondering about this vision of a woman who swept so gracefully out of the hotel.

If she was making too much of the moment . . . well, she deserved to, didn't she? There hadn't been any good moments in quite a while. They'd been through such a dark winter — the whole family, all of the Kopps — and Fleurette had wondered how she'd ever come out on the other side of it.

That was why this night, this small victory, shimmered as brightly as it did.

Her instructions were to wait for Mr. McGinnis to come around in his automobile. His motor was already rumbling toward her in the dark. She wished she could have just a moment more to herself, there on the sidewalk, under the tender pool of light cast by the dance of a gaslit lantern.

She looked like a woman with someplace to go, and she certainly felt like one, for the first time in ages. It was a shame that Mr. McGinnis was merely coming to take her home.

Couldn't she instruct him otherwise? Where did other people go at this hour? To the theater, and dinner after? To one of the massive dancing halls in the city? To the top floor of a very chic building, where women who were dressed just as beautifully as she looked out the windows to the rooftops beyond and held lightly on to the fragile

8

stems of their Champagne glasses?

It was a lovely dream, but it dissolved as Mr. McGinnis emerged from his hulking black machine to help her into her seat.

As he opened the passenger door, he grinned down at her cheerfully — no one, Fleurette thought, was as full of mirth and goodwill as a rosy-cheeked young Irishman like Peter McGinnis — and, taking her arm, said, "That was one for the books, Miss Kopp. The fellow was a champ about the whole business, and you handled him just right. Didn't flatter him, but you didn't put a load of guilt on him, either. That's just the way to do it."

He ran back around to take his place behind the wheel and closed the door, sealing them in just as the swirling wind brought a fresh smattering of snow.

She said, "He was a gentleman and a professional. I hope they all will be."

Mr. McGinnis glanced over at her, still grinning, but something about his eyes suggested that they might not all be quite so gentlemanly. He seemed to brush the thought away as he reached into his coat for his wallet.

"Now, let me see, I have a note, what did Mr. Ward say again . . ."

"Twenty dollars," pronounced Fleurette,

taking quite a bit of pleasure in it. To be able to command such a sum, for not even an hour's work!

Again Mr. McGinnis's eyes dashed uncomfortably across her face, but his smile stayed bright and pleasing. "Twenty it is. Buy yourself a nice dress."

"It's to go toward the funeral," Fleurette said. She tucked the bills into a little beaded purse, one she hadn't carried since before the war.

"I was sorry to hear about your brother," Mr. McGinnis said. They were rolling through downtown Paterson by now, toward home, or what passed for a home for Fleurette at this particular moment. "I would've been there to pay my respects, but —"

"But Mr. Ward was there to represent the firm, and we were touched that you thought of us." Fleurette said this a bit briskly and wished she hadn't brought it up. The condolences were hard to hear. They were only rote phrases, issued by people who could look at her tragedy from a great distance, but didn't have to live inside of it as she did.

Mr. McGinnis must've taken her meaning, because he drove along in silence for a minute. Then — being the kind of man who couldn't stand to let a lady sit mutely, staring out the window — he said, "Well! You're in the family business now, aren't you?"

"What do you mean by that?" Fleurette said sharply.

He looked a little stung, having expected a warmer reply. "Oh — I was only thinking — investigations, and legal matters, and . . . ah . . . detective work and the like."

Fleurette pulled her coat around her. "It's nothing to do with my family, and don't you say a word to them about any of this. It isn't their concern what I do. And don't forget to leave me at the corner. I'll walk the rest of the way."

"But I have to see you in!" Mr. McGinnis looked stricken at the idea of a woman leaving his auto unaccompanied.

"You can watch me go in from here," Fleurette said, as they arrived at the end of the street.

They parted cordially, Mr. McGinnis sending his regards to her sisters and Fleurette warning him once again to stay mum.

Francis and Bessie's house sat just four doors down. The kitchen light was still on. As she walked up, Fleurette could see through the curtains that Bessie sat alone at the table, looking over a newspaper.

11

She went in through the kitchen door and dropped a kiss on Bessie's cheek.

"Put this toward the funeral bill," she whispered, and pressed the money into her hand.

2

The funeral for which Fleurette was now paying in installments had been the bleakest affair imaginable, held graveside on an icebound January afternoon.

No one thought of waiting until fairer weather: the waiting had gone on too long already, because Norma had to be summoned home from France. The armistice had passed by then, the war had concluded, and Norma's duties were at an end, as far as anyone in the Kopp family knew, but nonetheless she'd been lingering in Paris. It had required an increasingly frantic series of letters, postcards, telegrams, and appeals to her former commander at Fort Monmouth to even locate her, much less to secure passage home at a time when every ship returning to the States was already overfull.

Owing to that delay, three weeks had passed from the day Francis's heart stopped beating to the day he was put into the ground. It was an unbearable length of time for the rest of them to wait. Funerals are for the living: they allow a beloved to be sent on his way decently and quietly, no matter the circumstances of the death itself. During the three weeks in which they were deprived of that opportunity, the Kopps lived in a state of agitated and unrelenting misery. Sending Francis to his grave wouldn't bring an end to their suffering, but it would be like dropping an anchor. It would hold them in place. It would give them something — a ceremony, a gravestone — to fix their tears to.

When the day of the funeral did at last arrive, Fleurette had turned up at the cemetery pinched and pale as an invalid, and still harboring a little death-rattle of a cough. In an effort to stifle it, she'd secreted away a tin of horehound tablets somewhere on her person, but they were well beyond her reach, as she was swaddled in the mufflers, scarves, and cloaks of half a dozen strangers, all of whom had thrust those garments upon her as she alighted from the carriage alongside the family plot. The way she stood unevenly, swaying among the mounds of gray snow, led everyone in attendance to fear that she might faint from the cold, so soon after her illness.

But it wasn't the weather that made her unsteady. It was the sight of a freshly dug grave, black and bottomless. It looked exactly like the very thing it was, a portal for the dead to pass through. She shuddered to even think of going near it.

The more she looked around, the more foreign and otherworldly it all seemed: the coffin, the strange red carpet placed underneath to protect it from the snow and dirt (as if it were not about to be consigned to snow and dirt forever), the crowd of neighbors and old acquaintances gathered around, the minister with his black book and dignified whisper, the rickety wooden chairs placed graveside, and beyond all that, the row upon row of stone markers under which Paterson's deceased resided.

It had been Francis's wish, whispered in Bessie's ear years ago as they sat together through the interminable funeral service of a neighbor, to skip the formalities when his time came, and to be remembered only at a simple graveside ceremony. Bessie had honored his wish. They would stand outside in the cold, stamping their feet to bring the feeling back into their toes, for as short an interval as was required to pay their respects.

15

The three sisters, by unspoken assent, stood clustered together for whatever brief remarks the minister would deliver. Fleurette took the center, flanked on either side by the familiar bulk of her siblings.

Her remaining siblings.

Constance stood to her left. She had a look about her like she'd been kicked in the gut and hadn't yet got her wind back. Her features sagged in a way Fleurette had never seen before. That very definite chin of hers had weakened and sunk into the folds of her neck, the great dark half-moons under her eyes had further settled, and there was now a weight pulling the edges of her mouth downward.

On her other side was Norma, stalwart and grim as always, her chin tucked into her regulation muffler and bits of hair escaping from a smart Army cap. She wore her uniform because she'd only just stepped off her ship the night before and couldn't be bothered with trying on the dress Fleurette had dyed black and tailored for her.

Bessie sat apart from them, inscrutable behind her veil. Fleurette understood now why widows wore veils at funerals. It was to give them a place to hide, a private room where they could retreat into silence and solitude.

Even her children couldn't reach her. Fleurette watched as Lorraine tried to lift her mother's veil, but Bessie only shook her head and pulled it down again. The children had to content themselves with sitting silently alongside her, each of them holding one of her hands, until even that was too much and she withdrew her hands to the inside of her cloak. Still each child clung to her, Frankie taking her elbow and Lorraine pinching a bit of fabric near her knee.

Fleurette herself could hardly bear to speak to anyone, but it was her duty to keep those in attendance away from Bessie. That was what Bessie had asked of her that morning: keep everyone away until the coffin was in the ground. She would face her fellow mourners after the burial, but not before. She feared she'd be sick if she had to say a word to anyone. Fleurette and her sisters were obliged to speak for the family so she didn't have to.

A lady approached — she might've been a neighbor or a churchgoer or a member of one of the innumerable committees on which Bessie served, they all looked the same in their long coats and fur hats — and Fleurette steeled herself.

"You must be the actress," the lady whispered. "Bessie's told me all about you."

Fleurette nodded at this and coughed a little. "I was on the stage," she croaked, "but I took ill last fall."

She patted Fleurette's arm, whoever she was, and made a sympathetic face. "I had hoped you might sing for us today. Bessie always says what a beautiful singing voice you have."

"I couldn't," Fleurette said, and coughed again as if to prove it.

The lady leaned closer. She smelled of a lilac perfume, applied heavily to cover the scent of mothballs coming off her black dress.

"I heard he dropped dead at his desk," she whispered. "It wasn't that awful Spanish 'flu, was it? Wouldn't it be just his luck to sit out the war and then the influenza comes all this way to get him?"

It was no wonder Bessie didn't want anyone near her! Was this how people talked at funerals?

"It wasn't the 'flu," Fleurette said. "His heart stopped beating. It was weak but nobody knew it. I hope that doesn't disappoint you."

The minister pronounced his brief words over the casket, words that neither Fleurette

18

nor her sisters could recall even a moment later. Then all at once the service was over, and the murmur of conversation started again.

Fleurette had expected to feel it in her bones when her brother went into the ground, forever banished from her life, no longer of this Earth but in it. But the lowering of the casket wasn't part of the ceremony. It was merely a job to be completed after. Most people turned their backs before the winches were secure, before the oiled wooden box began to groan and shift. There wasn't even a moment's pause to absorb the import of what was happening.

Instead she faced another round of pleasantries. People milled around, chatting like guests at a party. Before, they'd all been blank faces, unrecognizable and indistinguishable from one another, but now a few of them came into focus.

Norma stood off to one side, talking to the Wilkinsons, who had lived next door to Bessie and Francis since their respective houses were built.

Surrounding Bessie was a group of ladies with whom she volunteered at the library, including Mrs. Westervelt, mother-in-law to Robert Heath.

That meant that Mr. Heath had to be

19

there, too. Fleurette hadn't seen him since before the war. After he lost the election, and the new sheriff fired Constance, he dropped out of sight. Fleurette never knew why he'd slipped out of their lives. Perhaps it pained Constance too much to see him demoted from sheriff to ordinary mortal. But he would turn up for their brother's funeral. Of course he would.

Then where was he? She looked around for Constance and saw him at her side, the two of them walking down a little gravel path, their heads bowed together in conversation. They walked easily, as old friends. In their long black coats they were nearly identical from the back, save the difference in their hats.

With an old familiarity born of long nights spent waiting out a fugitive, and of afternoons spent going from house to house interviewing witnesses, Constance nodded at Mr. Heath when she spotted him through the crowd. She matched his stride as they took a turn around the cemetery.

"I didn't see you once during the war," Mr. Heath said.

"I was here, mostly. Down in Washington for a while, and sometimes away on assignment, but for the most part I stayed in

Paterson." Constance said all that in a rush, although she knew he wasn't asking about her every location. He wanted to know why they hadn't spoken in so long.

But he knew perfectly well the reason. Constance had been utterly crushed by the disastrous election of 1916, and the very public and humiliating loss of the only job she'd ever held or cared for. She'd recovered her dignity, eventually, and found even better employment for herself during the war — but her last association with Mr. Heath had simply wrecked her, and those painful memories were reason enough to stay away.

Besides, she'd always carried a small burden of guilt over his defeat. He'd lost the election in part because the public had turned against her. The newspapers were perfectly awful in their portrayal of New Jersey's first lady deputy. He'd always been stalwart in his defense of her, but he'd paid a price for it.

What could she possibly say to him now? And what did they have in common anymore?

"Well, I was in New York, mostly," Mr. Heath said. "Cordelia's father got me hired on at a plumbing outfit. They sold pipe fittings. It was my job to count them."

He said it so seriously, but Constance

21

almost laughed at the very idea of it. What was a lawman doing counting pipe fittings?

"Someone has to, I suppose," she said. "But you're not there any longer?"

He looked over at her and that old understanding passed between them. He couldn't stand a job like that, and she knew it.

"The Paterson Police Department has hired me on as a patrolman."

Then he was back to policing, after he'd sworn to his wife that he was through with it.

Constance said mildly, "What does Cordelia say?"

Mr. Heath rubbed the back of his neck. He didn't want to answer, did he?

"I thought she made you promise. You were supposed to stay away from any sort of position in law enforcement."

"She doesn't have to live at the jail this time," he said. "I'm an ordinary patrolman with a beat now. But if she didn't enjoy being married to a lawman, she doesn't like living with an office clerk any better. They had me sitting over a column of figures all day. I couldn't see the point in it."

"Well," Constance said, "I can hardly blame you. I wouldn't like a column of figures, either."

"It's a good group of cops in Paterson. If

you're interested, I could put in a word for you."

That would be useless, and Constance knew it. The Paterson Police Department might take on Mr. Heath, even with a little controversy in his past — as a lowly patrolman, what harm could he do? — but she'd never work in law enforcement again, at least not among people who'd been reading the New Jersey newspapers in 1916.

Thank goodness those old battles didn't matter anymore, now that she was off to Washington.

"That's kind of you, but I have a job offer from the new director of the Bureau of Investigation." She tried to sound casual about it, but in fact it still thrilled her to even mention the Bureau. "I've had to put it off for a few weeks. I can't very well run off to Washington with Bessie in tatters, and Norma only just off the boat. I'm keeping my room at the boarding-house in Paterson through the end of the month, just to make sure everything's settled here before I go."

"They'll be lucky to have you in Washington," Mr. Heath said.

"I'm the lucky one," Constance said. "I'll be training an entire class of female recruits. The Bureau's never done anything like it, but I convinced them to try." She heard the fervor in her voice, and the eagerness to impress her old boss, but remembered just then that she was at a funeral. This was no time for such talk. "It's a good salary. I'll be able to send something home every week. We want to see to it that Bessie and the children are looked after. Until that's settled, I'm staying right here."

"Of course," Mr. Heath said. "If they weren't provided for, will you let me —"

"No," Constance said sharply. "We'll take care of her. She's our responsibility. You have your own to look after."

"Miss Kopp," he said, that old formality between them sounding strangely intimate. "I'm someone you can call upon. Would you remember that?"

Fleurette watched Constance and Mr. Heath, and wondered what they had to say to each other. Funerals were funny that way, especially a funeral coming so soon after the war: people took the opportunity to get reacquainted even in this most miserable of circumstances.

She turned around — she could feel the press of friends and neighbors wanting to pay their respects to the bereaved — and found herself face-to-face with another man connected to Constance's old job, but who was he? She'd seen him before, but she couldn't place him.

He couldn't have been in law enforcement — he was too well-dressed for it. He wasn't terribly young or exactly what she'd call handsome, but he was interesting-looking, with a mop of curly hair that flopped across his forehead and into his eyes, and a lanky frame that wore clothes well. His suit was cut nicely, and the stripes flattered him, although they might've been a little too smart for a funeral. He looked like he wanted a highball in his hand.

Mr. Ward — he introduced himself straightaway — turned out to be a lawyer with whom Constance had dealings over the years.

"John Ward," he said, bowing a little as he shook Fleurette's hand. "What was your connection to the departed?"

"Sister," she said.

He dropped her hand and took a step back, appraising her. "You're a Kopp? You don't look anything like the other two!"

"I'm the youngest and the prettiest," she said — flatly, even somberly. Why did she put it to him like that? She wasn't trying to make clever conversation. He just seemed to require that sort of response.

Mr. Ward said, "I believe it. What sort of

name did they give you?"

"Fleurette," she said. "Kopp, of course. You're probably going to call me Miss Kopp."

"I'll give it a try. Awfully sorry about your brother, Miss Kopp. Condolences from the firm of Ward & McGinnis. We sent that horseshoe-shaped affair over there. Isn't it nice?"

She didn't bother to look: there were a dozen horseshoes done up in white carnations. What did a horseshoe have to do with putting one's brother in the ground?

"Where's McGinnis?" she asked.

"Petey's out on a job," he said.

"What do you mean, a job? Aren't they called cases, or trials?" Fleurette had the vexing sensation that she was flirting with him, without meaning to.

"A case, then," he said, "or at least, it will be if he can finish the job."

"Is he off chasing an ambulance?" she asked.

"We haven't had to resort to that yet," he said. "Petey's only after an adulterer."

"Oh, you're that sort of lawyer."

"Afraid so. It pays the most, you see, so what choice do we have?"

"And what does Petey do, catch them in the act?"

"Petey takes the pictures. Say, what do you intend to do with yourself, *après la guerre*? Are you in the family business?"

"And what's that, exactly?"

He gave a little shrug and looked over at Norma and Constance. "One's a soldier. One's a cop. They seem to like uniforms. Fighting crime, fighting Germans, that sort of thing."

"I did help Constance with a case during the war," said Fleurette, "but I'm in the theater."

"That much is obvious."

"What are you suggesting?" She was still wrapped in any number of scarves and mufflers, and her hair was pinned up under a demure black hat. There was nothing theatrical about her.

"Only . . . you've got a face for the stage, that's all," he said. "Even under that hat."

"Well, I don't have the voice for it. Not at the moment." She was still hoarse. Everything she said came out sounding like gravel. "I'm going back to seamstressing until I can sing again."

"That won't do for a girl like you," he said. "Say, wouldn't you like —"

She didn't hear the rest of it, because at that moment Norma came marching over and stood disapprovingly at her side.

27

(Fleurette wondered if Norma had always marched everywhere, even before the war, and remembered that she had.)

Fleurette said, "This is a lawyer friend of Constance's, Mr. Ward."

Norma looked him up and down appraisingly and said, "We've no use for a lawyer. Bessie's had enough, and so have I. We're going home."

3

At that moment, Fleurette did not yet have any inkling of the circumstances that would propel her into John Ward's employment. Of course there would be expenses connected to the funeral, and the doctor would eventually send a bill — she had a vague idea about all that — but she felt safe in her assumption that Francis had left his family provided for.

Surely if Bessie needed anything extra, she would say so, and then Constance would sort it out. Either Constance or Norma had always managed the sisters' finances, such as they were, between the bits of land around their farm that they leased or sold off from time to time, to the salary Constance earned as one sort of lady cop or another, to the barters for milk and butter that Norma negotiated with the dairy, and — well, whatever else was involved.

Fleurette didn't know what else might be

involved. She hadn't ever given it much thought, and now she didn't have to. She earned her own wages, and quite gladly used them to provide for herself. During the war she toured the Army camps as one of the Eight Dresden Dolls. Her room and board were provided, and any other small expenses came out of her own pocket. She kept herself in dresses and shoes, which was no small feat.

She did not, in other words, consider it her responsibility to look after any of her relations in a financial sense. It wasn't selfishness on her part: she felt she was being more than responsible by simply looking after herself, and not making anyone else do it.

Wasn't that enough?

When they returned from the cemetery, Fleurette fled to her room and sank into bed, grateful for the quiet and the dark. She'd been occupying Lorraine's bedroom as she recuperated from her bout of streptococci, forcing poor Lorraine to share a bedroom with her brother.

The room had been entirely taken over by Fleurette's possessions, which left no place to walk except from the door to the bed and back again. She'd wedged three trunks between the bed and the wall and stacked hat-boxes atop them, some containing hats but others filled with slippers, scarves, ribbons, pins, combs, stockings, and whatever other bits and pieces remained intact after her months of touring.

At the foot of her bed perched Laura in her enormous birdcage. The parrot had been having a rough time of it lately, between Fleurette's illness and the cramped quarters the two of them now shared.

Fleurette had acquired the bird while touring to entertain the troops last fall. A soldier named George Simon gave her to Fleurette, because the Army wouldn't let him take a green Amazonian parrot to France. She'd felt terrible about hauling a caged bird from hotel to train station to Army camp, but she later realized that Laura enjoyed travel and liked the variety of sights and sounds. She'd expected to give Laura back to her owner after the Armistice, but George had written to say that he'd extended his tour of duty overseas and had taken a Parisian bride. The bird was hers to keep.

Laura had watched worriedly as Fleurette recovered from her illness, but a sick girl isn't much entertainment for a bird. She'd grown bored and restless and, Fleurette feared, a little listless. She had started to pick at her feathers and tended to sit in broody silence, when before she would whistle and dance and even try to sound out a word or two.

Laura needed to get away from that tiny room. So did Fleurette.

Fleurette opened her cage and let the bird step out onto her arm. "Pretty Laura," she crooned. "Sing for Fleurette."

"Or-ette," she mimicked, or something that sounded very much like it. Fleurette dropped back onto the bed, and Laura walked up and down, picking at loose threads on the coverlet. She was the most magnificent creature, with emerald wings showing a flash of red at the tips, and orange eyes that saw everything.

Even Norma had been impressed with her when she arrived home the night before. She took her right off Fleurette's shoulder and turned her upside-down, which so surprised Laura that she spread her wings and her tail-feathers. That was exactly what Norma wanted to see.

"Healthy skin, sturdy ribs, good strong grip," she said, running a finger up and down Laura's underbelly. "You aren't giving her too much seed."

"Not at all," Fleurette said quickly. She

hadn't ever in her life wanted to impress Norma, but at that moment she very much wanted Norma to approve of her avian husbandry — and she did.

"That's a fine parrot," Norma said, handing her back. "Only this bird wants something to do."

Oh, Laura! Poor girl, trapped in this little room! Fleurette had been a miserable companion all that past autumn, sick in bed for weeks and weeks. Of course, back then she had every reason to think she'd recover, put herself back together, and work up a book of songs that she and Laura could sing on stage. She'd even been promised a contract — more than promised, she already had the contract, for three hundred dollars a week and bookings from Paterson to Chicago — and had only to sign it and return it to Mr. Bernstein, and then she and Laura could set off to make a new life for themselves.

Then Francis died, and all her plans had been pushed aside. But how much longer could she stand to sleep in this room, a room that Francis intended for his daughter? How much longer could she eat at his table, wash her face at his sink, and sit under the light of his lamp in the evenings? It was unbearable, living under his roof,

33

feeling her way around the edges of the enormous hole left by his absence, a hole so vast and dark that she felt as though she might fall in.

It sounded awful to say it — even to herself — but Fleurette had to get out. She'd been sick and miserable in that house for weeks already. Now everyone was sick and miserable. It was a house gripped by contagion and grief.

There was nothing Fleurette could do to help anymore. She had kept the children fed — if toast and sandwiches counted as food — on the days when Bessie couldn't get out of bed. She washed the windows, one afternoon, thinking that any ailment, even heartbreak, could be relieved by letting in the light. She answered the door when well-intentioned neighbors stopped by with their small gifts.

But Norma was home now, and in need of a place to stay until the farm was made habitable again. She could look after the family and the house, and was better qualified to do so anyway. Fleurette would be doing everyone a favor by moving out and making room for Norma to take over.

What she hadn't told Bessie, or her sisters, or even her parrot (because Laura was learning to speak and she was indiscreet) was that she had already found a room to rent. She wouldn't go far — just to a little boarding-house down in Rutherford, not even an hour away by train, just far enough away from Paterson to make a break from her old life, and close enough to New York to start a new one.

The boarding-house was a quiet one with only two rooms rented, run by a friendly and generous Mrs. Doyle, whose husband was dead and whose daughters had married and moved out west. Mrs. Doyle liked to have girls in the house, she told Fleurette, and she liked to cook for a crowd. Fleurette would be welcome to invite her friends for dinner. A parrot would make a charming companion. And if Fleurette wanted to practice her singing, her landlady would be delighted by the entertainment. She even kept a piano tuned in the parlor.

There it was: a little isle of contentment, a soft and welcoming nest for Fleurette and her bird, a place she could afford on just a little dress-making, until her voice returned and her act was ready to take on the road. A place where she could breathe untroubled air, for a little while.

Fleurette intended to tell Bessie and her sisters tomorrow. Her trunks were already packed, her deposit paid. Mrs. Doyle had given her a key.

She would leave just as soon as she decently could.

4

The rest of the afternoon following the funeral was a blur. The evening was called off entirely: everyone was in bed by seven, taking with them a book or a letter to write or a hot-water bottle wrapped in flannel.

Constance and Norma stayed overnight at Bessie's, sleeping on a mound of cushions and blankets in the sitting-room. Lorraine and Frankie shared a room as they had since Fleurette moved in. Fleurette slept soundly until quite late, as was her habit, and didn't make an appearance the next morning until Norma banged on her bedroom door with the edge of a frying pan still sizzling with eggs.

"Did they teach you that in the Army?" Fleurette groaned, as she stumbled down the hall behind her sister.

"In the Army you wouldn't be rewarded with fresh eggs for sleeping late. Sit down and eat before you set a bad example for the children."

Fleurette, still in her nightgown, dropped into a chair next to Lorraine, who said, "Aunt Fleurette has already taught us her wicked ways."

"Let's not have any talk of wickedness at the breakfast table," Bessie said. She smiled up at Norma as a fresh plate of toast appeared before her. "You must be exhausted. I never had a chance to ask about your crossing. I hear it's worse in winter."

"I've been both ways in winter, so I wouldn't know the difference," Norma said. "At least we didn't have the Germans skulking about this time."

"Did you see a U-boat?" Frankie asked.

"They do their best not to be seen," Norma said, and left it at that. There was no way to talk about Germans and submarines without eventually coming around to a story about soldiers lost at sea. Even Norma understood that they were all far too bruised and tender for tales of war-time suffering.

Norma had other reasons for wanting to steer the conversation away from her time in France: she didn't want to be asked about why she'd been hanging around in Paris after the Armistice. As far as her sisters knew, her official duties had ended. In fact, it took her commanders some time to locate her — not because she'd slipped away unannounced, but because no one could be found quickly in the chaos of winding-down operations and the avalanche of paperwork associated with it.

Had the telegram arrived just one day later, Norma would've missed it entirely. She was bound for Belgium with Aggie Bell, the nurse with whom she'd shared living quarters in France. The two had become close during the war, just as soldiers do, sharing a bond unlike any they'd ever known in their civilian days.

It had been Aggie's idea to stay in Europe. Like so many young women who found their first taste of freedom during war-time service, she had no interest in going home. She felt a dread of returning to an old life that would offer her little in the way of adventure. She'd come to love the chaos, the danger, and the frenzied pace of war-time, and feared that any sort of calm might sink her.

And Norma, begrudgingly, had to admit that she felt the same. What sort of existence would be waiting for her, back in New Jersey? Of course her sisters depended upon her immeasurably. Norma ran the household. She ran the farm. She ran things generally, because she was predisposed to do so.

But what would be left to run, after she returned? Fleurette was on her own. Constance could go to Washington or New York or anywhere she liked. Was Norma to return to an empty farmhouse and an abandoned pigeon loft? Without the war to prepare for — and she had been preparing, from the day the Archduke was assassinated — what did she have to look forward to?

Aggie had signed on to perform relief work for the refugees in Belgium. At the last minute she persuaded Norma, who spoke both French and German courtesy of her foreign-born parents, to come along and serve as an interpreter.

More importantly, she had persuaded Norma to stay with her as her companion and help-mate, to travel together and live as a pair, just as they had done for the last year. Their adventures weren't over, Aggie insisted. They belonged in Europe, and they belonged together.

That plea stirred something in Norma. It was a rare and fine thing to be wanted and appreciated by someone outside the family, someone she'd come to know on her own terms and in her own way. She agreed at once.

It was all settled — their tickets purchased, their trunks packed.

Then the telegram arrived.

Of course Norma had no choice but to return home. Aggie had to let her go, and to do so bravely. She'd been hardened to the tragedies of war and didn't shed a tear when they said good-bye on the train platform, one bound east and the other west. But she drew Norma into a tight squeeze, and whispered that she would write every week, and that she hoped Norma would come and join her, someday, when things were settled in New Jersey.

Norma didn't make any promises. When they pulled away from one another, Norma could still feel the impression Aggie had made against her, and could smell the particular sweet mixture of cold cream and milk soap that always clung to Aggie. By the end of a damp and chilly voyage across the Atlantic, that fragrance was gone.

Norma hadn't said a word about the plans she'd made with Aggie and didn't consider it her sisters' business. There would be letters from Aggie soon enough, telling about where she'd settled in Belgium and giving an address where Norma could write. Not in the first letter, but in the second or third, Aggie would ask if Norma's family could

41

spare her, and if she'd thought about returning to Europe.

But Norma knew the answer already. Of course she couldn't leave. One look at Bessie told her that the world had fallen apart, right here in Hawthorne. The Kopps were in ruins, and who but Norma would put them back together? Constance had one eye on a job in Washington. Fleurette would go skipping back to the stage any day now.

Someone had to stand by Bessie. Belgium would have to shift for itself.

The children finished picking at their breakfasts — neither one of them had much appetite — and Bessie shooed them away from the table.

"I want you ready for school in ten minutes," she called. It was her belief that the sooner the children resumed their old routine, the better. They'd been out since before Christmas. School had started a week earlier, and she didn't want them to fall further behind.

Once they'd disappeared down the hall, Bessie turned to Norma and said, "I hope we can make you comfortable here. I want you to stay as long as you like. It's good to have the house full of people."

"I can make room for you at the boarding-house as well," said Constance. "I'm keeping my room there until we decide . . ."

She let that trail off. It was just as well. None of them knew what had to be decided just yet.

"As long as I have a hot bath and a clean bed, it doesn't matter where you put me," Norma said. "But I'll get settled back home as soon as I can. Constance and I are going up to the farm this morning to have a look around." The farm, out in Wyckoff, had been sitting empty during the war. It was only five miles out of town, but it was an inconvenient journey on muddy roads. "Does the trolley still run out that way?"

"Oh, why don't you rest for a day first!" Bessie said. "Everything's been so hurried, since —"

"No, I want to go right away and find out what needs to be done around the place," Norma said, "and I see a few things I'd like to take care of here, too. I don't like the looks of those gutters. I'll get Frankie up on a ladder to clear them out. And what about your accounts, the bills and banking and so forth? Did Francis have charge of all that?"

Bessie shifted in her chair and put a hand over her stomach. Fleurette thought she looked queasy and wished Norma wouldn't go rushing into her affairs like that. But it was just like Norma to march from one thing to the next. If the funeral was over, it must be time for gutters and book-keeping.

"I'm sure I'll manage," Bessie said, in a voice both vague and kind.

As much as Fleurette didn't like to admit to having anything in common with her sisters, it was true that the three of them could each be sharp-edged and argumentative in their own ways. But Bessie was soft and tender, right down to her very center, even when Norma was at her most irritating.

It occurred to Fleurette just then that perhaps this was why Francis had married Bessie. She was nothing like the Kopp women. She was generous and accommodating and just better, in every way that would've mattered to him.

"Well, we're here to do whatever needs doing," Norma said.

"I know." Bessie pushed her chair aside and went down the hall toward her bedroom. Norma took Constance out on the porch to show her the gutters. Fleurette had hoped to make her announcement about the room she'd rented before breakfast was over, but she was still halfway through buttering her toast when everyone dispersed.

She would've gone out to speak to Constance and Norma about it, thinking that it might be better to tell them privately any-way, but just then she heard Bessie retching in the bathroom.

The door was not entirely closed. Fleurette pushed against it, lightly, and found Bessie doubled over next to the toilet, her hair hanging down around her face, hands over her belly.

Weeping. Heaving.

What a picture of misery! Bessie had such a warm glow around her, and was always so pleasingly put together, in a manner that Fleurette could only describe as welcoming and reassuring, like a pretty nurse, perhaps. When Francis first met her, and Fleurette was only a little girl looking up at her, that's what she thought: *My brother has fallen in love with a pretty nurse.*

But there she was in a heap on the floor, leaning over to press her cheek against the cool porcelain rim of the bathtub, sweat beading on her forehead. She looked up at Fleurette with an expression of horror that quickly gave way to apology. She didn't want to be seen like that. She didn't want anyone to have the burden of knowing how awful it really was for her.

Fleurette closed the door and locked it — what a blessing to women is a lock on the bathroom door! — and slid down on the floor next to her. There was a face-cloth dangling from the sink above them. She reached up and swished it under the faucet and passed it to Bessie, dripping and cold.

"Ahhhhh," Bessie sighed, running it over her mouth and around her neck. Then she pressed it into her eyes, and once her face was soothed a little, she dropped the cloth and turned to Fleurette. Her eyes were rimmed in pink and her lips swollen.

After a pause — as if debating how to put it — she said, "I'd forgotten what this feels like."

Still Fleurette didn't guess at her meaning! It was the last thing anyone might think of, at a time like that. But just as she opened her mouth to say some nonsense in return — "You've never lost a husband before, how can you know" — it came to her.

Bessie wasn't sick over Francis.

Well, she was, but this was something else.

As the realization dawned across Fleurette's face, Bessie smiled just slightly. A woman can't help but be a little proud of the creature she carries inside her, no matter the circumstances.

"Oh, Bessie," Fleurette whispered. "Are you sure?"

She nodded and reached out to take Fleurette's hand. They sat shoulder to shoulder as sisters, their fingers folded together. "It's been three months. You'll be letting out my dresses before long."

A baby — at her age! Bessie was forty. Frankie was her youngest, and he was already eleven. Lorraine was thirteen. What would Francis have thought about another baby in the house?

Somehow she managed to keep that question to herself, but she could only just manage to stop herself from asking one impertinent question before the next one popped into her head. Had Francis known about the baby? Was he conscious for even a few minutes there at the last, panting and clutching at his chest, thinking of the son or daughter he'd never meet?

And — here was the part Fleurette knew she really mustn't say aloud — what was Bessie going to do now? How could she manage, with a third child on the way?

While she was busy not saying any of that, she just stared at Bessie, at that sweet fallen face. Bessie was always composed when the rest of them weren't, but this time, she didn't even try to put on a brave mask. It was all there for Fleurette to see: the anguish, the great gaping loss before her, the despair of a woman left to look after two children alone, much less three. She had

47

the prettiest blue eyes, and when she cried, they were even brighter, the lashes wetter and darker.

"And you haven't told anyone?" Fleurette asked at last, grasping for any remark that wouldn't upset or offend.

Bessie squeezed her hand. "Not yet. Well, now you know. And Francis knew."

Fleurette took in a little gasp, not meaning to, but it hit her in the body, knowing that.

"That's good," she said. "It's good that he knew."

But was it?

"Oh, I'm not so sure," Bessie said. "I'm afraid I only added to his worries." Another wash of tears flooded her eyes.

"No, no, that's impossible! He wouldn't have worried," Fleurette said, quick as she could. "He loved babies. You remember how much he loved your babies when they were born. He'd sit at the dinner table with Lorraine on his chest. My mother was so shocked by that. She'd never seen a man handle a baby."

Bessie leaned back against the wall and sighed. "Your mother. She was so afraid he'd drop one of them."

"But he never did."

"No." Bessie pushed her hair back. There

48

was already a little gray coming in around her forehead.

From outside the bathroom door came a sound — a tiny, almost imperceptible sniff, a smothered sneeze, perhaps. Bessie cast a knowing eye at the gap between the bottom of the door and the floor boards. Fleurette looked over, too, and could just make out the shadows cast by one if not two pairs of feet.

Enormous feet.

Bessie shrugged. "You might as well let them in."

The doorknob rattled and Fleurette reached up, reluctantly, to grant her sisters admittance. They practically fell inside — comically, like two fools in a vaudeville show — and Bessie and Fleurette had to sit up quickly to avoid being trampled.

"I knew you didn't look right," Norma said, taking a seat on the toilet lid in the manner of a businessman sitting down to meet with his board. "When exactly is this baby coming and how are we going to manage it?"

"July, I expect," Bessie said. "It's enough time to get us moved, and settled —"

"Moved?" cried all three sisters, in unison.

Bessie sighed and pressed the cloth against her neck again. "I didn't want to tell you so soon after the funeral, but you might as well have it all at once. We did just fine on Francis's salary, but there's nothing coming in now. I don't like to depend on anyone, but I hardly have a choice. My sister has offered to take us all in. They have plenty of room and the children will get to live with their cousins."

"Didn't you tell us that you moved east to get away from your sister?" asked Norma.

"She didn't even come to the funeral," said Constance.

"And what about the children's school?" said Norma.

Bessie smiled a little at that. "They have schools in Illinois. And Della and I are older now. We'll get along just fine. They still live in my parent's old house in Springfield. There's plenty of room, and Della's husband is about to take over a medical practice from a doctor who's retiring. And you know, they're just far enough outside of town that they keep chickens."

Fleurette suspected that she said that last part for Norma, thinking that Norma would approve of a farmhouse with chickens.

Norma did not approve. She'd given up Belgium for this. She was digging in, already.

"Well, you're not going. You're provided

for right here. You have this house. You have us. And surely Francis left something. Wouldn't there be life insurance?"

Bessie put her hands over her eyes. The three of them waited, hardly breathing. Then she looked up at them and shook her head. "People used to come around selling life insurance. Francis would talk to them, but nothing came of it. I suppose I thought that if anything happened to him, I'd find some sort of work for myself, but nobody would have me now. Not with a baby on the way."

"But if you could live with Della in the countryside," Fleurette put in, not liking this idea at all but thinking that she should offer it anyway, "couldn't you live with us in the countryside? Let's all go out to the farm together and have a look around. We could turn the sitting-room into a nursery."

But Bessie wouldn't have it. "How are any of us to earn a dollar, out there in Wyckoff? Are we to raise three children on nothing but turnips and eggs?"

"What about our —" Fleurette understood so little of their finances that she hardly knew how to put it. "What about our little mortgages, from the parcels we sold?"

"The little mortgages are paid off, or else defaulted on," said Constance. "We have a few pastures leased, but —"

Norma said, "But we'll need that money to patch things up out there, once I have a look to see what needs to be done. Anyway, it doesn't matter. You're not about to run off to Illinois. The Wilkinsons are selling their house, did you know that?"

"Next door?" asked Constance.

Fleurette had an ill and nervous feeling about this.

"We'll sell the farm," Norma said, "and we'll move in next door and look after you."

"Oh, but you couldn't sell the farm," Bessie said. "Your mother intended that land for you girls."

"You're one of the girls that mother intended the farm for," Norma said. "She just didn't know it at the time."

Bessie was a bit weepy again (and now they all understood why: no one who is both pregnant and in mourning can keep a dry eye for more than a minute or two), but through her tears she continued to insist that they could not sell their land. "You've all made your plans for after the war," she said. "You have things you wanted to do. Fleurette's going back on the stage, Constance is bound for Washington, and you —"

But no one knew what Norma intended

to do, and Norma didn't offer an explanation.

"No one's going to Washington," she said, without so much as a glance at Constance. Of Fleurette's supposed return to the stage, she made not the slightest acknowledgment. "I'll speak to the Wilkinsons right now. They asked me at the funeral what they could do to help, and here it is. They'll lease the house to us when they move out, and we'll buy it when we sell the farm. I'll arrange it this minute."

"Oh, girls, I don't know," Bessie said, but it wasn't much of a protest. No one believed for a minute that she wanted to leave her home and drag her children off to Illinois.

"Well, we do know," Norma said briskly. "We'll be here every day to help with the children. There will be enough money after we sell the farm to buy the Wilkinsons' house and put some aside for all of us. With Constance working, and Fleurette —"

Fleurette didn't hear the rest of that, because all she could think about was that dear little room at Mrs. Doyle's slipping away.

She would have to set up housekeeping with her sisters, just as they had done before the war, only now she'd be in and out of Francis's house every day, unable to push

53

tragedy aside for even a minute.

But what choice did she have? How could she stand up and say that moving into the Wilkinsons' was fine for Norma, and fine for Constance, but that she was having none of it?

She could not.

Not with Bessie beside her, awash in tears and gratitude.

Having decided the matter, Norma went off to tell the Wilkinsons about it. Constance rushed the children off to school, leaving Bessie to compose herself in the bathroom.

Fleurette slipped back into her room, where Laura was waiting for her. She dropped onto the bed and her parrot watched her expectantly, as if she knew that something was afoot.

"We might not be going far after all," Fleurette said.

"Far," answered Laura, filling the word with music and longing.

5

Constance wasn't going far, either. She, too, felt a twinge of regret that she would admit to no one.

Norma had always been fond of making proclamations about Constance's life — what sort of books she ought to read, what she ought to make for dinner when it was her turn to cook, what sort of work would suit her best. When Constance ran the female section at the Hackensack jail, Norma knew every inmate by name and instructed Constance on the best way to handle each girl's troubles, without regard to the dictates of law or common sense.

"Hand that one back to her mother," Norma would say about a girl who'd been arrested for shop-lifting. "She has too much leisure time. That's her only problem."

"That's for the judge to say," Constance would tell her. "I can't just unlock the door to the jail and allow her to walk out because my sister told me to."

"Hmph," Norma would say. "The judge doesn't know a thing about it."

But Norma did. Norma knew precisely what was best for everyone in her immediate circle — and for any number of complete strangers, too.

So it came as no surprise when Norma announced that Constance would abandon her plans to return to the Bureau of Investigation and instead find something suitable in Paterson, just down the road from the little village of Hawthorne, where they would be living. Constance had suppressed a shudder, swallowed hard, and agreed.

What else could she do? Of course the job in Washington was gone — jettisoned like any other excess weight tossed off a lifeboat. It was unthinkable that she could leave now, with Bessie expecting a baby.

But it had been unthinkable before that, if Constance wanted to admit it. Even before she knew about the third child, there were the other two to consider. How had she ever imagined that this would work? Would she just return to Washington, begin her new job, and send a few dollars home now and again to keep the children in shoes? How much could she spare, after paying her own room and board in the nation's capital?

How had she ever expected Bessie to survive?

The fact was that it had taken some time to adjust to the reality of Bessie's situation. Before Francis died, Constance had, quite naturally, never given much thought to the prospect of her brother suffering an untimely death.

Even if she had considered the possibility, she would've assumed that Francis had made provisions for his family in case something happened to him.

But here they were, on the other side of the unimaginable, and there was no life insurance policy and surprisingly little in the bank.

There was no explanation, either. Why hadn't Francis been able to put anything extra aside, in all these years? He'd always been the one to lecture Constance on responsibility. How to explain the position he'd left his wife and children in?

It was unfair, of course, and pointless to quarrel with the dead, but it seemed that her relationship with Francis in death was going to carry on as it had in life. What had he been thinking? How could he have been so careless?

He'd always treated Constance, Norma, and Fleurette as if they were barely able to

57

look after themselves. Had he really expected that the three of them could look after his family if he was gone?

It didn't matter anymore what Francis expected. It was too late to second-guess him. All that mattered now was what was in front of them.

So the job in Washington had to go. Although she would never dare complain, it did pain Constance considerably to write to Mr. Allen at the Bureau of Investigation and tell him that she wouldn't be coming to Washington after all.

"If I could conduct Bureau business from here in Paterson," she wrote, "I would happily do so, but with the death of my brother, circumstances require that I remain near my family."

Mr. Allen replied at once with condolences and expressions of regret. While the Bureau did in fact employ a number of agents in other cities — someone had to keep an eye on Chicago, after all — any training program for new recruits, especially one as novel as a school for women, must be carried out in Washington, under his direct supervision.

"As I am only the Acting Chief," he wrote, "I don't expect to be here for more than six months myself, one of them already gone.

But if you are able to return to Washington before my departure, I would endeavor to find a place for you."

In this way, he closed the door to Constance's career at the Bureau as softly and kindly as he could. It was a punch in the gut to Constance, but she bore it. After Francis's death, every subsequent blow was just more of the same. What's one more wound to the already wounded?

Norma, of course, knew nothing of the toll this took on Constance, because Norma only looked to conquering the next task and the one after that. There was no room for regret in Norma's view of the world, only what was ahead.

So it was Norma who took it upon herself to find suitable work for Constance close to home. She read to Constance daily from the papers.

"The Hotel Hamilton wants a lady bookkeeper," Norma would say from behind her paper as soon as Constance appeared in the kitchen in the morning.

One day she called, "Here's one for a lady. Must be good with figures for general office work and stenography, and must have experience at silk concern."

Norma put the paper down. "Would putting a silk man in jail count as experience at a silk concern?"

"Isn't there anything besides book-keeping?" asked Constance.

"Saleslady for fancy goods and toiletries," Norma offered. "Other than that it's all factory work. Winders and starchers, mostly. Unless you want to be a housekeeper, but you've never kept your own house, so I don't know why you would keep anyone else's."

On it went, day after day, with little in the way of interesting prospects for Constance.

It was Mr. Heath — now Officer Heath, patrolling the streets of Paterson in his uniform — who suggested that she apply for a position as store detective at Schoonmaker & Company. Constance snorted at the idea.

"I tried that line of work before," she said. "Years ago, before you hired me. If I recall, I was told I was too tall and too conspicuous. If I applied today, I'd probably be told that I'm also too well-qualified."

"I know Mr. Schoonmaker," Officer Heath said. "He said he'd interview you himself at my recommendation. He's a businessman. He only wants people to stop walking out the door with his goods in their pockets."

"Well, I suppose someone has to guard the gloves," she said dispiritedly.

60

If anyone knew what it meant to take such an enormous step down in prestige and pay, it was Officer Heath.

"It'll get you through," he said.

"And that's all I'm after," she said.

She presented herself the very next day and had no difficulty in talking her way into the position. Mr. Schoonmaker, she discovered, had been a supporter of Officer Heath's during his tenure as sheriff. "I liked the way he ran that jail," he said. "Put it on more of a business-like footing. Had the inmates doing the cooking so they might learn a trade. Sent the able-bodied men out to my brother's farm in the summer and had them raise a crop. Kept the jail in potatoes and onions all winter long, did you know that?"

"I ate many a bowl of potato soup from the jail kitchen," Constance said. "I usually stayed overnight, in a jail cell alongside my inmates, and ate what they ate."

Mr. Schoonmaker nearly jumped out of his chair at that. "Now, you see, that's just the sort of idea I'm talking about! Let the inmates know they're not so different from the rest of us. How are they ever to join society again if they're treated as outcasts?"

"There's something to that," Constance said, "but first, we do have to show them the error in their ways, particularly if they're pocketing bottles off the perfume counter."

"When my father opened this store," Mr. Schoonmaker said, leaning comfortably back in his chair, having already made up his mind about Constance, "everything was kept in a case or behind the counter. You'd walk in and ask to see a pair of gloves or a box of handkerchiefs. There was no thought of just spreading the merchandise out where it could be fingered by anyone passing by. The old man would be shocked to see how we have it today, with dresses hanging on racks and shoes set out like apples at a market."

"I remember how it was in your father's day," Constance said, "but you're right to change with the times."

She let those words hang in the air, the implication clear. Changing with the times might include hiring a rather formidable-looking lady detective.

"Indeed," said Mr. Schoonmaker. "You'd be assigned primarily to hosiery and ladies' smalls. We're closed Sundays, of course, but Fridays and Saturdays are our busiest days. Expect to work late, because we need you here when the crowds are."

With that, she was hired on at the rate of eighteen dollars per week, only a few pennies less than she'd been earning before the war.

She resigned herself to guarding beaded purses and hosiery. What choice did she have?

6

Norma, for her part, took charge of the household as if she were running a small battalion. It was her firm belief that a pregnant woman should not under any circumstances manage the heavy chores, like laundry and mopping and rug-beating. Norma took on all of that, along with any small repairs that needed doing. Bessie allowed her to cook breakfast but would not otherwise relinquish control of the kitchen, to everyone's relief.

Apart from her indifferent cooking, Norma was in every way qualified to run a household. She stuck to a schedule and she kept everything in order. She did not, however, have an eye for decorating. She never bothered to put out the kitchen towels that matched the curtains, each of them sporting identical trim sewed on by Bessie herself, nor could she remember to put the worn checkered rug at the back door, where no one would see it, and to put the nice new striped runner at the front door, to please the guests. Once an item was clean, Norma put it back into use, regardless of color scheme or symmetry or the preferences of others.

Nonetheless, with six Kopps traipsing in and out and a seventh on the way, there was an inordinate amount of scrubbing, washing, rinsing, and hanging out to dry that had to happen every day. Norma simply stepped in and did it, and no one complained about mismatched towels.

She also took responsibility for the farm — the selling of it, in this case, rather than the operation of it. Since the funeral, she had been running around to appointments with builders, surveyors, and anyone else who might have an opinion about the most expedient and profitable way to offer the place for sale. The house, she believed, would be in good condition after a little sprucing up, and the barn was perfectly serviceable. The dairy down the road continued to rent parcels of land, which could bring in a little profit for any buyer who didn't mind having the neighbor's cows roaming around. There was a great deal to do: agreements to be signed, arrangements to be made, repairs to be undertaken or hired out, and a full-scale cleaning, top to bottom, inside and out.

She handled most of the work at the farm herself. Nothing suited Norma more than solitary drudgery. She didn't like helpers: she knew exactly what to do and how to do it, and couldn't be bothered to explain it to anyone else. Other people tended to leave things half-done, while she knew how to stay on a job until it was finished, and then move on to the next, and to do it all in such an orderly fashion that one task never interfered with the next.

She would never, for instance, undertake a painting project if there were windows to be caulked: better to do all the caulking and trimming and then to paint, and then to repair the shutters while they were down for painting, and hang them last. Others she had worked alongside — including her very own sisters — would go about such a project entirely backwards and set them back a month.

Her afternoons at the farm, then, were absorbing if not contented. It was difficult not to think of France, and the countryside there, and the villagers and farmers who were undoubtedly out themselves right then, undertaking the very same tasks, only with older and better tools and materials.

Norma thought fondly of the slate roof-tiles, some of them dating back centuries and held together with lichen and coal-dust, so vastly superior to her own wood shingles. In France one could outfit a barn entirely with metal fittings hand-forged by someone's *grand-père:* hinges, handles, nails, bolts, all of it. One could, for that matter, have any sort of metal pounded back into place the next time the farrier came around to shoe the horses.

It was all so sensible, the way country life was organized in France. They'd had centuries to work out their particular ways, and they stuck with them, even under the threat of war or modernity.

As Norma went around the farmhouse, adjusting doors that no longer closed properly, banging floor boards back into place, and scouring windows glazed in dust and mildew, she couldn't help but wish for a centuries-old homestead, built by great-grandparents who laid each stone with the certainty that the walls would shelter successive generations, who would live on past anything they could imagine.

That was not to be the case for their farmhouse. It would go to someone else, and the Kopps would move on. Norma didn't mind the idea of living at the Wilkinsons' — she never minded the most practical solution to any problem — but she could see now a transience to their way of living that was to be the new order of things: Francis gone, a baby coming, Constance back from Washington but probably not forever, Fleurette with one foot always out the door, Lorraine half-grown and Frankie Jr. not far behind her . . .

Her family looked, to Norma, like the inside of a train station, with everyone rushing off in a different direction on separate timetables. Even with a hammer in hand and a mouthful of nails, she couldn't fix them into place.

At night she thought of Aggie, and how Aggie said that she'd grown to love the tumult and chaos of war-time service. Nothing was the same from day to day. There was no dinner hour. A fresh influx of faces appeared before her every time the train came through. They'd invented new ways to bandage wounds, learned new treatments for diseases they'd never seen at home, and picked up a smattering of words in a new language.

Aggie came alive in the middle of such pandemonium. She never wanted to give it up.

What would have become of Norma, if

she had stayed in Aggie's whirlwind, and let it go to work on her a little longer?

She couldn't imagine. As the days passed, she saw no reason to try.

7

"We're going over to the Wilkinsons' to measure for furniture," Norma said. "You ought to come and have a look at the curtains. They'll need to be done over."

But Fleurette couldn't bear to go measuring for curtains. Innumerable projects awaited her: not just curtains but table runners, kitchen towels, upholstery, a spring wardrobe for — well, for all of them, including Bessie, whose dresses needed constant letting out, and the children, who got taller by the week.

And then there would be tiny gowns for a new Kopp baby, the one task Fleurette relished. She was, in her mind, already adorning a layette with rosebuds. This baby deserved a beautiful new beginning.

But measuring for curtains? She wasn't ready. She hadn't set foot inside the Wilkinsons' house and couldn't bring herself to do so yet. That was her future, boxed inside those walls. She would settle into it eventually — but not today.

"I'll look at the curtains later," Fleurette said. "It's time I went out to pick up some seamstressing."

That was how Norma put it, as if seamstressing had been left alongside the road and she had merely to go along with a bag and a sharp stick to collect it all.

But what good would seamstressing do them? How much could she expect to earn, at piece rates? And what of her expenses — fabric and thread and notions?

It occurred to her, as she walked along Hawthorne's little business district, that Norma hadn't given these questions any consideration. She had merely dropped Fleurette into the slot that belonged to her, that of reliable seamstress and dutiful youngest sister, laboring for pennies.

Fleurette was constitutionally opposed to living her life according to Norma's dictates and couldn't help but wonder if there was another way. Why not put together an act, as she'd planned to all along, and convince Mr. Bernstein to start booking her into theaters? Perhaps a slightly better salary could be negotiated, one that would pay more of her touring expenses, leaving her with an entire paycheck that she could send home, as long as she was willing to dine on tea and crackers every night, and she was.

Surely, under such a scheme, she could contribute more to Bessie and the children's upkeep than she'd earn taking up hems and dropping waistlines in Paterson.

As she hopped on board the street-car, this newly invigorated version of her future came into ever sharper and brighter focus. Wouldn't her sisters be happy not to have her underfoot? Wouldn't Bessie be pleased to see her return to the theater? Bessie — having come from more cheerful and less judgmental stock and therefore able to exude such unencumbered goodwill toward others — always expressed unblemished delight at seeing her female relations pursuing their ambitions. Surely she would approve.

And although Bessie would need an extra pair of hands around the place, would she really need three extra pairs? Lorraine was old enough to help with the baby. Norma would always be around — what else would Norma do, but look after things — and then there was Constance, available for whatever needed doing when she wasn't on duty at that dull little department store in Paterson.

Fleurette was becoming convinced that such an arrangement would benefit all of them. She would send her remittance home faithfully and, more than that, she'd send little gifts for the baby (booties knitted backstage), and newspaper clippings and programs for Lorraine to paste into a book of keepsakes. She'd be the glamorous aunt in the theater.

It wasn't that she didn't want to offer comfort and companionship to Bessie and the children. Of course she did. But how much comfort did Fleurette have to give, when she was so miserable herself?

And what a relief it would be to return to the stage! The theater was a wonderful place to become someone else entirely. At the theater she could put on a disguise. She could wear a costume, paint her face, and play a part. That's what the audience paid for. They came to see an imaginary girl, singing her pretty songs, throwing out her clever lines, living in a candy-colored painted backdrop.

Fleurette wanted desperately to be that imaginary girl. She wanted anything but the life that her sisters were busy taking measurements for at that very moment.

She found Freeman Bernstein at his office in Fort Lee, where he usually spent his afternoons taking calls and answering letters. He chomped habitually at a cigar and shouted into the telephone, which meant that she could both hear him and smell him before she knocked at the door.

"My stars, it's Miss Kopp!" he shouted when he saw her, putting the receiver down in mid-sentence. "And where is your fine feathered friend?"

"In rehearsals," Fleurette answered gaily. Here was a taste of the world she loved! She was back in it already.

"I hope you've brought me a song list," Mr. Bernstein said. "And where are those publicity pictures?"

"I'll have it all to you next week," Fleurette said. "I have just —"

But then she dissolved into a coughing fit and was obliged to grope around in her pockets for a lozenge. She turned away so that Mr. Bernstein wouldn't see the tears running down her face, tears brought on by the coughing but also from the maddening frustration of a voice she couldn't control.

"You might need more than a week," Mr. Bernstein said quietly, once she'd settled down. "Do you suppose you can sing me a line?"

What choice did she have but to try? She stood tall, gathered her breath, and reached for a familiar line.

There's a little bit of bad in every good little girl . . .

But her voice wouldn't come. She choked on the exhale. Freeman put his cigar down with the air of a man admitting defeat.

"I have just a little trouble controlling my breath," Fleurette said, coughing discreetly into her handkerchief again. "It's getting better, truly. It's just those high notes . . ."

When she saw the look on Mr. Bernstein's face — the resignation of a doctor delivering bad news — she dropped into a chair across from him and waited, already defeated. Here was yet another person pronouncing her fate.

"Look, sweetheart. I've seen girls bounce back from a thing like this. You can, too. But don't sing. In fact, don't even think about singing. Go do something else. Keep yourself busy. Give it a few more months. Wait for better weather. It's too cold and dry right now. Let's see how you do in the spring."

In the spring? She hadn't been on the stage since September. She'd already waited an eternity. Now she had to wait for the snow to melt?

But what could she do? She'd failed the audition. Mr. Bernstein wasn't about to put a girl on salary who couldn't find the notes.

It occurred to her then that Mr. Bernstein might have a line on a better class of seamstressing work. A costuming job at the movie studios in Fort Lee would be profitable and infinitely more interesting than the more mundane business of alterations. Besides, the actresses would bring her their own dresses for tailoring, and even the cameramen and the directors would come to her if they needed a cuff repaired or a pair of trousers let out.

Last time she'd worked at the studios, she'd had more business than she could handle. Why not pick that back up again, until her voice came around? And was it too much to hope that one of those directors might offer her a part in the pictures?

"I suppose you're right," she said. "All I need is a little more rest, and something to keep body and soul together for a while. What do you have for me at the studios right now? Not on the stage, but in the costume department?"

He sat back in his chair and blew out a long, discouraged breath. "Listen, sweetheart, the moving pictures are moving. They're going out to California."

"California? All the way out there? But the actresses are here," Fleurette said.

"The actresses are going, too. Looks like 1918 was the last good year for Fort Lee and the movie business. We had a coal shortage like everybody else, and we couldn't keep those studios heated. Everybody's been out with that damned Spanish 'flu. Who wouldn't want to go to California? Get some sunshine, make a picture on the beach."

"On the beach?" Fleurette tried to imagine it. Didn't actresses perform on a stage?

Freeman shrugged. "I don't know what they're doing out there. All I know is, they're not doing it here. Not right now."

"I wonder what Mr. Edison thinks of that," Fleurette said.

"Ask him yourself, sweetheart," said Mr. Bernstein. "I'm sorry, but I've got nothing for you. Come back to me when you can sing."

Come back to me when you can sing.

She made a dejected figure as she slunk out of Mr. Bernstein's office and waited again for the street-car, counting her tokens. Her aspirations had been so small that she almost pitied them. A fledgling stage act, opening in third-rate theaters. If not that, then a sewing table in the corner of a cavernous studio, where she'd work furiously at turning a nursing costume into a dress meant for a shepherdess and back again.

What modest ambitions they were, yet she'd pinned so much on them.

All she wanted was her own future, the one she'd dreamed of all along, not the one dictated to her by tragedy and loss.

She wanted the Francis-shaped hole in her life to get smaller, not to grow so large that she couldn't see the edge of it.

But that was selfish, wasn't it? No one in her family could get away from their grief. Why should she?

The street-car rolled up eventually and took her back to Paterson, where she lingered dispiritedly along the city's main streets, taking an appraising look at the dress shops and tailors, wondering if she might get hired into a shop for a month or two. There was no profit to be made in taking in mending: that was work any woman could do for herself and her family and would, now that men were back from the war and women returning home. A shop would put her on salary, at least, and she wouldn't have to bring in her own materials.

Just as she was considering that, she turned a corner onto Hamilton and nearly walked right into John Ward.

"Miss Kopp!" he cried, as if meeting an old friend. He took a deep bow and tipped his hat. There was something so jolly about Mr. Ward: she couldn't help but be cheered by him. "What brings you out this afternoon?"

"Work," said Fleurette, "or the lack of it."

"Isn't there always work on the stage for a pretty girl?"

"It's dress-making I'm after," Fleurette said, "at the moment."

"Not my line," said Mr. Ward, "but could you do something about the elbows on this jacket?"

He whipped off his suit jacket and presented it to her like a gift. It wasn't just the elbows that were frayed: the cuffs were an embarrassment as well.

"Yes, it's terrible," Mr. Ward said, before Fleurette could make a pronouncement. "Take it, please, before it destroys my reputation."

How strange, to see a man in his shirt-sleeves, right there on the street! But that was the sort of man Mr. Ward was: unembarrassed and unencumbered by convention.

"I can patch the elbows and replace the cuffs," Fleurette said, "but isn't there a Mrs.

79

Ward to look after your things?"

"Yes, let's not tell her about this little dalliance with my cuffs," Mr. Ward said. "Say, if you could use some extra work, we've lost our girl."

"Your girl? I'm not a secretary."

He shrugged and gave her a half-smile. "We can always find a secretary. It's just that most of the girls who apply aren't suited for the other part of the job. And if they are, they have the damned annoying habit of marrying the client, and then we lose them."

"But you don't think I'm at any risk of getting married," Fleurette said. She was a little offended by the insinuation, although the last thing she wanted at that moment was a husband telling her what to do.

"You Kopp girls don't seem like the marrying types," he said, "but I've been wrong before."

"There's no such thing as a Kopp girl," Fleurette said. "There's Constance, and you know what she's like."

"I'm afraid I do."

"There's Norma, and you'd rather not find out what she's like."

"I'll take your word for that."

"And then there's me, and I don't take after either one of them."

"Who do you take after? Was there a saucy aunt or a granny with a noteworthy past?"

Now Fleurette was smiling. He brought it out in her. She said, "I can only hope so. Are you going to tell me what the rest of the job entails?"

"Well, Miss Kopp, in the divorce game, the only thing that matters is the collection of evidence. That and the fee, of course."

"Yes, I take it the fee matters a great deal to you."

"That's why it's called work," he said cheerfully. "They have to pay you to do it. Anyway, we're looking to hire a girl to help with the evidence. Sometimes, you understand, the couple wishes to part ways, but there's nothing to put before a judge. No one's run off with the milkman, or taken up with the stenographer. The poor wretches simply don't want to be married anymore. Can you see the difficulty that poses?"

"Judges are awfully particular about finding fault and placing blame," she said.

"Exactly. Sometimes, neither party's at fault. But one of them can pretend to be! Do you follow?"

"I'm beginning to," Fleurette said warily.

"Of course you do, you're a bright girl. Now, in ninety-nine cases out of a hundred, the husband will sacrifice his reputation, if

81

it means putting the unpleasantness of an ill-conceived marriage behind him. All that's required is a pretty girl and a man with a camera."

Fleurette took a step back. What was he proposing? "If you think I'm going to jump in a man's bed for money —"

"No, no, Miss Kopp! It's nothing like that. The whole business could happen in your mother's parlor, it's that cordial. All we need is a girl in the arms of the man. Why, we don't even need to see her face! It's nothing but a bit of play-acting, don't you see? You only have to pretend to be the other girl, so the wife can act shocked and sue her husband for divorce."

"Do you mean that you want me to be . . ."

Fleurette wasn't sure what to call it, but Mr. Ward supplied the term.

"A professional co-respondent. A lady" — he nodded at her and emphasized the word *lady* — "who is hired to serve as the second respondent in a divorce lawsuit filed by the wronged wife. The first respondent being the husband, of course."

"That's a fancy title, but it sounds like the sort of thing Constance's jailbirds would've been mixed up in," Fleurette said.

He shrugged at that. "One or two of them

might have," he said, "but that wouldn't land them in jail. I wouldn't ask you to break the law. I'm a lawyer myself, remember?"

"I'm not sure what that has to do with it," she said, "but this isn't exactly the sort of play-acting I do."

He was still grinning down at her, flashing that winsome smile of his. "Take the jacket anyway. Think about it while you stitch me up."

8

Mr. Ward's offer stayed on her mind.

It was tawdry, Fleurette knew that. It was illicit. It might've even been illegal, despite his assurances to the contrary. (Did he actually tell her that what he was proposing was legal, or had he merely said, in response to her question, that he was a lawyer? That was just the sort of verbal sleight of hand that a lawyer would get up to.)

There was also the question of the soon-to-be-divorced men themselves. Was she to be left alone for hours and hours with a strange man, waiting for the photographer to pop in, trying to steer the conversation in a direction that would keep his mind off the very thing that they were pretending to do?

And what of those photographs? What happened to them? Wouldn't they go before a judge? How could she be sure she wouldn't be recognized? Even with her back to the camera, wouldn't the judge start to notice a sameness to the pictures in the divorce cases that came before him? If all the girls in the pictures presented as evidence by the firm of Ward & McGinnis showed a woman of the same height, with the same general hairstyle, the same slope of the shoulders — wouldn't that start to look suspicious?

The solution presented itself even as she was trying not to consider the problem too closely: a disguise. That's how she'd handle it.

She would wear a wig, and a different hat every time, and perhaps a cut of dress that made her shoulders broader, her figure a little more generous. Sometimes she might stand on a footstool, if it could be left out of the picture, to appear taller.

And of course, she'd have to tailor her manner of dress to the man in question. A wealthy man wouldn't leave his wife for a dowdy matron in a poplin house dress, nor would a railroad worker have the luck or fortitude to land a glamorous young woman in silk and furs. And each of her characters (already she was thinking of herself as playing a part) would require a false name. She couldn't very well go around answering to a name like Fleurette Kopp in Paterson. Everyone would know that she was Constance's sister, and that would only invite trouble.

By the time the elbows on Mr. Ward's jacket had been patched, his cuffs replaced, and the buttons re-stitched for good measure, Fleurette had allowed herself to be carried away by the idea. Once she'd taken up the practicalities, she had a hard time shaking it. Could she justify a new pair of shoes, for instance, to give her a little more height? And how would she come by the wigs? Might Freeman Bernstein have a line on a collection of them, perhaps in an abandoned closet in Fort Lee, discarded by actresses who'd left their old war-time styles behind for a sleek new Californian bob?

Then she landed, of course, on the question of money. Nothing in the way of compensation had been discussed. But for a job like this, her expenses would be considerable and her risk high.

What guarantees could Mr. Ward provide that the police would never break into the room where she was posing as a disreputable woman with a married man? What assurances would she have that the men would never be drunk or brutish?

It didn't occur to her, at that moment, to name a price that she felt would be fair for such a job. She was hardly accustomed to working at all — she'd only been at it a few years — and when an employer such as Freeman Bernstein named a sum, she simply took it. It was quite an achievement to land any sort of work at all. Demanding more money than the amount offered wasn't, as yet, in her repertoire.

Even her seamstressing work didn't require her to do much in the way of fixing a price for her services. Before the war, everyone knew, more or less, what the going rate was for an alteration, an adjustment to a hemline, or a new collar. She'd charge a quarter here and fifty cents there, just as everyone else did, and in that manner might hope to earn as much as ten dollars per week.

The war had changed that, of course. Everything was upended now. Prices had flown sky-high for certain goods owing to shortages, but at the same time no one had any money in their pockets and simply went without such niceties as a hired seamstress. It just wasn't a lucrative occupation at the moment.

For that reason, the idea of working for Mr. Ward had its appeal. She enjoyed turning over in her mind exactly how she'd go about it. Her version of events sounded quite adventurous: late-night assignations, disguises, false identities, and dashing divorcés.

But she might still have returned Mr. Ward's jacket to him, collected her dollar, and gone on her way, had she not found Bessie at the kitchen table late at night, shuffling through the bills.

Bessie looked a little better, now that her secret was out and her plans settled. The children had been told that they were to expect a new brother or sister, and took the news with grace if not with a bit of confusion. "How can we have a baby without a daddy?" Frankie Jr. had asked, and Bessie had just slicked his hair down and told him that Francis would always be his father, and he would be the baby's father, too.

Her color had improved and the morning sickness had abated somewhat. Still she looked tired and drained of her old good cheer, as she pushed papers around on the kitchen table and tallied sums in a green ledger still filled with Francis's handwriting.

"Is everything all right?" Fleurette said, sliding into a chair next to her.

"It will be," Bessie said, trying to turn a reassuring face to her. "Only . . ."

But that was as far as she could get before she crumpled again. The tears took over, and she put her face in her hands. "I'm sorry," she said, her head down. "I'm so tired of crying."

Fleurette pushed the bills and the ledger out of the way. "Why don't you let Constance manage all this? She'll handle it perfectly and you won't ever hear a word about it."

Bessie laughed a little at that. It was enough to let her raise her head again and wipe her eyes. "It isn't the numbers I mind," she said. "It's what they add up to. Look at this. A hundred and sixty dollars for the funeral. Forty dollars for the doctor. Heating oil. Lorraine needs shoes. Frankie barely fits into his coat."

"I'll have a look at that coat," Fleurette muttered, but she saw the difficulty.

"I had no idea we'd been living so close to the bone," Bessie said. "Francis never mentioned it. Whatever we needed, it was always there."

"We'll take care of it," Fleurette said, although she had no idea how they would.

The question hung in the air, so clearly stated that neither of them needed to say it aloud.

How many women would it take to replace one man's salary?

9

That settled it. Two nights later, Fleurette went out of the house wearing a very good dress concealed under her plain coat.

Mr. Ward, she had discovered, kept a closet of ladies' coats, dresses, hats, and wigs for the women in his employ to wear on their jobs. The garments had been purchased, over the years, by the women themselves and reflected the styles of the moment. They would've been lovely dresses two or three years ago, but tastes had changed since the war and everything had to be done over. Waists had to be let out to accommodate bodies newly liberated from corsets, hemlines raised to show not just ankles but a glimpse of calves, and bits of lace and dowdy wooden buttons removed from necklines and wrists.

None of this bothered Fleurette, of course. A pile of seamstressing work was exactly the cover she needed to explain the hours she'd be away from home and the money coming in.

And what a lot of money it would be! Mr. Ward had laughed as he tossed her a dollar for the repairs to his jacket and offered her twenty for an hour's work at a hotel.

Twenty dollars! At this rate . . . . Fleurette could hardly calculate what her new wages would buy, or the speed at which the money would accumulate.

Sneaking out of the house was perhaps the riskiest part of the entire operation. She felt like a spy, up in her room putting on her disguise — but not the kind of spy Constance had been during the war, stomping around in factories and printing shops. She was the glamorous kind, with a mission that might involve a glass of Champagne taken in the line of duty.

But first she had to get past her sisters.

Bessie had gone to bed early, now that she had plenty of female relations to take care of the children and the washing-up. Norma was paging noisily through a magazine on farm management, and issuing her opinions as though anyone in the house wanted to hear them. ("You'll never keep goats in a pen like that, and I ought to write and tell them.") Constance, who stopped in most evenings although she was still living at the boarding-house, sprawled on the sofa, her enormous feet propped up in a manner that Francis never would have allowed, snoring underneath a well-worn paperbound book called *Department Store Merchandise Manual,* Volume 2.

What tedium! Fleurette would've worked for Mr. Ward for free, if it meant getting away from those two for a night. As she walked out — tiptoed, practically, not wanting to disturb either one of them — Norma looked up from her magazine long enough to say, "Where on earth are you going at this hour?"

Constance, jolted from her sleep, gave a giant snort and looked up too. "You aren't leaving, are you?"

"I'm going to see a lady for a fitting."

"A fitting, in the middle of the night?" said Norma.

"It's only seven."

"I'll walk with you," said Constance, "as soon as I can find my boots." She began rooting around under the sofa for them, still groggy.

"I'm only going to the street-car. I'm late as it is," said Fleurette, and practically ran out the door.

Petey — Mr. McGinnis, but Mr. Ward called him Petey and Fleurette couldn't help but do so herself — was waiting for her around the corner, just out of sight. He didn't like her walking after dark any more than Constance did: he stood alongside his automobile, watching for her anxiously.

"Good evening, Miss Kopp," he said as she came into view. "It's chilly tonight, but I've brought a blanket —"

"Let's get going," Fleurette said, diving into the auto. "My sister's right behind me."

Petey knew how to make a discreet get-away. Hawthorne was not much more than a village, and it took only a right turn and then a left before they were out of town and rolling toward Paterson.

Once inside the city, Petey left his auto down the street — not wanting to be remembered by the hotel's valets and porters — and soon the two of them were walking down an alley behind the Metropolitan Hotel in downtown Paterson, picking their way past the fish bones and milk bottles. Petey pushed open the kitchen door, and they were inside.

It was Petey's responsibility to put enough coins in the hands of the bellhops and dishwashers to grant Fleurette safe passage into the hotel. The Metropolitan had no ladies' entrance and no plans to install one, but that was just as well: according to both

Ward and McGinnis, a ladies' entrance was much more closely chaperoned than a service entrance. This was the safest way for an unescorted woman to walk in.

The kitchen staff at any hotel are accustomed to a certain amount of illicit trade strolling past the fry station: a hotel that doesn't have a regular supply of liquor, cash, jewels, and pretty girls sneaking in the back isn't serving its customers well. As such, not a single head turned when Petey and Fleurette hastened by.

It occurred to her, as she raced past the kitchen boys, Petey's arm around her, her head turned demurely away under the brim of a jaunty navy blue hat, that she'd been a fool to think that patching elbows and cuffs would get her anywhere. Seamstresses worked at one rung of the economic ladder, but here was another rung entirely, one populated by attorneys and wealthy clients wanting out of their difficulties.

In her good blue silk, with a bit of stylish green embroidery at the neck and the wrists, she was one of them. What a delicious rush it gave her to feel like someone else entirely for a night!

Petey knew the back passages of the Metropolitan well: it was a favorite hotel of the firm. He took her up a narrow set of stairs used only by housekeepers, and stopped in the stairwell, panting a bit, at the fourth floor.

"You all right, miss?" he asked, looking her over. They hadn't had a chance to speak since he smuggled her in through the alley.

"I'm just fine," she said, although in fact, that high fizzy feeling was spilling over into trepidation. The moment was at hand, the game was about to begin. Could she really do it?

Until then she'd been thinking only of the preparations: the costume, the alterations to her hairstyle (Should she go ahead and cut it? She hadn't dared yet), the placement of the hat so that her face could easily be hidden, and the choice of a *nom de plume.*

She was handy with invented names. When Constance was working at the Bureau of Investigation, during the war, Fleurette had happily taken up the task of choosing covert names for her sister. Winifred Sedgewick had been a favorite. Henrietta Nutting was, she felt, particularly inspired. Fleurette had participated in one of Constance's spy operations herself and chosen the name Gloria Blossom. She'd always been partial to the name Gloria and thought Blossom would be easy to remember as it was so closely connected to her own name. But she soon found that choosing a name similar to her own didn't matter: what mattered was practicing the name, over and over, saying it aloud, and using it in conversation, until it rolled off the tongue effortlessly.

The name she'd chosen for tonight's performance (already she liked to think of them as performances, and the names merely stage names) was Ella Bennet, the author of an old dress-making guide whose instructions were no longer of any use to her.

Her version of Miss Bennet could be a secretary destined for greater things, she decided, who along the way had fallen in love with a junior executive at the firm. He was married, but it couldn't be helped. They'd fallen hard for one another.

She'd enjoyed every minute of those preparations — the costuming, the hairstyling, the choosing of a name and a demeanor and an invented past — and even relished the adventure of dashing through the kitchen and up the stairs. How long had it been since she'd done something half as exciting? She'd missed having any sort of intrigue in her life.

But now, as they stood in the stairway, the truth of what was about to happen dawned on her. She would walk into the room and a man would be waiting. What took place after that was not entirely under her control.

"Tell me again about Mr. Lyman," Fleurette said.

Petey nodded briskly. Reassuring the girls was part of the business. "He's in advertising. Forty years of age. Enough good years ahead of him to think he can do better than what he has now."

"What he has now? Are you referring to his wife?" Fleurette asked.

Petey put his fingers together under his chin, almost as if he were praying to her. "The wife wants to be released from her marriage vows as much as he does, miss. He's doing the honorable thing by taking the blame himself. If he had a girl on the side already, he wouldn't require our services."

"If neither of them want to be married to the other, a judge ought to set them free," Fleurette said.

"But they don't. It's the law. Adultery and willful desertion are the only ways out. Desertion takes too long and it's a harder case to win."

"All right. And how long will I be alone with him?"

"Three minutes on the dot." Petey reached into his vest and held up a pocket watch, placing it next to her ear so she could hear it tick. "Think of a song that runs to just three minutes. Let that run through your head."

"I suppose he can't get up to much mischief in three minutes," Fleurette conceded.

"He can't get up to any mischief, or he'd have to answer to me. And he'll escort you right out the front door. He put his wife's name in the guest registry, so nobody will think anything of him walking out with a woman. But keep your head down anyway."

"And you'll meet me outside?"

"I'll be waiting."

With that, Fleurette had received all the reassurances she could possibly ask for. It was time to go to work. She summoned up a little nerve. (She might've borrowed a bit of Constance's, if she wanted to admit it, which she did not.) Nonetheless she squared her shoulders and made ready to march in, looking braver than she felt.

"Then let's meet Mr. Lyman," she said.

Mr. Lyman greeted them at the door, as jovial as a host at a dinner party. He was an altogether pleasant-looking man, with kind eyes and just a smattering of silver in his hair. He was quick to smile and greeted them with the air of a natural entertainer.

"My co-conspirator has arrived," he said, giving Fleurette a wink and Petey a handshake. "Will you both come in and . . ." He cocked his head at Petey, as if suggesting that a cigar and a whiskey soda might be on offer before the proceedings got under way.

But Petey was looking up and down the hall, ever mindful of his obligations.

"Three minutes," he said, and pointed back toward the stairway to indicate where he'd wait. His watch was already in his hand.

Mr. Lyman stepped aside to allow Fleurette to enter. The lyrics to "Your Lips Are No Man's Land but Mine" were running through her head: that one went for about three minutes if one sang it at a brisk pace. She had its tempo fixed in her head: the song had already begun.

The room was a welcoming one, done up in deep green and dark wood. At the foot of the bed — she tried not to stare at the bed — was a settee just spacious enough for two.

"Mr. Ward — he's your employer, is that right?" Mr. Lyman inquired. Fleurette nodded. "He knows his business. He likes this hotel because of the way the rooms are arranged. Never stayed here myself."

"Nor I," said Fleurette.

"Well . . ." Here Mr. Lyman paused and

99

rubbed the back of his neck, searching for a way to say it. "He likes it because we can sit here" — pointing to the little tufted settee — "and you'll have your back to the door, and I'll be looking up at the door, over your shoulder, like this . . ."

Here he mimed a look of surprise so lively and comical that Fleurette laughed. This pleased him and he winked conspiratorially at her. "Is that a good face? I've been practicing it."

"It's just right," Fleurette said, "only don't smile, not even a little. Think of something that genuinely frightens you."

"Another twenty years with my wife?" Mr. Lyman asked.

"Worse," Fleurette said. "Your shoelace is caught on the track and a train is coming."

He let out a mock gasp. "That is terrifying."

"We ought to get ourselves settled," Fleurette said.

It occurred to her that Mr. Lyman was not her host, but her client. She could tell him what to do. After tonight, she would be the more experienced of any pairing on one of these jobs — or would some of her clients have been through one divorce already? How much of this sort of thing went on anyway?

Mr. Lyman took his seat obediently. Fleurette sat next to him, her back squarely to the door.

"I'll turn my head just so," she said, tilting to the left, "and you can look up at the door over my shoulder. We're to hold quite still until Petey — until Mr. McGinnis takes three or four pictures."

They were quite close now, their knees almost touching. Mr. Lyman's face was so near that she could smell cigarettes and peppermint. "How old are you anyway — Miss Bennet, is that it? I don't suppose that's your real name?"

"Old enough," she said. "Petey wants a bit of the bed in the picture. He thought it would look more convincing if you threw your jacket down, right there at the corner."

Mr. Lyman obliged. It gave Fleurette a little shiver to have a man undressing so close to her. It wasn't an altogether unpleasant shiver — she'd decided by then that Mr. Lyman meant her no harm. She could feel a warmth coming off of him now, and saw the bulk of his shoulders, the hair at his wrists. She noticed he didn't wear a ring.

"Mr. Ward told me to take it off," he said, following her eye down to his hands. "He said I ought to look like I'm trying to deceive. I'm to put my left hand around here" — he moved carefully, slipping an arm around her but barely touching her back — "so that we can be sure the hand is in the picture."

Just then she heard a footstep in the hall. Mr. Lyman smiled down at her. "I'm going to take you in my arms, you know," he said, his face even closer now. Fleurette became a little entranced by the lines around his eyes. "Don't let it shock you. I haven't had a complaint yet from a girl."

"You have only to convince the camera," Fleurette answered.

Mr. Lyman looked down at her playfully and swept her into an embrace just as the door opened. They were pressed together — heart to heart, as it were — and Mr. Lyman's rough chin brushed her neck as he turned to look over her shoulder. She shivered a little at the sensation and thought Mr. Lyman might've laughed at her reaction.

"You've been caught," Petey said roughly. Fleurette couldn't see him but guessed that he'd had to remind Mr. Lyman to look terrified. She heard the shutter click twice — three times — then a fourth — and all at once she was released from Mr. Lyman's embrace and left alone on the settee to smooth her dress.

The door had already closed behind Petey. The performance was over. Fleurette felt an urge to rush off stage.

"Well, that's all there is to it," Mr. Lyman said. He shrugged on his jacket and looked around the room. There was a little table in the corner and seating for two. "I could send up for some supper, if you like, or . . . ." He looked longingly at the bottles and glasses and ice bucket on the sideboard.

"Mr. McGinnis is waiting for me," Fleurette said. "You're to escort me out through the lobby, but don't actually leave with me."

"I wouldn't think of it," he said. "And where do you go tonight? Back to a room you share with three other girls?"

"It isn't as bad as all that," Fleurette said, but she didn't offer any other details. The less he knew about her, the better.

"Then let's be on our way," he said, and helped her into her coat.

That was the end of her assignment. Mr. Lyman ushered her briskly through the lobby, speaking to her in a low voice so that she had a reason to keep her head turned toward him, the brim of her hat low, and a muffler up high under her chin.

"Who's the next fellow?" Mr. Lyman asked, bending down to her ear.

103

"I don't know if there will be a next fellow," Fleurette said. Was she really going to make a habit of this?

As they neared the doors, she felt him slip something into her pocket.

"I suspect Mr. Ward doesn't pay you enough" came his final words to her, and then she was out on the sidewalk, and Petey was rolling up in his automobile.

Later that night, alone in her room, after she'd handed Bessie the first twenty dollars she'd earned, she remembered what he'd said and pulled an envelope from her coatpocket.

Mr. Lyman had given her another twenty dollars. It was only her first time, and already she'd doubled her salary.

10

"I've just never heard of a seamstress making calls at night before," said Norma at breakfast the next morning.

"I told you already," Fleurette said. "Some of my ladies do their committee work for the relief charities during the day. And some of them have jobs now. You haven't been home long enough to see it, but the offices are filled with girls these days."

"The men are going to want those jobs back, once they're home."

"They might not. It'd be awfully dull compared to what they saw in France."

"Hmmph," said Norma. She steadfastly continued to resist any attempt to bring the conversation around to France. "Nevertheless, if you go out at night, you ought to tell us where you go, and when you'll be back."

"We didn't know where you were for the better part of a year, and you did just fine," Fleurette said.

Norma lifted an eyebrow and began to compose a response, but just then Bessie wandered in, and she let it drop.

Sunday mornings had become a leisurely affair in the recently reconstituted Kopp household: Norma awoke early, supervised the children's breakfast, and stole into Bessie's bedroom with dry toast and tea, which was all she could face at that hour. Fleurette slept late, as was her habit, and Constance turned up around ten and finished any scraps left on the breakfast table.

"I slept better last night than I have in weeks," Bessie said, shooting a meaningful glance at Fleurette.

Was it to be a secret between them that Fleurette had put twenty dollars toward the funeral bill? Fleurette realized that she wasn't sure how and when she'd be expected to make her contributions to the household coffers. Every penny she'd ever earned, until now, went directly into her own purse, where she could spend it as she pleased. Would Norma tally up their expenses and demand a particular sum each week?

Fleurette shuddered at the thought. She'd managed to get by just fine without Norma's constant scrutiny during the war. What exactly would the arrangements be, going

106

forward — financial and otherwise?

Bessie dropped into a chair next to her and gave her a squeeze on the shoulder. If she could simply slip a few dollars to Bessie every week, and see her burden lightened a little at a time, that would suit her just fine.

Constance arrived just then, banging in through the kitchen door with the news that she'd survived her first week at Schoonmaker's and required bacon, fried eggs, and a fresh batch of biscuits to mark the occasion.

"And how many shop-lifters have you put in jail so far?" Norma said.

"None, just yet," Constance said, unwinding her muffler and lifting the lid of the coffee-pot to see what was left. "Mine is more of what you might call a preventative role."

"Which means you go around glaring at people, and scare them off before they can steal anything," said Norma.

"Without discouraging them from buying. Yes, that's about right." She said it in as cheerful a voice as she could muster, but Fleurette saw right through it.

"You're not fooling anyone," Fleurette said. "It sounds dull and inconsequential."

Constance didn't take the bait. "It's here in Paterson, and that's what matters. I'll

107

look for something else once the farm is sold."

"Don't count on the farm just yet," Norma said.

That put a halt to the conversation.

The farm was Norma's responsibility. Since the funeral, she'd busied herself with appointments at builders, surveyors, and anyone else who might have an opinion about the most expedient and profitable way to offer the place for sale. At the rate Norma worked, there was every reason to think she'd have it settled within a matter of weeks.

"I thought the house only needed a little sprucing up," Constance said. "And the barn's perfectly serviceable, isn't it? What else is there to do?"

"It hardly matters what we do to the house," Norma said as she buttered another biscuit. "We won't get nearly enough for it. There are four other farms for sale within thirty miles of ours. They've all been waiting until after the war to sell. Judging by what they're asking, on a per-acre basis, we can't hope to bring in more than two thousand."

"Two thousand, for eighty acres with a home and a barn?" asked Constance indignantly.

"That's only if someone wants ours more than any of the others," Norma said. "How many people are looking to buy a farm just now?"

"I'm not moving back there, if that's your idea," Fleurette said.

"You won't have to," Norma said. "We're going to divide the land into smaller plots, each one suitable for the construction of a new home, and sell them off one at a time. That should bring in closer to four thousand dollars. We'll have enough to buy the Wilkinsons' house and still have something left in the bank."

"But that'll take months," Constance said.

"If we can count on anything, we can count on delays, paperwork, and unanticipated expenses," Norma said. "And we'll owe rent to the Wilkinsons for considerably longer than we expected. But there's no way around it. We'll just have to live close to the bone."

"Aren't we already?" Fleurette said, feeling the extra twenty dollars Mr. Lyman had given her slipping away.

"Exactly. We're used to it, after the war. If we can just continue on a war-time footing, for another year or so, we'll be fine."

"A year!" Fleurette put a hand over her mouth as soon as she said it, but it was too late. Bessie looked mortified.

"You girls are giving up too much," she said. "I can't ask this of you."

It took all three of them to reassure her. "No one has given up more than you, in losing a husband," said Constance.

"And the children, losing their father," Fleurette added.

"And don't forget that the farm is as much yours as ours," Norma said. "We'll see it through."

Bessie didn't look convinced, but before she could say another word, a knock came at the door. Norma glared at the clock: it was half past ten. "I don't know how you get anything done with all these salesmen at the door," she muttered, but she went to answer it anyway, and returned a minute later with an old and weary-looking man in tow.

"Mr. Griggs," Bessie said, pushing herself to her feet. "Girls, you remember Mr. Griggs. Francis's boss."

He nodded and waved at them to stay seated, which they did. None of the Kopps were in what could be called a hospitable frame of mind, having only just begun to grapple with the prospect of another year of sacrifice and war-time living. Visitors were a nuisance generally after a funeral, but now their hospitality was entirely exhausted.

Mr. Griggs looked a bit unsure of himself in the presence of so many unaccommodating women. "I'm sorry to intrude. I didn't have a chance to speak to you at the funeral, and I thought it best to wait a decent interval before . . ."

"That's fine, Mr. Griggs," Bessie said. "Please do sit down. Can we offer you anything? We were just about to put on another pot of coffee."

"No, thank you," he said.

He was a wiry man bordering on frail. Fleurette had the impression that he used to travel to China every year to buy baskets (that was his business, he imported baskets from China), but that became impossible during the war. Francis used to say that Mr. Griggs just didn't have the stamina for such a long voyage anymore and thought that he — Francis — might be asked to go in his place next time.

It occurred to Fleurette that Mr. Griggs was the last person to see Francis alive. What a way to die — to simply drop at his desk, in the middle of an ordinary day of work, and to have his boss looming over him in the final minutes.

They all sat watching him, waiting for him to say what he'd come to say. Fleurette hoped vaguely that he'd brought his check-book. Perhaps Francis was owed a bonus, or the firm had taken out some sort of insurance?

"We're just so terribly sorry about Francis," Mr. Griggs began. He had to clear his throat several times to get through it. "He seemed perfectly well right up until — well, until the last moment. It was all so very fast. We don't believe he suffered at all. I want you to know that."

"You told me so at the time," Bessie said. "He was surrounded by people who cared about him. That means a great deal to me."

Mr. Griggs seemed to be determined to deliver some sort of prepared speech. "And he was very much at the center of everything we did, as you must know."

"Yes, of course," Bessie said. "He was entirely devoted to your company. You've been so good to him over the years."

"Well, he was good to us, too," Mr. Griggs said.

Norma had even less patience for plati-tudes now than she did before the war. She stood up as if to indicate that his visit was over. She could be quite formidable, even in the way she let the kitchen chair scrape the floor as she rose.

"If you're missing him so much, maybe

112

you'd like to offer his job to one of us," she said, a little too forcefully. "Didn't Francis keep the books? Constance can do that. Any one of us could drive a truck, or sweep the floor, or take orders, or —"

"Oh, but I've found a position already, and I'm sure Mr. Griggs —" put in Constance, but Norma wouldn't hear it.

"There's a baby on the way," Norma pronounced, causing a startled Mr. Griggs to sweep his eye over the four of them, perhaps uncertain as to who, exactly, was to be the bearer of the next generation of Kopps. "So we don't have time for condolences. We need the work. Tell us what exactly Francis did down there, and we'll sort out who can do it. His salary can just keep coming to this address as before."

Poor Mr. Griggs looked as though he'd walked into the wrong house and couldn't find his way out. He took an uneven step backwards and said, "I can see I've come at a difficult time. Perhaps I might call on you again, once you've . . . ." But whatever he meant to say trailed away, as he fumbled for his coat and hat.

The Kopps uttered their half-hearted good-byes and he was gone.

113

11

It wasn't the year of miserly living that most worried Fleurette. It was the possibility that a year might turn into a lifetime. How many stories had she heard of penniless widows, of destitute spinsters? Poverty was like a leak in a boat: once the hull was punctured, it started to list, and to take on water, and soon it became impossible to right.

Although she'd never realized it, the farm had always been, to Fleurette, a source of great untapped wealth that would act as a sort of bulwark against misfortune. Over the years she'd felt trapped by it, and yoked to it, but she'd also felt the solidity of it beneath her feet. Eighty acres has a pleasing heft to it, like a pocketful of coins.

But what good could it do them now? It had not escaped Fleurette's notice that Norma had been vague about what, exactly, the proceeds from the sale would mean for them, eventually, beyond the purchase of the Wilkinsons' house. Would there be enough left to keep Bessie and the children fed and housed for years to come?

It seemed unlikely.

It seemed equally unlikely that Constance's salary could furnish any sort of comfortable existence for all six of them — seven, once the baby arrived.

And surely no one believed that Fleurette's seamstressing wages would do more than pay the egg and butter man.

With buttons and hems and eggs and butter on her mind, she paid another visit to Mr. Ward.

"It's about time you turned up," he said when she appeared in his office. "I was about to resort to throwing pebbles at your window. Petey says he knows some Morse code and we thought we might try signaling from the roof across the street."

"You'd never get a Morse code signal past Norma," Fleurette said. "You'll just have to wait for me to drop in."

"I wasn't sure if you would. Some girls don't find the work to their liking."

"That's why it's called work. You have to pay me to do it. Didn't you say that?"

"It sounds like something I'd say. But Mr. Lyman wasn't so awful, was he? I wouldn't mind a cuddle with him myself, if he bought me dinner after."

"He was very nice," Fleurette said. "Are they all like that?"

"They ought to be," Mr. Ward said vaguely. Fleurette thought again that everything Mr. Ward said could be interpreted two ways.

"And did the pictures come out?"

"Works of art, every one of them," Mr. Ward said. He pushed them across his desk and Fleurette studied them. She thought she looked quite dramatic, even from the back. "Girl Caught in Scandal," the caption could read. She would've enjoyed making a scrapbook of them, except that her sisters would find it. Criminals like to keep a record of their misdeeds — she remembered Constance saying that. She couldn't fall into such an easy trap. With a good deal of reluctance, she handed them back.

"Do you have another Mr. Lyman for me?"

"Well, how does a Mr. Finley sound?" he asked, shuffling through the files on his desk. "He has something to do with shipping and, would you believe it, his wife has run off with a sailor."

"Then why aren't we trying to get a picture of Mrs. Finley with the sailor?"

asked Fleurette.

"Because, I remind you once again, my client is doing the honorable thing," Mr. Ward said. "He doesn't want to see his wife photographed *in flagrante delicto,* and her name dragged through the papers as a common — well, as a woman who would run around with a man who is not her husband. He loves her still, you see."

"I wonder why," Fleurette said.

"Some of them do," Mr. Ward said. "Now, this fellow isn't the type to take a room at the Metropolitan. Since Mrs. Finley has already left the premises, you're to pay him a visit at his home. He just lives over in —"

"In his own house?" Fleurette said. "Isn't that awfully *familiar?*"

"Shocking, isn't it?" Mr. Ward said mildly. "If you think a judge looks unkindly on a married man entertaining a lady in a hotel room, you should see what he'll say about inviting such a lady into the marital home. Right there in the sitting-room, next to the family portraits, the vixen's dainty feet pushing the missus's knitting-basket under the settee. It's an outrage, wouldn't you agree?"

"I suppose it doesn't matter where I go," Fleurette said, "as long as Petey's quick with the camera."

117

"It's even better this way," Mr. Ward said. "Petey'll be inside already, rummaging around in the kitchen, most likely enjoying a glass of Mrs. Finley's cooking sherry while the two of you get comfortable. You'll be in and out in a minute."

It wasn't a minute. Mr. Finley came to the door a ruined man.

Petey had seen it before: he took one look at the man's crumpled face and said, "There now, Mr. Finley. It's like a jab at the doctor's office. Treatment hurts worse than the disease. Not that I'd say" — here he cast a flattering eye in Fleurette's direction — "that an evening in Miss Crawford's company would hurt at all."

Fleurette was Rose Crawford that night. She liked to pick her last names from the city directory, and she chose first names from among the theatrical notices. She was partial to any sort of floral name as she thought they suited her. She'd be Lily next, and thought she might make a convincing Iris, too.

Mr. Finley remembered his manners and rushed to assure Fleurette that it wasn't her company that upset him so. "Oh, it isn't you, of course. Only now that you're here, I think of my dear Agatha and . . . well, this

118

is her home, too, and to think that it's come to this . . ."

He turned away and dabbed at his eyes. Petey and Fleurette edged into the room: they'd had to practically force themselves inside because Mr. Finley was too distracted to play the part of host. Already Fleurette missed her first client. Mr. Lyman had known how to take charge of the situation and seen to it that Fleurette enjoyed herself.

But now it became obvious that Fleurette would have to be the one to take charge.

"What a lovely home, Mr. Finley," Fleurette said, hardly glancing around at the embroidered cushions and chintz curtains. She shrugged out of her coat. "Where would you like to hang this?"

When a man is out of his depth, it's always good to give him some simple task to accomplish that will allow him to regain his footing. Fleurette had learned this lesson in the short time she'd spent traveling with a vaudeville troupe, shifting from train to cab to hotel to theater and back, always with a driver or porter or usher to contend with. She'd acquired a knack for telling a man exactly what needed doing and then praising him for doing it. Men liked that.

It worked perfectly on Mr. Finley. He snapped out of his reverie and reached at once for Fleurette's coat. "May I take your hat, too, miss?"

Fleurette had a very particular idea about how her hair ought to look when photographed from the back in Mr. Finley's parlor. "I'll just run to the powder room first, if you don't mind," she said, "and Mr. McGinnis will tell you exactly where he'd like us to sit."

Having left the two of them to work out the arrangements, Fleurette dashed down the hall into a tiny bathroom that had obviously only just recently been emptied of a woman's toiletries. A glass shelf still held the circular imprint of a powder-puff box, and a little enamel tray was sticky with the residue of perfume bottles recently swept up and taken away. In the medicine cabinet, Mr. Finley's razor and soap remained crowded on the bottom shelf, alongside his hair tonic and a salve whose purpose Fleurette did not wish to investigate. The other shelves stood empty.

She unpinned her hat and made the necessary repairs to her hair, which she'd done up in an arrangement that might've been becoming in 1912. Her idea about Rose Crawford was that she wasn't a widow but lived as one: she'd been abandoned by a suitor years ago and found herself unable to love another, until she noticed Mr. Finley and he noticed her. They'd been living in some proximity, Fleurette had decided, as neighbors or fellow churchgoers or perhaps (Fleurette liked this version of events best) Rose Crawford worked in a dull and dusty office near Mr. Finley's place of employment, and they passed each other frequently on the street.

Mr. Finley hadn't, of course, thought to so much as nod in Rose Crawford's direction when he was still a married man. It was only after dear Agatha ran off with a sailor that he even glanced her way, and saw her looking at him . . .

On the strength of that fine bit of fiction, Fleurette had worked up a hairstyle and a plain little dark green dress with the saddest excuse for a lace collar she could conjure. Poor Rose Crawford, pinning her dearest hopes on the misty-eyed Mr. Finley! She allowed her shoulders to slump forward a little as she returned to the parlor, as had become Rose's habit after so many years bending over a typewriter.

"There she is," Petey said, hardly looking her way. He was all business now: he'd put a dainty wooden table at an angle, with a picture of Mr. and Mrs. Finley in a brass frame prominently displayed, to further outrage the judge.

The sofa was long enough to allow two people to sit entirely apart and never touch, so Petey placed a pillow where he wanted Mr. Finley to sit, and another, right next to it, for Fleurette.

Mr. Finley watched all of this with the air of a man observing a plumber going about his work. He seemed inclined to offer a suggestion or two, but held his tongue.

"We'll be finished in no time, Mr. Finley, and you can enjoy your evening," Petey said.

Mr. Finley looked around morosely. "There's nothing left to enjoy. If my Agatha were here —"

"Why don't we take our seats," Fleurette put in, before Mr. Finley launched into another soliloquy over his departed Agatha. She arranged herself on the cushion Petey had placed for her, leaving Mr. Finley no choice but to settle down next to her.

She recalled, a little wistfully, how Mr. Lyman had given her a thrill when he swept her up in his arms. Looking back on it, she thought it generous of him. He had put her at ease with a dash of harmless flirtation, and he'd been sure enough of himself to know how she'd take it.

Should she do the same now, for poor Mr. Finley?

No. She couldn't stomach the thought. After all, she was the one being paid to do a job. If that job involved bestowing any gestures of affection upon the client . . . well, she didn't like to think what that sort of job might be called.

There wasn't time anyway. Petey stood in the doorway between the parlor and the kitchen, took one last look around, made a few more adjustments to picture-frames and cushions, then dashed away to retrieve his camera.

"Remember," he called, "you're to take her in your arms, look over her right shoulder, and give me a little shock and fright. Don't overdo it."

Fleurette was close enough to Mr. Finley now to smell the wintergreen hair tonic she'd seen in the bathroom. He was a thin-featured man, with a sallow complexion and eyes flattened into their sockets.

He wet his lips. Fleurette feared she was in for a kiss.

She turned her head just slightly — making it easy for him to offer his expression of shock and fright over her shoulder — and leaned toward him just a bit so that he could get his arms around her. He hesitated at first, but when he heard Petey's footsteps, he put a hand on her shoulder and then —

Mr. Finley burst into tears.

He didn't just get a little damp along the eyelashes. He issued forth a sob, his chest heaving, a most pitiable moan gurgling up from his throat.

To make matters worse, he clutched at Fleurette and pressed his face into her shoulder. She was at once sticky from his tears. Mr. Finley was the sort of man who rocked back and forth when he cried, and he rocked Fleurette along with him, as a child would a doll.

This wouldn't stand. She wasn't paid to console a man through the end of his marriage; she was paid merely to help usher the proceedings along.

And she knew already that Mr. Finley wouldn't be pressing an envelope containing another twenty dollars into her palm as she left. There were limits to how far Fleurette was willing to go for her wages, and Mr. Finley had exhausted them.

"I beg your pardon!" Fleurette said, quietly but firmly. She glanced over her shoulder at Petey, who'd come in from the kitchen with his lens trained on them, but now stood with the camera dangling resignedly from its strap.

"Yes, let me help you up, Mr. Finley," said Petey, grasping the man's arm and pulling him to his feet. "Why don't you take a minute to compose yourself?"

Mr. Finley looked back and forth at the two of them as if he'd almost forgotten they were there. "I hope you'll excuse me. It just came over me." He'd managed to find a handkerchief by now, and dabbed at his eyes.

"Go and take a minute to yourself," Petey said, ushering him toward the powder room. "Straighten your tie and run a comb through your hair. You'll feel better."

As Mr. Finley disappeared down the hall, Petey dropped into a chair across from Fleurette and rolled his eyes. "Some of them just aren't ready," he said. "They go marching into our office with a head full of steam, but by the time we get here, they've gone soft."

Fleurette wondered just then how many times Petey had done this before, with any number of her predecessors. "How did the other girls handle it?" she asked.

Petey said, "Some of them took pity on the fellows and tried to sweeten them up. But some girls just couldn't watch a man cry. They called the job off."

"Did they collect their pay anyway?"

"You've heard Mr. Ward. No picture, no paycheck. We can't guarantee that the pictures will win the day in court, but we do promise to get them done. For that we get paid."

Fleurette tallied up what remained of the funeral expenses and the doctor's bill. She might not make a career out of coaxing weeping men out of powder rooms, but she decided that the least she could do for Francis was to see his final account settled.

With that in mind, she went on down the hall to have a word with Mr. Finley.

It was accomplished more easily than she would've imagined. Mr. Finley wanted to be persuaded. He was in fact eager to be rescued and resuscitated. Mostly, Fleurette suspected, he wanted a sympathetic feminine ear of the sort Mrs. Finley had, until recently, always provided.

"It's just terrible what you've been through," murmured Fleurette through the bathroom door — Fleurette, who at that moment had little sympathy for someone whose beloved had only run off on an adventure and not been lowered into the ground in a casket.

The door opened at once. A pink-cheeked Mr. Finley looked all too eager to hear more along those lines. "My dear," he whispered, "you have no idea."

"Oh, but I do," said Fleurette. "Someone you thought would be with you forever has simply vanished. Your whole life is upended. To go on living without her is intolerable."

"It is, it is!" said Mr. Finley. "I just can't —" He waved his arm around at the house. "I can't just go on as I was before. Everything I did was for her. Everything I said, every . . ."

He fumbled for a handkerchief. Fleurette feared he was going to break down again.

"Which is why you must win her back," she said.

This startled him so that he forgot entirely about his tears. That had been Fleurette's aim exactly.

"However could I?" asked Mr. Finley. "She's made her choice. She knows exactly what she's left behind, and as for what the other fellow has to offer . . ."

Fleurette sighed. There was no hope, in other words, of Mr. Finley making any adjustments to himself. Dear Agatha could take what he had to give or look elsewhere. Clearly Agatha had chosen.

Nonetheless she plunged on, fishing not for an answer to Mr. Finley's woes, but for her twenty dollars. "She's only gone off with another man because she knows you're right here waiting. But what if you weren't? What if she had reason to believe that another woman was threatening to take her place?"

"But I would never . . ." Mr. Finley said, and then he took her meaning. "The photographs!"

"That's exactly right," Fleurette said. "Once you have the pictures, don't they have to be sent on to Mrs. Finley's attorney, so that she might file for divorce? You won't be turning them over to the judge yourself, will you? Isn't the idea to pretend that Mrs. Finley is the wronged party?"

In fact, Fleurette wasn't sure what, exactly, happened to the photographs after they were printed, but she seemed to have more or less guessed correctly, because Mr. Finley embraced her idea immediately.

"Of course! The photographs are for her to put into evidence! But we don't have to send them to her attorney."

"That's right. You could send them to her," Fleurette said, "and tell her that your friendship with a certain girl in the office has blossomed into something more, and that the lady was eager to pose for a picture and move the matter along, provided her name is left out of it."

"Oh, but I wouldn't want Agatha to think I'd found someone else and forgotten all about her!" Mr. Finley said.

By now Fleurette was leading her client down the hall, back to the sofa.

"She won't think that," Fleurette assured him, "but if the pictures are convincing enough, she'll wonder about it, and she'll have to come back and see for herself."

12

"What a triumph!" shouted Mr. Ward. "I should be tossing roses at your feet and demanding an autograph!"

"I collected my pay," said Fleurette coolly, "and that was all the reward I expected."

"Still," said Mr. Ward, settling behind his desk and tapping his pipe, "you saved that job. Petey couldn't have talked him into it, but you did."

"I shouldn't have needed to," said Fleurette. "He wasn't prepared."

She allowed the implication to hang in the air: Mr. Ward was the one who should've prepared him.

He pretended to squirm under the pressure, but it was only a game to him. "Men are fickle and weak, haven't you learned that by now? Why don't you let me make it up to you with a" — here he fumbled with some papers on his desk until he fished one out with a flourish — "a Mr. Theodore

Packard, of Park Avenue. Would you mind a little trip into Manhattan?"

Fleurette would not mind at all. Mr. Ward explained that Mr. Packard was an older man, of a prominent family, too well-known among the New York lawyers to hire any one of them for a bit of clandestine work. For her time and trouble, Fleurette was promised an extra five dollars, a good supper, and a pleasant evening.

She looked forward to it inordinately. Since Norma had delivered her grim news about the difficulty selling the farm, Fleurette had done her best to stay out of the house. There was nothing but downcast faces and hushed conversations over columns of figures. Even the children sensed it, and stayed in their rooms. A few weeks had passed since Francis's funeral. When they should have been climbing out of their grief, just an inch at a time, they were instead sinking.

A nice evening in New York, in the company of a wealthy and well-behaved man, would do a great deal to buoy Fleurette's spirits. This job was coming to mean more to her than she liked to admit. The money was a tremendous help (she continued to slip everything she earned into Bessie's pocket, having decided not to turn a dime over to Norma until she demanded it), but what mattered more was the theatricality of it — the costumes, the hairstyles, the false identities. What a relief it was to be someone else for a night! To be out among people, and involved in their affairs, took her mind off her worries in a way that hours spent in front of a sewing machine never did.

At the sewing machine, she could brood and worry all day long. In Petey's automobile, on the way to New York, she kept her chin up and her mind on the job ahead.

"I hope it isn't too much of an inconvenience to go all this way," Petey said on the drive into the city.

"An inconvenience? I'd live in Manhattan if I could," said Fleurette. "Does Mr. Packard really live on Park Avenue? I hope it's the nice part."

She didn't know, particularly, if there was a part of Park Avenue that wasn't nice, but she'd spent a little time with some New York society girls before the war and she knew how New Yorkers liked to draw their fine distinctions. If there was a fashionable block on Park Avenue, there would have to be an unfashionable block, too.

"I believe Mr. Packard will live up to your expectations," Petey said.

He did indeed. The Park Avenue apartment was a penthouse, the fireplace marble, the hot and cold taps in the bathtub (which Fleurette inspected thoroughly but did not presume to touch) made of gleaming brass or perhaps gold, for all she knew, and the windows — well, the windows were marvelous, because they looked out over Central Park, to the flickering lights of the city beyond.

There simply wasn't a better view in the world.

It was in front of this view that she did, in fact, enjoy a nice supper with Mr. Packard, a silver-haired gentleman of perhaps sixty, who dressed immaculately in the sort of suit that men of his generation wore in the evenings. The clam cocktail was the best she'd had, the guinea hen done to perfection, the cheese soufflé almost enough to make her want to learn to cook. (Petey, waiting downstairs in the butler's pantry, was sent Virginia ham with pickles and rolls, and insisted that he preferred it.)

There were frail goblets of Champagne, a tray of cakes that rivaled Bessie's, and, at the end of the evening, a tiny wooden box that set Fleurette to quivering when she imagined its contents.

"They say the smaller the box . . ." Fleurette began, but Mr. Packard waved away her speculations.

"It's just something Mrs. Packard left behind," he said. "If she misses it, her next husband can buy her one just like it in Pennsylvania."

"I wouldn't leave all this for Pennsylvania," Fleurette said dreamily, looking around the enormous room where they'd dined together and posed for their pictures.

Mr. Packard laughed and said, "The difficulty with this place is that you'd have to live with me, too. I come with the furniture."

Fleurette was so embarrassed that she dropped the box. "Oh, I didn't mean to suggest that it was only the apartment that mattered."

"It's always the apartment," Mr. Packard said, bending over to retrieve the box. "Here, don't forget your emerald."

She didn't look inside that box until she was home, well away from Petey and any possibility that Ward & McGinnis might lay claim to a percentage. She waited until she was back in her cramped bedroom, and even pushed a trunk against the door for extra protection against her intrusive sisters.

Then she pressed her palms against the box, as if squeezing a magic charm, and opened it.

Inside was a sharply cut emerald, a perfect little rectangle set into a gold pin, gleaming and elegant.

"Look at this, Laura," she whispered, holding it up to the bird's cage but not (she knew better by now) putting it so close that Laura could reach it with her beak.

Laura slid across her perch and cocked one mandarin-orange eye at it. "Pretty," she said.

"It is pretty," said Fleurette.

Laura was acquiring new words every day, now that she and Fleurette sat talking to one another for hours at a time in Bessie's sewing room.

"Laura," said the bird. "Pretty."

"Pretty Laura," said Fleurette absently, her eyes more on the emerald than her parrot.

"Laura. Pretty. Green," said the bird, and Fleurette understood: the emerald was the same color as Laura's feathers. If she didn't put it away now, and stop talking about it, Laura would be describing the pin to Norma by morning.

It was difficult enough, keeping secrets in this house. It was even more perilous with a talkative parrot watching her every move.

At least they weren't to be crowded together

much longer. The Wilkinsons had moved out, the Kopps would start paying rent, and already Constance and Norma were next door, scrubbing the kitchen sink and pushing rugs around. Fleurette went over, with some reluctance, to have a look at her new home, the setting for what seemed to be an endless, yawning future with her two older sisters.

Three Spinsters, they could name the house, if they were the sort of people who named houses.

The Wilkinsons' house (this was, in fact, what they called the house, as it didn't seem like their house at all) was identical to Bessie's, only reversed, with the front door on the left instead of the right. There was the same sitting-room in the front, and behind that a kitchen and a little hall leading to the bathroom. Upstairs, under the eaves, were three snug bedrooms.

In this house Fleurette would also be expected to do her sewing on the little enclosed porch that served as a sewing room at Bessie's, but she was relieved to find that the Wilkinsons had expanded theirs, added proper walls, and installed a door leading out to the side yard.

Fleurette thought it would make a fine space for a sewing room. In addition to the outside door, there were windows all around so that Laura could enjoy a view, and room in the corner for an armchair and a footstool. She could practically live in that room, as long as there was a lock to keep her sisters out.

Just as she reached over to test the doorknob, Norma walked in with a yardstick and started taking measurements. "We'll put Mother's old curio cabinet in front of that outside door," she said. "You can put your thread and notions and things in it."

When Fleurette objected, Norma saw at once her reason for it and said, "You don't need your own private entrance. You'll come and go through the front, like the rest of us."

"It's for customers coming for fittings," Fleurette said. "They won't want to walk in the front door and find you sitting around in your slippers."

"I'll hardly have time to sit around," Norma said.

"Won't you?" asked Fleurette.

Norma seemed not to hear and went on with her measurements, making notes and jotting down diagrams.

The question of what, exactly, Norma would be contributing to this venture was one that grated at Fleurette. She was, at that moment, bringing in more money than anyone else, with assignments from Ward & McGinnis coming at the rate of two or three per week. ("We liberated France and now everyone wants to be liberated," Mr. Ward liked to say of the post-war rush on divorces.)

Constance earned a steady paycheck at the department store, which would satisfy her share of their obligations, and she'd certainly take a better position if one came along. Employment was, of course, out of the question for Bessie with a baby on the way.

Then why, exactly, was Norma exempt from the obligation to find a job? Before the war, Fleurette would've considered Norma unemployable, what with her disagreeable nature and unwillingness to follow instructions or consider another person's point of view — much less the direct orders of an employer.

But hadn't she gone to France, and served with the Army, and followed orders and done what was expected of her? Had she not in fact served with some distinction, and been awarded a medal by the mayor of the village in which she was stationed?

What, then, prevented Norma from taking employment in a shop or an office like her sisters were expected to do?

To be fair, Norma was, at the moment, entirely occupied with the task of moving their old belongings out of the farmhouse and into the Wilkinsons' house, and selling or disposing of anything they wouldn't bring with them. Then there were the repairs to the farmhouse, and the work with the surveyors and the lawyers, and negotiations with the various parties currently leasing pastures from them.

It required a great deal of effort on Norma's part, Fleurette admitted that — but what was to come after? Why was Norma bustling around Fleurette's sewing room, arranging her things and deciding how she should run her affairs, but no one had a word to say about Norma's affairs?

The question of whether Norma was to support the household or be supported was thrown into sharp relief when Fleurette traipsed back over to Bessie's house to find her in the kitchen, staring down at a dozen eggs and three russet potatoes.

She wasn't just staring at them: she was glaring at them, her chin down and her arms folded across her chest.

"Whatever have they done to offend you?" asked Fleurette.

"They're not pork chops, or green beans,

which was what I intended to feed you for supper," Bessie said.

Fleurette looked at the clock. It was only four o'clock on a Saturday. The markets were open. This must've been Bessie's way of saying that she didn't feel well enough to do her shopping.

"I'll go," she offered. "There's plenty of time."

"Oh no, it isn't the time," Bessie said. "It's . . ." And then she started to sniff, and to put a handkerchief against her eyes, and although Fleurette understood that a pregnant widow shouldn't be expected to have a dry eye for months, she did wonder how the pork chops, or lack of them, brought this on.

Fleurette pulled out a chair and nudged Bessie into it. "You could turn the kitchen over to us, you know," she said, although she quaked at the thought. "Constance is an awful cook and Norma will put cabbage, potatoes, and sausage on the table seven nights a week, but we'd manage."

Bessie smiled into her handkerchief. "It does me good to stay busy. It isn't that. The trouble is . . . Oh, I hate to tell you, after everything you girls have done . . ."

"Now I'm getting worried and you have to tell me," said Fleurette.

Bessie sighed. "All right. I went over to Belsky's just now and . . . well, our account is past due. Mr. Belsky said he hated to bother me about it at a time like this, but he hasn't been paid in months, and . . . Oh, Fleurette, he said it in front of everybody! I didn't know what to say. I just ran out."

"How could he speak to you like that, after what you've been through? Of course the accounts will be paid. We just have to sit down, and . . ." Fleurette realized that she didn't really know what needed to be done. Where was Constance, at a moment like this?

"He said he hadn't been paid in months. Since August, he said."

"But that's impossible! Wouldn't you have known?"

"Francis never talked to me about money," Bessie said, "but something strange did happen over the summer. He used to give me an allowance to run the house. I'd buy groceries, small things the children needed, all of that. But then he stopped. He wanted me to go on charging to our accounts, and he said he'd go around and pay them all himself once a month. I told him that didn't seem easier at all. How would I know how much I had left to spend? But he insisted on doing it this way."

141

"And he never said why?" Fleurette asked.

"Oh, I tried to get it out of him," Bessie said. "We had such a fight about it one night. I said that it made me feel like he didn't trust me to handle a weekly allowance. He said that I should trust him to take care of the family. It was just awful. We just didn't talk about it again after that. We couldn't."

"So you had no idea what was owed when he died?" Fleurette said. "I wish you'd told us."

"Well, I knew we'd have to reckon with some bills, but I was waiting for you girls to get settled next door. I thought surely I'd have another month or two to sort it out."

"How much do you owe?"

Bessie sunk her chin into her hands. "It's over twenty dollars. All I could think to do was to come back here and see if we had anything at all that I could pass off as supper for tonight."

Fleurette stood up and looked around for her coat. "I'll go and see what I can do."

Bessie started to object, but Fleurette said, "I had a little put away before all this started. And now I've got my seamstressing. Give me your grocery list and I'll take care of it."

Bessie sighed and wrote out a list. "Please

don't bother your sisters with this. I just want a night to think about it. I can't imagine why Francis would've done a thing like this. I'm just . . . I'm not ready to answer any questions about it yet."

Fleurette snatched the list away. "There's no reason to tell them at all. It's probably some sort of book-keeping mistake. I'll speak to Mr. Belsky and sort it out."

Bessie stood and smoothed her apron. "You're right. I'm making too much of it. Do you suppose you could pick up some rolls at Penfield's too, if there are any left?"

It was the first bit of shopping Fleurette had done for Bessie, in all the weeks she'd been living under her roof, and it came as a relief to find another way to be of use. She would make a payment against the account, arrange to pay the rest a week at a time, and return home with a fat parcel of pork chops. If only all their troubles could be so easily undone.

But their troubles, she was about to learn, went quite a bit beyond the price of porkchops.

At the butcher's — Belsky & Son, where Bessie had traded for fifteen years — Mr. Belsky (the elder) weighed the chops and, as he did so, asked the name on the account.

"Kopp," Fleurette said.

Mr. Belsky looked down at her, one bloodied hand on the scale.

"Francis Kopp? Are you a relation?"

"Sister," said Fleurette.

Mr. Belsky eyed her a minute more, his heavy gray eyebrows furrowed, jowls hanging down like a hunting dog's. "Sister of the deceased," he said.

"That's right," Fleurette said, steadying herself.

He wrapped the chops and tied them with string. "Did Mrs. Kopp send you?"

"I've come to make a payment on the account," said Fleurette.

With the news that she could pay, his countenance changed, and he gestured for her to follow him to the register. He looked around first to see that no one was listening, then leaned over the counter and said, in a low voice, "Like I told Mrs. Kopp, the account's been delinquent for six months. I didn't like to tell a widow that, but the longer we let it go on, the worse it'll be for her."

"It shouldn't have gone on this long."

"Well, it wasn't easy for anyone, with the war on, and we just knew your brother

144

would catch up again when it was all over. But now . . ."

"But now he never will," Fleurette said. "I don't blame you. Only I can't imagine why my brother couldn't pay his butcher bill. How much is owed?"

Mr. Belsky made a great show of paging through his ledger, but Fleurette suspected he knew the sum to the penny.

"Twenty-three dollars and seventy-eight cents," he said, and showed her the page, with Francis's name at the top and sums going down a column in ever-increasing amounts.

"I'll buy the chops myself," Fleurette told Mr. Belsky, "and pay you five dollars a week on the account, starting now."

Mr. Belsky frowned and looked over his page of figures again. "The last time I saw Mr. Kopp, I told him that the war was over and it was time for him to pay the balance in full."

"If only Mr. Kopp were here to pay that balance," Fleurette said, "and to meet his third child, to be born in July. I don't suppose Mrs. Kopp told you, but it'll be apparent in a few weeks."

Mr. Belsky went as red as his blood-smeared apron and rushed back to the meat counter to wrap up half a pound of liver.

"With my compliments," he muttered. "Five dollars a week will do just fine."

The baby — as yet unnamed, unseen, and not yet definitively fixed in Fleurette's mind — was nonetheless earning its keep. Fleurette took note of that.

She would've returned home shaken but nonetheless pleased at having sorted out one of Bessie's small difficulties, except that she soon learned that the difficulty was not so small. Francis owed money all over town. At Penfield's — the bakery — and at the green grocer, and even at the druggist and the dry goods store, every account was delinquent. Hawthorne's business district was only a few blocks long. It was not at all difficult to walk up and down the street and tally the damage.

Taken together, over two hundred dollars was owed. Out of kindness to Bessie, not one of the merchants had sent a bill to the house — but they were all eager to be paid.

Fleurette walked as if in a dream from one shop to another, putting down a dollar here, two dollars there, against every past-due balance.

What, exactly, had Francis been doing with his earnings if he'd stopped paying his bills? If the merchants knew, they weren't telling. All anyone would say was that the war had been difficult, that they didn't want to trouble a widow, and that the Kopps had been customers of such long standing that they were willing to be patient.

By the third or fourth such conversation, Fleurette stopped asking for an explanation and approached the matter coolly, as a business transaction. She had no more need of condolences.

It occurred to Fleurette, as it often had since her brother's death, that he would miss everything from now on. He would miss watching Lorraine turn into a young woman, and Frankie Jr. grow into the very image of his father. He would miss his third child entirely. He wouldn't see Europe at peace again, after talking of nothing but the war for the last year of his life. He would not, for that matter, even see spring again.

The world would just continue to turn without him. Whatever the next week brought, or the next year or the next decade, Francis would not be a part of it.

And now this. He wouldn't live to see his debts retired. He wouldn't know that it was Fleurette, the perpetual thorn in his side, the young and irresponsible one, the one who defied him and argued with him — he would never know that it was she who went door-to-door, reaching into her purse, mak-

ing one small payment after another against
all that had been lost.

13

Mr. Ward said, "You're back at the Metropolitan this week. This time I'll be your accomplice."

"Why, what's Petey doing?" Fleurette asked. She didn't like the idea of working with anyone but Petey. The two of them had their methods, their unspoken agreements, their secret signals.

"Petey has the night off," Mr. Ward said. "Mr. Thorne is an old friend of mine. He wants me to handle this one myself."

"And what kind of man is Mr. Thorne?" asked Fleurette, already thinking of her wardrobe.

"The kind who likes pretty girls," said Mr. Ward. "Do yourself up."

Fleurette did herself up. She couldn't even walk out of the house in her full regalia: although her dress was well-hidden under a plain wool coat, her satin evening slippers had to be buried at the bottom of a carpet bag, along with stockings, a very fetching velvet turban with a peacock feather tucked into the brim, a full complement of face powders, lip-sticks, and hairpins, and a handkerchief soaked in a rather scandalous perfume called Narcisse Noire, a gift from a client who complained that his wife didn't appreciate Parisian style. She intended to tuck it into her bosom when she arrived at the hotel and remove it again before she returned home, in the hope that her sisters wouldn't smell it on her.

With these and many more accoutrements, she arrived at Mr. Ward's office a full hour before they were due at the Metropolitan and busied herself with her preparations in his bathroom. While she put herself together, Mr. Ward lounged at his desk, his feet up, the sports page folded over his knee.

"Come out here and help me pick a pony," he called, just as Fleurette was rolling her stockings on. Her dress hung on a hanger behind her: she'd step into it again after she finished with her powders and paints.

"There's no racing this time of year," she called back.

"There is in Havana. Say, have you ever been to Havana? The ponies run all year long. We could catch a steamer tonight."

This was to be the banter between them for the next hour, she could see that. He wouldn't be so brutish as to barge in on her when she was in a state of undress, but he certainly seemed to want to hear from her while she was in such a state.

"What if I read the names aloud and you tell me the one you like? Girls seem to have a knack for picking the right horse just from the name. How does Naturalist sound to you?"

"Unseemly," said Fleurette.

"What about Lottery?"

"Too risky."

"Mother-in-Law?"

"You made that one up."

"It's right here in the paper if you want to come see for yourself."

They continued in this manner until she emerged, ten minutes ahead of schedule, in a state of simmering allure. She wore a slim, wine-colored dress of Georgette crêpe so translucent that it had practically no neckline at all: if not for the glittering sprays of beadwork, it would almost disappear. The ensemble was designed to move and shift and show a bit of collarbone here, a protruding hip bone there. She'd piled her hair up high but loosely because she knew how it brought out her eyes. She wore Mr. Packard's emerald pin as a pendant, hanging low from a long chain. That little flash of green against her burgundy dress spoke of something Fleurette had only sensed in the air since the war had ended — a bit of carelessness, a touch of defiance, a note of hedonism, in the way women were about to start dressing themselves.

She was exactly right about that. In her slouchy, sheer, bejeweled state, she was, in fact, a woman of the coming decade, not the one fading into the past.

Mr. Ward knew just how to respond to the sight of a woman emerging from her dressing-room: he turned once, started, turned again, jumped to his feet, sent his pipe flying, tumbled over his chair, and regained his footing with the comic grace of a dancer.

"Miss Kopp, you're going to break up half a dozen more marriages just walking down the street," he said, "including mine, if you'll have me."

"I won't," she said. "Will this do for Mr. Thorne?"

"It will if he survives the shock," said Mr. Ward. "I wonder if the Metropolitan keeps a doctor on staff."

"Is he terribly old?" Fleurette asked, a

little disappointed at having gone to all the trouble. Any twenty-one-year-old is attractive to a man of advanced years. Why bother dressing up?

"It isn't that he's terribly old, it's just that you're so terribly beautiful," said Mr. Ward. "Let's not keep that dress waiting any longer."

He whisked her down the stairs and into his automobile. In fact, the hotel was only seven or eight blocks away, as nothing was very far in Paterson's downtown. But they'd need an auto if they had to get away quickly. Besides, Fleurette was too sumptuously attired: she'd attract attention. Mr. Ward brought her in through the kitchen entrance, as usual, and in a matter of minutes the two of them were standing in front of room 513 at the Metropolitan.

It was always Petey who knocked, so Fleurette waited for Mr. Ward to do so. Instead he fumbled in his pocket for a key.

"Why do you have the key?" said Fleurette. "Isn't he here already?"

"He's downstairs," said Mr. Ward. "We have to conduct a bit of business first. I'll send him up and give you two a minute to get settled, then I'll be right in with the camera. Isn't that how Petey handles it?"

"More or less," Fleurette said, a little uncertain.

Nonetheless she followed him into the room. It was just like all the others: the same heavy curtains, the same good thick carpet, the same two chairs around a little round table, the same settee at the foot of the bed. She found the sight of it comforting: the rooms had grown familiar to her, and she felt every inch the professional as she paced around, making little adjustments.

"Petey likes us to sit here," she said, indicating the settee, "with my back to the camera, of course. When you come in, he'll look over my shoulder, like this." Here she took Mr. Thorne's position and made an expression of mock surprise at the intruder.

"That's the face that convinces the judges," Mr. Ward said. "I'll send him up in two shakes. Say, did we settle on a name for you this time?"

In all her excitement over her costume, Fleurette had forgotten to choose a pseudonym! What did it matter, as long as it was one she could remember? "Gloria Blossom," she said. It was a name she'd used before, but not with Mr. Ward. She'd used it on a clandestine case with Constance during the war. No judge would recognize it.

Mr. Ward bowed. "Miss Blossom. It's a crime to keep you waiting."

"Then hurry," she said.

The wait was longer than she expected. There were no books or magazines with which to pass the time. She would've read Mr. Ward's racing sheet if she had it. She thought to step into the powder room and touch up her hair, but she'd left her combs and creams in Mr. Ward's automobile. So she waited and watched a little clock on the bedside, as ten minutes passed, then twenty, then thirty.

At last a key rattled in the door, and a sweaty and inebriated Mr. Thorne stumbled in. "He said you'd be waiting for me!" the man shouted, before the door fell shut behind him. "Gloria, is it? I knew a Gloria once. Now, come over here and tell Billy all about the time we met, because like I told Jack, I don't remember a thing about that night."

Mr. Thorne was an absolutely enormous man, as tall as Constance and twice as broad. Fleurette never would've agreed to be alone with him if she'd seen the state he was in. What had Mr. Ward been thinking, pouring drinks into him before allowing him upstairs?

"I don't believe we have met before,"

Fleurette said mildly, trying to stifle her alarm. "You and I are here to do a job. If you could take a seat here —"

He grinned at her and took her hand. "Let's both take a seat." Before she could pull away, he dropped down to the settee, forcing her off-balance and very nearly yanking her into his lap.

In the scramble — Mr. Thorne reaching clumsily for her and Fleurette fighting to regain both her balance and her dignity — her hair came undone. Down it fell, the pins and combs springing loose.

"Mr. Thorne! Look what you've done." She didn't dare crawl around on the floor to retrieve the pins: he'd be on her in a second.

Where *was* Mr. Ward?

"It's better like that," Mr. Thorne said, looking greedily at her hair, which now, Fleurette realized in a panic, made her look even more like a woman ready for bed. He rocked back and forth in a manner that suggested that he was about to launch himself off the settee and back at her.

Fleurette put a hand out. "Stay where you are." The authority in her voice surprised her: it sounded like something Constance would say.

Through some miracle he obeyed. It was

perhaps the miracle of drink: Fleurette could see his eyelids drooping, the soporific effects going to work on him.

"But if I'm over here," he mumbled, "and you're over there . . ."

Fleurette was by now looking around the room, gathering her things. She could do without the twenty dollars this time. She wasn't about to go near the man again, even if Mr. Ward walked in with his camera at that instant.

She would've slipped quietly away and brought the evening to a discreet close, except that Mr. Thorne roused himself and staggered to his feet just as she lifted her coat from the coat-rack.

"Now, Gloria, don't run off." He had the most enormous mouth, thick lips, wet with spittle, and he pursed them appallingly as he leaned toward her.

"Don't you dare," she said, but he was past hearing. He leaned in for his kiss and put a hand at the back of her neck.

She didn't have a minute to think, but she didn't need it. Constance had shown her what to do. She'd shown a whole group of girls, back at a training camp before the war.

"If you're shorter than him, it means you're underneath him," Constance had said. "And if he's pulling you toward him,

157

then he's already supplying the force. Go straight up and in with the heel of your hand" — and here she pantomimed it, pushing the heel of her hand up into the underside of an attacker's nose.

"It's the most delicate part of the nose," she said. "Go in with everything you've got. Even if you don't break it, he'll step back. That's when you hook his leg with one of yours. He'll fall, and you might go with him. Go ahead. Once you've landed on top of him, you can stomp on a hand or an elbow or a knee. You'll be able to break something."

Fleurette didn't recall Constance's instructions so much as she felt them. She let Mr. Thorne pull her close, and she brought her hand up as he did, slamming her palm into his nose as if she was aiming for the back of his head — as if she was aiming for the other side of the room.

That was all it took. He yelped and stumbled back, losing his footing.

He fell like a tree. Fleurette did not, in fact, go down with him.

Instead she ran out the door, down the back stairs, through the hotel kitchen, and directly home.

14

It was a shame about the carpet at the Metropolitan. If the floors had been tile, or even an unforgiving oak, Mr. Thorne's skull might've cracked in two.

As it was he suffered only the mildest bump on the head and a dizzy spell that dissipated when Mr. Ward burst into the room, camera in hand, to find his client in disarray and his employee vanished.

Mr. Ward didn't need Mr. Thorne to explain what had happened. The hairpins scattered around the carpet, the ostrich-plumed hat still resting on the hat-rack, and the bloodied nose of Mr. Thorne himself told all.

What sort of apology was a woman due, after an ordeal like that? What sort of explanation was in order?

Whatever it was, Mr. Ward did not go personally to deliver it. He sent Petey.

This posed any number of difficulties for

Petey. There was no easy way for him to approach the Kopp household without the risk of exposing the entire scheme to Norma and Constance (whose wrath Petey quite rightfully feared). If Fleurette had managed to keep her association with the firm of Ward & McGinnis a secret, Petey would only make things worse for her by turning up on her doorstep.

But every lawyer has his tricks. Petey waited until Constance left for work (Constance, with her law-and-order tendencies, being a greater threat than Norma, or so he believed) and tipped a delivery boy, making his rounds for a nearby druggist, to slip a note in the letter slot at the Kopps' front door.

The note was sealed in a business-like envelope. The sender, carefully typed in Petey's most professional manner, was Van Pelt's Fabric & Notions.

The note inside read: "Meet me at our usual spot. I'll wait until eleven."

Fleurette did, in fact, make him wait until eleven: he deserved that. When she arrived at their meeting spot around the corner, next to a little park where Petey often collected Fleurette or dropped her off when they did a job together, she refused to get into his automobile. She simply stood next to it, arms folded, as somber and forbidding a creature as she could be, in a dull gray coat and the same black hat she'd worn to Francis's funeral.

Petey didn't like the idea of having this discussion in public, as there were people out and about, and neighbors sitting just behind curtained windows. But when he stayed at the wheel a second too long, Fleurette shrugged and walked off, leaving him no choice.

Next to him on the front seat was the bag Fleurette had left in Mr. Ward's auto the previous night. He grabbed it and chased after her. Fleurette snatched it away from him and kept walking.

"Mr. Ward sent me," he began, but Fleurette shot him such a look of ferocity that he stopped.

When she turned to face him, Petey saw her as she was, stripped of paint and artifice, without a costume, with no role to play. Her lips were pale, her cheeks colorless, her hair not even pinned, but merely tied in a knot with a hat slapped on top.

"I know what Mr. Ward did," she said, "but what did you do? Where were you last night?"

"He didn't tell me anything about it, miss, I swear. I wouldn't have left you alone with a fellow like that. We could've found another way."

"Another way to do what? He could've killed me!"

Petey ventured a smile. "Or you could've killed him. That was quite a punch you landed, knocking down a fellow that size."

"Oh yes, I'm sure if I'd killed a man, we'd all be doing just fine this morning." Fleurette said that a little too loudly, and looked around to make sure no one had heard. She turned and marched into the park, which was empty save an old man tossing bread crumbs at birds.

"And what do you mean, we would've found another way? Another way for Mr. Thorne to get what he was after? Because it wasn't pictures he wanted last night."

"No, it wasn't," Petey said, "and Mr. Ward should've told you the truth about that. Our client is Mrs. Thorne."

Fleurette had been storming along at a furious pace, but she skidded to a stop at that. "Mrs. Thorne," she said, turning it over in her mind. "Do you mean to say that she wanted pictures of her husband with another woman, but he —"

"He didn't know about it," said Petey. "You see, Mrs. Thorne knows exactly what sort of man her husband is. What he tried with you last night —"

"He's tried with others," Fleurette muttered.

"And Mrs. Thorne never had the nerve to sock him in the nose like you did. But she did want a divorce. She needed a picture of him with a girl — any girl, you see, so long as a judge was convinced — but she didn't want Mr. Thorne to know that she hired the photographer. She wanted us to set him up. I guess she was afraid of him."

"I guess she was," Fleurette said tartly. "Wouldn't Mr. Thorne suspect, when Mr. Ward barged in with the camera?"

"That's why she chose Mr. Ward," Petey said. "He and Mr. Thorne know each other. She thought Mr. Ward could make it seem like a joke — them having a drink downstairs, then he goes upstairs to meet a girl Mr. Ward told him about, and after a few minutes Mr. Ward jumps in with the camera, treats it like a prank . . . That was the idea anyway."

"Do you mean to say that Mr. Ward told him that I was a —" Fleurette could hardly summon a word to describe it.

Petey sighed and rubbed at the back of his neck. "He told Mr. Thorne that you were a girl they both knew, from some wild night they'd had together. He said that you'd taken a liking to him — to Mr. Thorne, that is. And that you were waiting upstairs, hoping to meet him."

"Well, that's despicable. And now Mr. Ward sends you as his messenger."

"To be honest, miss, he was afraid to come himself. Those sisters of yours give him the jitters."

"They ought to." Fleurette wondered what Constance would say if she knew what Mr. Thorne had done. But there was no way to tell her without explaining why she'd been going into hotel rooms with men for money.

It had seemed like a game, when she began, but now she could see that it was someone else's game entirely. She was just one of the pieces, to be moved around on the board for points.

Just as she was thinking of points and score-keeping, Petey pulled an envelope from his coat-pocket. "Mr. Ward sent this," he said, sheepishly, handing it over but looking down at his feet as he did so. "He said you deserved it."

"You mean I earned it," Fleurette said, tearing open the envelope. There was fifty dollars inside. She crumpled it and slammed it against his chest. "Is this the going rate for getting groped by a man twice your size in a hotel room? Well, I didn't agree to that job, so I won't take the money." She stomped on. The park was so small that they were only making circles around it, but Fleurette felt she had to keep moving.

"I told him you wouldn't accept it," Petey said, huffing along beside her.

"Did you also tell him that if he can afford to pay me fifty dollars now, he could've afforded it a month ago?" Fleurette was shouting now. "I'm not doing this for my own entertainment." She stopped and pointed down the street, in the direction of Bessie's house. "My brother's dead. His widow has another child on the way. Last week she didn't have any money for food. Food, Petey! Food that you put on the table and eat so that you can live."

Fleurette glared at him as if she expected an answer. Petey opened his mouth to say that he understood what food was, but thought better of it.

It didn't matter. She spat the words out. "We are four women and three children. There is no father looking after us. There is no husband. I'm not doing this for pin money."

"No, ma'am," muttered Petey.

Fleurette was thoroughly spent by now. She also felt lighter, having gotten it all out.

"You tell Mr. Ward that I'm the wrong girl

for this job. But if I ever hear of him setting up another girl like that, I won't tell Constance. I'll come after him myself."

15

Norma and Constance were accustomed to Fleurette's moods and didn't find it out of the ordinary that she sulked and hung about the house and contributed none of her usual chatter at meal-times. It was the belief of all three Kopps that a good sulk had restorative qualities: it was a way of shutting down the engines, blowing out the accumulated grime, and allowing hot metal to cool.

In fact, Constance, observing Fleurette's mood, remarked to Norma that she wouldn't mind a nice long sulk herself. Norma told her to wait until Fleurette's was over, because the Wilkinsons' foundation might collapse under the leaden weight of two Kopps giving in to their darker tendencies at once.

Fleurette was not immobilized: she remained at her sewing machine, making over her professional co-respondent costumes, one last time, into everyday dresses that she could wear herself. (She gave no thought to returning them to Mr. Ward. Most of them were half-disassembled anyway and of no use to him.)

Once she had her own wardrobe in order, she enlisted Lorraine's help in hand-lettering a set of cards advertising her seamstressing services, to be posted in shops around town.

"The first notices I put up were on ordinary letter-writing paper and they simply fell apart in the shop windows," she told Lorraine, although she hadn't, of course, posted any notices at all and merely said it to perpetuate the fiction that she'd been running a legitimate seamstressing operation all this time.

Regardless, the new batch was made on heavy cardstock, carefully lettered in a modern script that Lorraine copied from a magazine, and the two of them had a fine Saturday afternoon together in Paterson, going door-to-door and posting their notices.

It was good to get out with Lorraine. There had been such a flurry of activity since the funeral that no one had thought to take the children on any sort of outing, or to try to relieve their cares in any way beyond the everyday, practical matters that consumed the adults' every waking hour but mattered little to the children.

"Mother keeps telling us how glad she is to see everything go back to normal," Lorraine said, when they stopped for egg creams after they'd posted their notices, "but nothing's normal anymore."

"No, it won't be, not without your father," Fleurette said. "Do you know that I was about your age when my mother died?"

"I hadn't thought of that," said Lorraine.

"I hadn't either, until just now," said Fleurette. "She'd been ill for a while, so we were prepared . . . although I didn't feel at all prepared at the time. I think I only believe that now in hindsight. But I do remember Constance and Norma talking about how we'd go on living as we always had, and how good it would be for me that nothing had to change. But of course, everything changed. Every little moment in the day was different without her. The whole household had revolved around her, and then it didn't. Everything I did was in relation to her — whether she would like it or not, whether she would approve, whether she would find out . . ."

Here Lorraine laughed, a little too knowingly. What had she been hiding from Francis or her mother? Fleurette realized she

169

ought to keep tabs on the girl. They were closer in age: Lorraine might tell Fleurette a secret that she wouldn't tell her mother or her older, more law-abiding aunts.

"That feeling didn't stop for a long time," Fleurette said. "It didn't seem right to stop taking her into account. I thought that's what I had to do, if we were to keep everything the same."

"And did you?" asked Lorraine. She was looking at Fleurette hungrily, desperate for whatever crumbs of insight Fleurette could offer. She had such deep dark eyes, so like Fleurette's. As Lorraine got older, she came to resemble Fleurette more and more. The two of them could've been sisters.

How could she tell Lorraine the truth — that in fact, she had, in some ways, forgotten her mother? That without meaning to, she had lost the sound of her mother's voice, and could only recall her face as she'd seen it in those last days, when she was so ill?

What had her mother looked like when Fleurette was five, or ten? Those memories were gone.

And did Fleurette still take her mother into account? Did she recall her expectations, her wishes, her demands?

She did not. That was the truth of it. Her

mother belonged to another era. She did not live to see what had become of them, and what they'd had to do to survive. She didn't live to see Constance wear a deputy's uniform, or Fleurette appear on the stage, or Norma set sail for France. She didn't live to see Europe torn apart by war.

She did not, thankfully, live to see her son put into a grave. Nor would she see her third grandchild born.

What could Mrs. Kopp possibly have to say about the world they lived in today, or about the predicament that her daughters now found themselves in?

Fleurette couldn't imagine it, and she had to admit (to herself, she would never say it aloud) that she hadn't much tried.

The same would happen to Lorraine someday. Five years would pass, or ten. The world would be different in ways that none of them could foresee. And Francis wouldn't belong to that world. He would belong only to the past.

Fleurette pushed the last of her egg cream over to Lorraine. "You don't have to wonder how you're going to feel. It'll just happen. You'll be swept along into the rest of your life, and you'll know where your father fits into it."

Lorraine spooned the last of Fleurette's

egg cream from the bottom of the glass, and in that way that the young have of turning from weighty matters to more practical ones without breaking stride, she said, "At least I have my room back now that you've moved out. Although I wish Mother would tell us what she's doing in the basement."

What Bessie was doing in the basement became clear that very afternoon, when Fleurette and Lorraine returned from Paterson. In the Wilkinsons' kitchen they found Norma leaning over the sink, peering through the window.

"Who are these men coming to visit your mother?" Norma asked Lorraine when they walked in, without taking her eyes off the house next door. "There've been three of them this afternoon. One every hour."

"Are they tradesmen?" said Lorraine. "She's been working on something in the basement the last few days."

"If she needed a tradesman, she should've asked me," said Norma, who was never satisfied unless she had a facility to take charge of. She considered both Bessie's home and the Wilkinsons' to be hers, and kept vigilant oversight on all aspects of the houses and grounds. A sticky door, a crack in a window-pane, a missing roof shingle, a

172

wobbly fence — all of it fell under her purview. Norma had always found it reassuring that things could reliably be counted upon to fall apart, and she could just as reliably put them back together.

What, then, were the male visitors for?

"Is this how you're going to spend the rest of your days, spying on Bessie?" Fleurette asked. "Because if you're as bored as all that —"

"There he goes!" said Norma, and all three of them crowded around the window to watch.

A middle-aged man in an ordinary brown tweed suit lifted his hat to Bessie and then walked down the street, in the direction of the train station. He carried no case or papers of any kind.

"He's not a tradesman," said Norma. "No tools."

"Could he be a lawyer or a banker?" said Fleurette.

"I would've guessed he was a salesman, except he didn't have his case," said Lorraine.

Constance, returning from work, banged through the kitchen door just then. "Who was that man leaving your house?" she asked Lorraine. The three of them shrugged.

Once Constance understood that he was

173

not the first man to have come and gone that afternoon, she said, "Well, I suppose if Bessie wants us to know, she'll tell us."

But Norma was already putting on her coat and sliding into a pair of old barn shoes that she kept at the kitchen door for the express purpose of trekking back and forth to Bessie's house to find out what was going on.

"There's no point in being coy about it," Norma said. "Lorraine has a right to know if there are strange men coming in and out of the house."

Lorraine, wisely unwilling to be caught up in her aunts' schemes, looked desperately at Fleurette for help.

"Maybe Bessie deserves her privacy," offered Fleurette, herself a great champion of keeping secrets from one's relations.

"If she wanted privacy, she'd smuggle him out the back," pronounced Norma, and off she went, with Constance, Fleurette, and Lorraine following reluctantly but curiously in her wake.

16

Bessie was a terrible liar.

"I thought we'd take in a boarder," she said, as brightly as she could under the glaring countenances of three sisters-in-law and a daughter. "I'm already cooking for a crowd, and with the rent from a boarder, I'd cover our entire grocery bill, plus the heating oil in winter."

"Then I suppose that's what you've been doing in the basement," said Norma, with the air of a detective in a penny matinee.

"Are you really going to let one of those men live in the basement?" asked Lorraine in horror. "And he'd sit at our table at dinner?"

"Couldn't you find a lady tenant?" said Constance.

"If you have a room in the basement, I might rent it," Fleurette said, if only to take the attention away from Bessie, who was wilting under the questions being fired at her. "Can I go see it?"

"I haven't fixed it up yet," Bessie said.

"I should hope not, in your condition," said Norma.

"I've only cleaned it," Bessie continued, "and advertised that I'd furnish to suit."

"I saw that advertisement and wondered who in their right mind would rent a room without knowing something definite about the furnishings first," said Norma, displaying as always her perfect recall of every column inch of the newspaper, even the classifieds.

Bessie was standing her ground, but just barely. Fleurette admired her for trying.

"With the first and last month's rent," Bessie said, "I can put some money down on a suite of good second-hand furnishings, and pay the rest over time. That is, if there aren't any extras at the farm I could use."

Constance stepped in before Norma could grouse about the idea. "I'm sure there are still some odds and ends at the farm," she said, "but why are you so worried about the grocery bill? We ought to sit down and work out exactly how we'll handle our finances until the farm sells. We could do it now, if you'd like."

Bessie exchanged hardly a glance with Fleurette, but Fleurette knew what it meant:

176

Constance and Norma remained entirely ignorant of the delinquent accounts all over town. They hadn't any idea that Bessie's credit extended only as far as Fleurette's pocketbook would allow.

And — Fleurette realized with a sickening drop in her stomach — without a salary from Mr. Ward, she would no longer be able to make her rounds, dropping two dollars here and five dollars there to keep the bill-collectors at bay.

"Why don't we go next door," Bessie said, glancing at her daughter. "There's no reason to bore the children with any of this."

"But you were ready to bore us with a man in the basement," Lorraine said.

"Keep an eye on Frankie," Bessie said, and led the way back over to the Wilkinsons'.

Fleurette followed with a sense of dread. How did Bessie intend to make a confession about the unpaid accounts without revealing Fleurette's part in it? And then how would they explain where the money had come from? There would be no sneaking the details past Norma — she'd see the entire situation for what it was, tally the sums in her head, and deduce at once that Fleurette couldn't possibly have earned enough from seamstressing to satisfy so many creditors.

On the short walk next door, Fleurette began to spin any number of scenarios in her head and to scrutinize them for plausibility. Could she claim that she'd had some money set aside from her travels last year? (Unlikely, as Fleurette had never saved a penny in her life.) Perhaps Freeman Bernstein owed her back wages, and she'd finally forced him to pay? (That would at least fit nicely into Norma's view of Mr. Bernstein as a man who couldn't be trusted.) Or could she claim to have picked up some small item of value during her time on the stage, a bauble from an admirer, that she sold after Francis died?

A bauble.

What happened to the emerald that Mr. Packard gave her?

She had worn it as a pendant on that disastrous night with Mr. Thorne. It had hung low and loose around her neck. Where was it now? She didn't remember taking it off that night. She'd rushed home, gone straight to her bedroom, torn off her entire ensemble, and stuffed it into the bottom of her wardrobe. She couldn't bear the sight of that crumpled dress and hadn't wanted to go near it as long as the memory of that terrible night still had a hold on her.

Was the emerald still there, among the dress and stockings and her ruined slippers?

They had by now reached the Wilkinsons' house. Bessie, Constance, and Norma were taking their seats around the kitchen table. Norma reached for the household ledger-book she kept in the cupboard and adjusted her spectacles with the air of a presiding judge.

Fleurette couldn't sit still without knowing what had happened to her emerald. How much could she have sold it for, if only she'd had the presence of mind to do so right away? As she thought back on Mr. Packard's lovely apartment on Park Avenue — the good pictures in their gilt frames, the grand marble bathtub, the regal silk-lined drapes — she knew he hadn't given her a cheap trinket. What a fool she'd been, to wear it around like a piece of costume jewelry!

But she couldn't go hunting for it now. Her sisters were watching her expectantly, waiting for her to take a seat.

So she sat, resigned to whatever explosions might come when Bessie told the truth.

But Bessie didn't want to talk about the grocer's bill.

"I've had a letter from the bank," she

began. "I didn't want to tell you about it because I didn't want to bring you yet another problem until I had a solution."

"But we are the solution," said Norma.

Fleurette thought she caught a flicker of doubt across Bessie's face.

It occurred to her, for the first time, that perhaps Bessie was a little dubious of the idea that she could entirely rely upon her sisters-in-law. Fleurette couldn't blame her for having second thoughts about their arrangement.

"All right, then," Bessie said. "According to the bank, Francis took out a mortgage against the house. He'd been making the payments in person at the bank every month. They'd like to know when those payments will resume."

She said it as flatly and calmly as she could, but Constance and Norma were in an uproar at once. Over the cacophony Bessie eyed Fleurette levelly. Only the two of them knew the rest of it — the unpaid bills all over town.

Francis had been in some sort of trouble.

Bessie waited while Constance and Norma sputtered and stammered their outrage. Hadn't they sold off a substantial parcel of their farmland, years ago, so that Francis could buy the house? How could he have borrowed against it without so much as a word to Bessie? What did the bank have to say for itself?

It was on the bank that Norma pinned her grievances. "This has to be an error. Have you been down there to speak to them yourself? We'll go directly to the manager on Monday."

And this, from Constance: "If he mortgaged the house, where did the money go?"

"I wish I knew," said Bessie. "The letter tells me nothing, except that the payments come due at the first of every month and I'm two months behind already. I thought that if I could take in a lodger, I could show them that I have a plan . . ."

"You don't need a plan, and you certainly don't need a man living in the basement," said Norma. "This is nonsense. Francis would never mortgage his home. The bank has made a mistake." Norma said it with the profound certainty that she usually reserved for mistakes made by politicians, reporters, and lawyers.

Bessie didn't look at all persuaded, but what choice did she have? They could spend the rest of the week-end arguing about what Francis would or wouldn't have done, or what sort of error the bank might plausibly have made, but their opportunity to speak to the bank manager wouldn't come until Monday, and their opportunity to speak to Francis was gone forever.

Constance and Norma were still huffing over the very idea of their brother landing in such a mess, but Fleurette knew better, and she could tell from the heaviness in Bessie's countenance that she knew better, too. Something had gone terribly wrong in the last year of Francis's life. Whatever it was, there would be a substantial price to pay.

As soon as she could decently excuse herself, Fleurette slipped upstairs to rummage around in her wardrobe. There was her lovely sheer Georgette crêpe, crumpled in a ball, a few of the beads missing, and her skirt, splattered at the hem with mud, and her pretty satin slippers, ruined after she'd run all the way home.

Of Mr. Packard's emerald she found no trace.

17

"Petey told me you'd come around," called Mr. Ward when she appeared at his office door on Monday.

"No, he didn't. That's the last lie I want to hear from you." Fleurette had come dressed for business, in smart gray wool. (How beautiful that emerald would look, against charcoal gray!)

"When have I ever lied to you?"

"That entire job was a lie and you know it. Do you think I would've put myself in harm's way like that?"

"Now hold on, Miss Kopp. Would I have left you in a room with Mr. Thorne if I didn't know you could handle him? How'd you do it, exactly?" He was on his feet now, all smiles and easy grace, practically waltzing over to her. "A girl your size, how'd you land a punch hard enough to knock him over? Go ahead, you can try one out on me if it'll make you feel better."

He offered his nose, still grinning, still winking. "You know, I've never hit a man myself. I have the hands of a piano player, you see" — and he fluttered his fingers, long and elegant.

"I'm not going to show you my tricks," Fleurette said, "in case I need to use them against you someday."

Mr. Ward sighed and leaned against his desk. "In case Petey didn't get the idea across, I never intended for Mr. Thorne to be alone with you for more than the blink of an eye. I was supposed to be ten paces behind him. I was going to play it like it was all a game, Petey told you that, didn't he? But the hotel manager stopped me on my way up and asked to see my key. Trouble was I'd just given the key to Mr. Thorne. I don't know why that manager was suspicious of me."

"Yes, why would anyone be suspicious of you?"

"I had to do quite a song and dance to get away from him, and then I ran up those stairs so fast my heart nearly gave out."

Fleurette flinched at the mention of a heart giving out — the visage of her brother clutching at his chest before he dropped had become a familiar nightmare — but she steeled herself and said, "You would've

184

deserved that, too. Why didn't you just tell me you were playing a different game with Mr. Thorne?"

"You wouldn't have played along."

"So you forced me to."

He hung his head, but he looked up at her almost immediately, seeking forgiveness. "Was any harm done? Mr. Thorne took quite a punch, but you came out all right, didn't you?"

"And what if I hadn't?"

He threw his arms up in a gesture of hopelessness. "You can yell at me all afternoon if you like, but I'll bet you've come back for your jewelry."

"You have it! Why didn't you give it to Petey?"

"I didn't have it at the time," he said. "I didn't know you'd lost it until the hotel telephoned. A porter brought it over this morning, after I described it. You're lucky I have such a good memory."

"Then someone else found it?"

"Apparently there's still such a species as an honest housekeeper. It must've flown under the bed in all that mayhem."

"Then I'll take it and I'll be on my way."

"I suppose you've decided to collect your pay, too," said Mr. Ward.

It had felt so gratifying to throw that

money back at Petey — but what a lot of good it would do them now! Where did it belong, in her hands or Mr. Ward's?

"I'll take my pay, but it's going to cost you double," said Fleurette.

"Yes, of course," said Mr. Ward, fumbling with his wallet. "In fact, I sent Petey over with fifty. Didn't he tell you? You earned it."

"I said double. You owe me a hundred."

He looked up with an almost comic expression of astonishment. If he'd had a pipe between his teeth, it would've dropped to the floor and sent sparks up. "A hun—"

There came a knock at the door just then and Fleurette jumped, thinking, somewhat irrationally, that her sisters had found her.

But the woman who entered was entirely unknown to her. She couldn't have been more than thirty, but she looked frail and fatigued beyond her years and wore a narrow-shouldered disappointment of a coat. If Mr. Ward had hired this woman to take her place, Fleurette would warn her away from the job. It was obvious she'd never be able to handle the Mr. Thornes of the world.

"Mrs. Martin," Mr. Ward said, jumping to his feet. "I hope you had no trouble finding the place."

"Not at all," she said, but her eyes were

on Fleurette.

Mr. Ward looked back and forth at the two of them. "Mrs. Martin is in quite a predicament," he said, by way of introduction.

Then she was a client, not a prospective employee.

"I'll collect my things and be on my way so you two can talk," Fleurette said pointedly to Mr. Ward, thinking only of the jewelry and the money.

But Mr. Ward rushed around to the other side of his desk and pulled two chairs closer for Fleurette and Mrs. Martin. "Miss — ah, Miss Blossom is my associate," Mr. Ward said. "I asked her to come and hear about your situation for herself. I believe she'll be able to help us."

Mrs. Martin looked at Fleurette with a great deal of relief: perhaps she wanted to meet the woman who would be photographed in her husband's arms.

But Fleurette wanted nothing to do with it. "I'll come back later," she said, reaching for her coat.

"I wouldn't ask you to stay," said Mr. Ward, still quite pointed in the way he looked at Fleurette, "except that Mrs. Martin is in such a difficult position and from what I hear, she could use our help right away. Isn't that true, Mrs. Martin? Now,

Miss Blossom and I have a bit of business to finish, but we can do that after. What's most important right now is that you tell us how we can help you after all you've been through."

Mrs. Martin sniffed and sat down. Fleurette, reluctant but resigned, took a seat next to her.

"Thank you, ladies," said Mr. Ward. "Now, Mrs. Martin, I have your letter, but it would be so enlightening to hear it in your own words. Why don't you tell us both what happened?"

Mrs. Martin looked worriedly between the two of them and said, "My husband's taken up with a girl in the theater. He intends to run off with her, I know it. He'll leave me without a penny."

"He's a scoundrel and a fool to leave a woman like you, Mrs. Martin," Mr. Ward said. "How do you feel the firm of Ward & McGinnis can be of help to you?"

"Please call me Alice," Mrs. Martin said. "I never thought I'd be here, talking to a pair of strangers about divorce. But I believe it's inevitable now. I just want a judge to rule in my favor."

"And to make sure Mr. Martin pays his support," Mr. Ward added.

"Ah . . . yes, that too, I suppose," Alice

said, but it sounded to Fleurette like that had only just occurred to her.

"All you require is the evidence."

"Will that be a problem?"

"Well, it's always a bit of a problem, which is why a firm like ours is called in to handle it, isn't that right, Miss Blossom?" asked Mr. Ward.

Fleurette gave no reply. She was only biding her time, waiting for the meeting to end so that she could be on her way.

"Am I to understand that he goes to the same places with this girl and won't be hard to find?" Mr. Ward asked.

"Oh, he's not at all hard to find," said Alice, "if you can get in. That's the trouble. The girl's in the theater, and he only ever sees her there, on Wednesday nights. They have their little — well, their little trysts, or whatever you might call them, right there in her dressing-room."

"The theater? Is that so? Our very own Miss Blossom has a bit of experience in the theater. She has quite a way with costumes and disguises, too. If anyone could slip backstage undetected, this young lady could do it."

"But how would I get Petey backstage?" asked Fleurette, already putting the operation together in her mind, even though she had no intention of taking another dollar from Mr. Ward. If she could dress as one of the chorus girls, she wouldn't have any trouble convincing a guard that she was a new understudy . . .

"You'll take the pictures this time," said Mr. Ward, easily, as if it fell within the normal course of business.

Fleurette was about to object again, or simply get up and walk out, when Mr. Ward turned to the subject of money.

"I believe you'll find our fees to be completely fair, Mrs. Martin," he said, although he was pitching his voice at Fleurette. "We charge one hundred dollars to take the pictures. If you are satisfied with them — and only if you're completely satisfied, Mrs. Martin — it's another hundred to file the petition for divorce with the court, with the pictures entered as evidence. Then there's our time in court. As long as Mr. Martin doesn't put up a fight, you can expect the case to be disposed of with no more than a brief hearing. How does that sound to you?"

"All right, I suppose," said Alice. "I'd been told to expect to pay five hundred dollars for a divorce."

Five hundred dollars? And Mr. Ward had only been paying her twenty? Fleurette sat up a little straighter at that. Mr. Ward noticed.

"Well, you can expect to pay some court fees," he said, keeping an eye on Fleurette. "And of course it could be higher if we had a lengthy trial, like the ones you read about in the papers, but that hardly ever happens unless there's a large family fortune to be haggled over. I don't believe you're afflicted with one of those, are you?"

Alice shifted uncomfortably and said, "I only wish I was. Think of the trouble that would've saved me."

"Money's just a different kind of trouble," said Mr. Ward. "We can start right away, if you like. You'll pay the hundred dollars now, directly to my associate, for her expenses. I'll collect the rest when I have pictures to show you. Does that — ah, does that pose any difficulty for you, Mrs. Martin? It gets tricky if you don't want your husband to know that any money's missing."

"I suppose I have a few things I could sell," she said. "Little trinkets he wouldn't notice."

"A silver tray here, a bracelet there? That's just fine. Now, if you could just put down the particulars about the theater . . ."

There was more to it than that, but

Fleurette wasn't listening. She was calculating.

This couldn't be another trick, could it? She'd heard the client's story for herself. Mr. Martin wouldn't try to get his hands on her. He already had a girl. There was a good reason to send her to take the pictures instead of Petey: she'd have an easier time slipping backstage.

And a hundred dollars! Was he serious about paying her all that, or did he intend to keep a share for himself? She'd walked in with little hope of retrieving her missing jewelry and hadn't even intended to demand that he pay her a hundred dollars for her trouble with Mr. Thorne. That had occurred to her only at the very last minute, on a rising tide of outrage.

What if she walked out with two hundred dollars, along with the emerald?

She could pay off every merchant in Hawthorne. Bessie could start fresh, with her credit restored. Norma and Constance would never have to know.

She might even have enough left over to make a mortgage payment, although Fleurette hadn't any idea what was owed or how she'd pull that off without her sisters finding out.

If nothing else, she could slip a few needful items to Bessie and the children: new school clothes, a pair of shoes here and there . . .

Even if she never saw Mr. Ward again (and this was her intention, still, after what he'd done), this single job — this simple, straightforward, and not at all dishonest job — would ease Bessie's troubles considerably.

"That's just fine, Mrs. Martin," Mr. Ward was saying, as Mrs. Martin handed him an envelope and he counted out the bills. "This goes directly to Miss Blossom for her trouble —"

And there he was, handing an envelope of cash to Fleurette, which she took automatically, as anyone would do —

"And we'll get those pictures this Wednesday, if we possibly can. Is there anything else we can do for you today?"

Alice looked back and forth between them, a little startled, as if she hadn't expected to have conducted her business so briskly. "No. I suppose that's all, then."

18

"You see, it isn't always such a terrible thing, working for Ward & McGinnis," Mr. Ward said, when Alice left. "That little envelope full of cash has cheered you up considerably."

"As long as there aren't any unpleasant surprises."

"I can't vouch for Mr. Martin, but it sounds like his interests lie elsewhere. Of course, if you feel it's too much of a risk, I could give this one to Petey."

"I can handle it myself," said Fleurette, snatching up the envelope.

"I never doubted it."

It was no consolation for the way she'd been treated, but to walk out of Mr. Ward's office two hundred dollars richer, to say nothing of the emerald hidden under her blouse, did leave Fleurette feeling victorious. She went directly to Belsky's to pay off the account, and then stopped at every other merchant to whom the Kopps owed money, bringing Francis's debt to zero.

Money can't solve every problem, but it solved this one. Fleurette walked down the sidewalk with a fine feeling of satisfaction: it was all she could do not to brush her palms together, briskly, as Norma did when she was finished pounding a fence-post.

At home, she met with glum faces all around. The bank manager had refused to see Norma and Bessie without an appointment, and his secretary insisted that no appointments were available for a week. Norma was ready to draw up placards and stage a demonstration on the bank's threshold, but Bessie convinced her to wait.

"We'll go back tomorrow, and the next day," Bessie said. "He can find one minute in his busy day to speak to us. We'll be persistent, but polite."

Norma never would have brooked such an objection from Constance or Fleurette, but gave far more leeway to a widow expectant with child. "All right, we'll try polite and persistent, but if that doesn't work, we'll just be persistent. And we won't give that bank one dime in payment until they give us the explanation we're owed."

"Of course we won't," Bessie said.

"And if they don't like it, they can speak

to our attorney," Norma said.

"Do we have an attorney?" asked Fleurette, wondering what use a man like John Ward could possibly be in negotiations with a bank.

"We will hire one, if they give us any trouble," said Norma.

Petey didn't mind at all that he had to turn his camera over to Fleurette and teach her how to use it. "I've been telling Mr. Ward that we could use a girl photographer," he said later that night, when she slipped out to meet him in his automobile. "There are some places I just can't go. A chorus girl's dressing-room is one of them."

"Then you don't mind that I'm taking your salary?" asked Fleurette.

"Miss, I'm a partner in the law firm, although Mr. Ward doesn't treat me like one. Half of everything he collects belongs to me."

"Of course," muttered Fleurette, although in truth, she had no idea how a law firm operated.

"Most lawyers hire a photographer when they need one," he said, "and the photographer brings the girl, if there's going to be a girl. But we had a receptionist who said she'd like to be the girl, if we'd pay her extra. I already had a camera, so . . .." He shrugged. "We keep more of the fee that way. But if Mr. Ward would rather have you do the pictures, we just pass the cost on to the client. You see how it works."

"I do now," said Fleurette. She was starting to see that working for a lawyer was not much different from working for a vaudeville showman: whatever she pocketed was only a percentage of what the man hiring her put in his pocket. Neither the legal profession nor the theatrical business was designed to make money *for* her, they were both designed to make money *off* her — off her talents, off her time. She was paid; someone else profited.

Nonetheless, she was willing if not eager for the job. A bit of spy-work was in order first. On Tuesday she took the train into Manhattan, dressed in nondescript black so she wouldn't be seen or remembered. She walked right up to the theater where Mr. Martin visited his chorus girl and waited around at the stage door after the performance, like any autograph-seeker. In this way she had a good look at the costumes the girls wore. They were of a sturdy blue satin, the skirts pleated so they flew up when the girls danced. Fleurette memorized the ensemble with a single glance and knew she'd have no trouble at all putting together a reasonable facsimile.

The next night, she presented herself at the stage door and met little resistance from the man standing guard. She'd been around enough stage-hands to know just the right tone to take: she must be harried and act as if she already belonged inside.

"I'm the new understudy, didn't they tell you? I have a letter from Mr. McCallister —" Here she rummaged in her bag for a letter she didn't actually have from the director, his name easily obtained from the programs dropped in the street outside the lobby.

"Never mind about the letter," said the man at the door. "You're late. You'd better hurry."

With that she was inside.

What a familiar pleasure it was to be backstage at the theater again! There was no better feeling in the world than to be behind the curtain, amid the chaos of scattered costumes and discarded pots of face-paint. What she'd missed most of all about the theater was the camaraderie of a traveling troupe, the fresh scandals and old jokes, the rising sense of anticipation as the audience filed in, the sliver of danger that hangs in the air around any live performance, knowing that something might go awry, half hoping that it does, if only to keep things fresh . . .

Perhaps it would do her voice some good to be around theater people more often. Maybe she wasn't so much taking a rest as atrophying. Would it hurt to audition for something like this — a light musical, just one of the chorus, nothing too taxing? Perhaps that was just what she needed to build herself up again.

There were enough people scuttling about that no one noticed her at first, but she had to get herself hidden, and quickly. She could claim to be a new understudy to one or two people, but as soon as they started checking around, she'd be sunk.

Fortunately, there were any number of curtains and backdrops where she could conceal herself. Once the entire cast was on stage, she could have a look around the dressing-rooms to see if Arthur Martin was waiting in any of them. His wife had described him as short, round, and balding, with quite unmistakable black horn-rimmed glasses. He didn't sound like the sort of man an actress would carry on with, but perhaps, Fleurette reasoned, he had compensatory charms.

Once she found him, she had only to lurk

nearby, camera in hand, and wait for the right moment. There was no such thing as a door with a lock on it in a place like this: the dressing-rooms were nothing but curtains with paper-thin walls that didn't even go all the way to the ceiling. She'd have no difficulty getting into the room. Whether she'd have enough light to take a recognizable photograph was another question.

As to how she'd get out again, with a furious Mr. Martin chasing after her . . . for that, Fleurette might have to rely more on wits than speed.

She could pretend she was a friend of one of the other girls, taking pictures for a lark, and had popped into the wrong room by mistake.

She could put her acting skills to the test and pretend to be a fan, desperate for a picture of Mr. Martin's love interest.

Or perhaps she would outrun him — she was small and nimble, after all.

Perhaps.

Fleurette realized, as she considered her options, that there was a reason Petey didn't mind letting her take the job, and it wasn't because a man would have a harder time sneaking backstage.

It was because getting the picture was a nearly impossible task. And there were no easy exits. The stage-hands would know every possible hiding-place. If she was caught, here in the theater district, a police officer was easily summoned.

It was a mad scheme and unlikely to work. But she'd taken the money and spent it already. What else could she do but try to finish the job?

It was nonetheless with a sense of relief that she realized she wouldn't have to.

As she crouched in her hiding spot behind a half-unrolled painted backdrop, she heard a girl call from a dressing-room, "Arthur! Come and see how I've expanded my diaphragm!"

Another sang out, "Listen to my triplets! Koo-koo-koo!"

A third said, "He's helping to loosen my larynx. You'll get him next."

Could this be Arthur Martin? How many Arthurs could there be backstage?

Soon enough she heard him answer back in a deep, sonorous voice, a well-cared-for and cultivated voice. "I'll be right with you, Madeline! Let me hear your vowels. Hold your diaphragm like I showed you."

As Madeline proceeded with her vowels, Fleurette risked a peek from behind the backdrop. The dressing-rooms stretched in a row away from her: in the dim light, she could just make out a figure moving between them. He stopped to knock at the post holding up the curtain between two rooms, and when the curtain parted, he was greeted with enough light that Fleurette could be certain.

Short, rotund, balding, with heavy glasses. Arthur Martin didn't have a love interest in the theater. He had students.

Well, perhaps he had both. She waited to see if he treated any one of the girls differently from another. Elizabeth was made to practice sustained passages. Anita was introduced to the idea of lip strokes, and shown how to sing *wa, wo, we,* up and down the scale.

Fleurette couldn't help but follow along. *Wa, wo, we,* with the lips pursed as if to whistle, and then drawn quickly back, causing the suction of air. Why hadn't she ever been shown that before?

She was by now so distracted by Mr. Martin's lessons that she'd forgotten about the photographs. There wasn't the slightest hint of impropriety in his manner toward his students. Fleurette was entirely convinced that she'd been sent on a fool's errand. She couldn't guess at Alice's reason for accusing him and did not, in fact, take any time to think about it just then. She was too intent on hearing what Mr. Martin had to say.

"Hand on your larynx, Martha! Is it entirely relaxed? Is it merely an instrument of the diaphragm?"

Fleurette put her hand on her own larynx and thought that it hadn't properly relaxed in months.

Mr. Martin continued his rounds, listening to scales, dispensing exercises, and exhorting every girl to sing with ease and abundant breath, and to never strain to be heard. "Remember, especially when you're dancing, that your abdomen dances with you! That's why I want you walking when you practice, or rehearsing your steps along with your songs. You can't abandon one for the other."

Abandon one for the other. Perhaps that's where Fleurette had gone wrong. All those tricky dance steps — it was easy to forget about the voice when everything depended on leading with the left foot. Had she ruined her voice not through illness but through improper singing?

The piano player was starting now. The lights went down in the theater. She could hear Mr. Martin saying his good-byes.

The girls hurried to their places and the show began. Mr. Martin stood for a moment and watched — she could only see his shoulder, and a foot tapping just under the curtain — and then he turned to leave.

Fleurette slipped away from her hiding-place. "Mr. Martin!" she whispered.

He turned and waited, taking stock of her costume. (It was a very convincing costume.)

"I don't believe we've met," he said, bowing slightly. He didn't whisper, so beautifully controlled was his voice that he could send it near or far with no effort at all.

"I'm only an understudy," she said. "Laura" — how desperate she had to be, to choose her parrot's name as her pseudonym! — "Underwood."

"An understudy called Underwood. You were meant for it."

"I hope I'm meant for the cast," Fleurette said. They were by now near the back door and had no need of whispering.

"Not with that voice, you're not," he said.

She put a hand over her throat. "But you haven't even heard me sing."

"I don't have to," he said. "You've had an illness, haven't you? Or an ulceration."

"Both," she admitted.

"Your voice is thin and unsupported. You're trying too hard to protect it. Put your hand here" — and he placed his own hand over his throat. Fleurette did the same.

"You're squeezing it like a lemon, aren't you? Going around all day with it clamped shut. Trying to protect it from getting hurt again."

"I hadn't thought of it like that," admitted Fleurette. "I'd been told to rest it, and I thought I was."

"But you can't hold a note, can you? It cracks up and falls apart. Or you start to cough."

Fleurette was practically in tears by now. She nodded but couldn't answer.

"We can't do anything about it now," he said. "I can't hear you properly with the show going. I don't know if you ever get to Paterson . . ." He fumbled around in his pockets until he withdrew a card. "I give lessons on Tuesdays and Thursdays."

"And you teach here as well?" Fleurette thought she ought to at least be sure of her assumptions about Mr. Martin.

"These girls can't afford lessons, or they can't be bothered to take the train all the way to Paterson, but they pool their pennies and have me come around on Wednesday nights and give them a little — well, punching up, I suppose you'd call it."

That sounded like a reasonable explanation. Didn't Alice know what her husband was doing?

"It's good of you to come all this way for them," Fleurette said.

"Oh, I'm out most nights, at one theater or another," he said. "Hazard of the job. Go on, take my card, and come see me when you can. You're going to need to build yourself back up again before you go on stage."

She took the card. ARTHUR MARTIN, it read. VOCAL EXPRESSIONIST.

19

Having failed to obtain her photographs, Fleurette decided not to report back to Mr. Ward just yet but to first pay a visit to Alice.

She knew she wasn't exactly authorized to go around speaking to Mr. Ward's clients. But hadn't he praised her before for salvaging a job, when poor weepy Mr. Finley was too heartbroken to have his picture taken?

She saw no reason why she shouldn't try again, with Alice, to salvage a ruined job. Perhaps the girl in question had moved on to another show. Or maybe — and this would be a disappointment, in terms of the fee, but a relief to Alice — he wasn't having an affair at all, and the whole sorrowful business had been a misunderstanding.

It was unlikely — Alice had seemed awfully convinced of her husband's infidelity — but how else to explain it?

Mr. Martin's address was on his card. It appeared to be not an office, but a home address. It wouldn't be at all unusual for a voice teacher to work out of his living room. She wasn't sure how she'd speak to Alice alone, but she took a chance and strolled by the following afternoon.

She could hear a student singing scales to a metronome from half a block away. The sound didn't come from the house, though, but from a cottage in the back not much bigger than a garden shed. With Mr. Martin so obviously occupied, Fleurette knocked at the front door.

Alice answered almost immediately. She was dressed to go out. When she saw Fleurette, she took a step back in surprise. Fleurette took the opportunity to step inside, a trick she'd learned from Constance. In an investigation, don't wait to be invited in. (Was this an investigation? Fleurette felt it might be.)

She found herself in a sitting-room that was unexceptional in every way, except that it was outfitted with an upright piano and the walls were hung with autographed programs and playbills. Here lived a person devoted to the theater.

"Mrs. Martin, I'm sorry to bother you at home," she began.

Mrs. Martin was still standing at the door, her pocketbook under her arm. "My husband's here," she whispered. "You shouldn't have come."

"As long as we can hear them singing, we know where they are," Fleurette said. "I came to tell you what happened. I went to the theater last night as you asked. There was no girl. Well, there were plenty of girls, but they were his students. You know that, don't you? He goes to the theater to visit his students."

Mrs. Martin glared at her. For such a mousy woman, she could be quite fearsome. "Of course he goes to the theater. He's surrounded by young girls all the time. Your job was to get a picture of him with one of them."

"One of them?" said Fleurette. "Don't you mean to say that you wanted a picture of him with the girl he's threatened to run off with? The one you intend to name as corespondent in the divorce case? If she exists at all —"

"Of course she exists," Mrs. Martin said.

"Then she's no longer at that theater. Or she wasn't there last night. He was only backstage for ten minutes, and I watched him. His conduct was above reproach. He was obviously there on a professional basis. If you can tell me where else I might find him and his girl together, I'll go again. But

I can't take a picture of a girl who isn't there."

The singing stopped just then. Mrs. Martin looked at the clock. "They're about finished. You should go."

"Why don't we both go," Fleurette said. "You look like you were on your way out anyway."

They heard footsteps at the back door. Mrs. Martin sighed and stepped outside. Fleurette followed.

Mrs. Martin walked at a furious pace. They dashed down the street and around the corner. "I thought you lawyers could get a picture of anything. I pay your fee, and I get a picture of my husband with a girl."

"Oh, you mean . . ." But Fleurette didn't know how to put it.

"Yes, exactly," Mrs. Martin said. "Doesn't Ward & McGinnis do that sort of thing? When I saw you in his office, I assumed you'd be the girl. Isn't that how it works?"

What Fleurette wanted to say was *Yes, but you didn't ask for that.* But if she let it be known that such a service was available, Alice would simply demand it and that would be the end of it. Poor Mr. Martin, who appeared to have done nothing wrong, would find himself on the receiving end of a divorce suit. But why?

Fleurette had the feeling that Alice wasn't telling her everything. She wasn't about to proceed until she knew what Alice was holding back.

"Mrs. Martin, I do want to help. Mr. Ward is your lawyer. He wants to gather all the facts and do the very best he can for you. Can you tell me how you found out that your husband was having an affair? Have you seen the girl? Do you know anything at all about her?"

Alice was even more agitated now. "I've told you what I want from you. If you can't do it, then I'll take my money back and give it to another lawyer who can."

Fleurette wasn't about to tell her that the money had already been spent. "No one can take a picture of a woman who doesn't exist, Mrs. Martin. Are you sure there isn't something you're not telling us? You do know that we want to help."

Mrs. Martin didn't answer. She wheeled around and walked away. This time, Fleurette let her go.

20

The next morning, Fleurette picked at a late breakfast while Constance read another of the innumerable department store protocol manuals she brought home from work.

"I don't know why you bother with those books," Fleurette said. "They're only paying you to follow the ladies around and make sure they don't slip anything into their pocketbooks. You don't need a manual to tell you how to do that."

Constance hardly bothered to look up as she answered. "Mr. Schoonmaker has been dangling the possibility of a promotion, if I'll learn something of the business. He has an idea to put someone in charge of inventory generally. I wouldn't just be looking out for thieves. I'd be managing everything — how it's received, how it's stored, how we keep track of what goes in and what goes out. He wants to put the business on a more modern footing."

Fleurette pushed her plate away and squinted at Constance. "That has to be the dullest thing you've ever said. Truly, I don't think I've ever heard a more deathly boring string of words come out of your mouth. You don't really intend to become an inventory manager for a department store, do you?"

"I intend to take a promotion if it's offered and to bring in more money if I can," Constance said. "Isn't that what we're all doing?"

"Yes, but . . ." Fleurette thought better than to argue. She'd found a very lively line of work, even if it did come with its hazards. She wouldn't mind fending off the occasional Mr. Thorne if it meant that she never, ever had to think about inventory management at a department store.

"Your talents are wasted, that's all I'm saying," said Fleurette.

"My talents can wait," said Constance.

Could they? Fleurette thought again of Francis, struck down at his desk. What had he put off until later? What ambitions had he deferred? Fleurette realized she didn't even know. It had never occurred to her to ask.

Norma and Bessie banged through the kitchen door just then, having been up especially early to catch the bank manager on his way in.

"That Mr. Tichborne doesn't own the bank," Norma groused, as she hung up her hat and took Bessie's right off her head. "I intend to find out who does and complain to him. To treat a grieving widow like she's some sort of — of — disinterested party is unforgivable. I'll have him dismissed."

"It isn't how he treated me, but what he had to say," Bessie put in. She spoke slowly, as if the shock of it still hadn't registered.

"To insist that he'll only speak to our lawyer is in itself illegal," Norma said. "It must be. But if he wants a lawyer, he'll get one. Don't we know an attorney?"

"I thought one came to the funeral," said Bessie.

"That was John Ward," said Norma. "I don't know that he'll do us much good."

Fleurette dropped her spoon and ducked down to retrieve it. Norma seemed not to notice. "We'll have someone write a letter," she continued. "Do you know I believe Mr. Tichborne was terrified to have a pregnant woman sitting across from him?"

"You didn't have to tell him," said Bessie, smoothing down the front of her dress. She was at that in-between stage where no man would dare to guess whether she was pregnant or merely stout.

"I wanted him to know what we're up against," said Norma, "and I wanted more than three months."

Constance pushed her store manual aside and said, "Three months for what? Do you mind telling the rest of us what the banker said?"

Bessie sighed. "Sit down, Norma. You can't pace around all day."

"Oh, I intend to pace around," Norma said, "until I work out what Francis did with all that money."

"Then he did take out a mortgage," said Fleurette.

"About six months ago," said Norma. "He borrowed fifteen hundred dollars against his own house."

"Fifteen hundred? That has to be a year's salary," said Constance.

"Almost," said Bessie.

"But — why?"

Norma said, "That's what they won't tell us. They want us to believe that it's not our business what he did with the money. It's only our business to pay it back."

"Wouldn't the bank have records?" asked Fleurette. "Unless he walked out with a bag of cash, there must be something that shows where the money went. He didn't keep it,

215

did he?"

"He didn't keep it in the bank, if that's what you mean," said Bessie. "We had almost nothing in our account when he died."

"Then he must've paid it to someone," said Constance. "I can't believe the bank manager doesn't know."

"Oh, he knows," said Norma. "He just doesn't want to tell us. He doesn't think he has to. Francis was the bank's customer, and now Francis is dead. Bessie has the account now, but as far as Mr. Tichborne is concerned, that's an entirely different matter."

"But the mortgage is still owed," said Constance. "So it's not a different matter."

"I explained it to Mr. Tichborne in precisely those terms," said Norma, "but he's a banker. He wants his money."

"He agreed to delay for three months," said Bessie, "but then we're expected to start making those payments."

"And if we don't?" said Fleurette.

Bessie opened her mouth to answer, and then looked through the kitchen window at her own house next door.

Norma answered for her. "The bank can take the house."

"But that's impossible!" said Fleurette.

"You've lived there since you were married. It's bought and paid for."

Bessie turned back to look at her. "I'm afraid it isn't. Not anymore."

She was near tears already. Fleurette didn't dare ask another question.

But there was no stopping Norma. "We can file suit, and we should. Francis must've put that money somewhere. It could be on deposit at another bank. He could've bought a piece of property. Fifteen hundred dollars did not just vanish overnight. We'll find out where it's gone, we'll take it back, and we'll settle the mortgage. I can't believe Francis intended to leave you with a mess like this."

"Francis didn't intend to leave me at all," said Bessie quietly. Fleurette reached over and rubbed her shoulders.

Norma dropped her elbows on the table and put her chin in her hands. "He wouldn't have squandered the house, that's all I know." She looked up at the calendar tacked on the wall. "Six months ago. That would've been August. I was in France, obviously. I had no idea what he was up to. But you were here. Can't you think of anything he said, any sort of opportunity he might've mentioned? A friend going into business, a house for sale, anything at all? He didn't go out and buy war bonds with it, did he?"

Bessie shook her head. "I found all the war bonds in his desk."

"I'm going to have another look at that desk," said Norma.

"He never said a word about money to me," said Constance. "I suppose we could ask his friends and his associates at work. He was always volunteering with some committee or another during the war. Those were mostly businessmen. One of them might remember something."

"Oh, let's don't start asking his friends. I don't want to spread this all over town," Bessie said.

"No, that's right," said Norma. "If word gets around, we'll be questioned every time we walk down the street. This is between us and the bank."

"Well, my shift starts at noon," said Constance, pushing away from the table. "I ought to get ready. But if you change your mind, just say the word and I'll go speak to a few people. Discreetly."

"Not yet," said Bessie. "I'd rather find another way. Is there any coffee left?"

Norma was already reaching for the morning papers. "Fleurette will make another pot."

Bessie made a show of pushing herself up, but Fleurette put a hand on her shoulder.

"Stay where you are."

Constance disappeared down the hall while Fleurette busied herself with the coffee. Norma paged through the newspaper, reading aloud as she always did.

"It says here that divorce petitions have nearly doubled since the end of the war," Norma announced. Fleurette kept her eyes on the coffee.

Despite the lack of interest from anyone in the room, Norma went on. "They're suggesting that divorces aren't really any higher if you consider the fact that they were lower last year, when the men were in France. They're just catching up now."

"Oh, that's awful," said Bessie. "Fleurette, dear, I wouldn't mind one of those molasses cookies."

"Bring the whole tin," said Norma, without looking up from her newspaper. "These don't seem like divorces that were put off because of the war. They seem like fresh affairs. Here's an Amanda Ballard, filing suit against her husband, G. W. Ballard, who was seen at a hotel that shall not be named because it is such a regular advertiser, in the company of the co-respondent, a Miss Gloria Blossom. Now, according to this, Mr. Ballard is no returning war hero. He's fifty-two —"

219

Fleurette nearly choked. She didn't dare look around to see if Constance was within earshot. Norma wouldn't recognize the name Gloria Blossom, but Constance would: it was the only pseudonym Fleurette had used when she worked on Constance's case during the war.

For a full agonizing minute Fleurette waited. But Constance didn't reappear.

She listened for footsteps, the sound of drawers opening and closing, a faucet running, anything that might tell her whether Constance was upstairs or downstairs.

Had she really missed it? She must have. She would've come running in if she'd heard that name. It was so obviously phony, and Fleurette had used it for weeks last fall. There was no forgetting it.

But who was G. W. Ballard? Fleurette couldn't recall the case. It occurred to her that the clients might've also been acting under an assumed name. Perhaps the men might also have wanted their identities kept private. It made sense: Mr. Ward had every reason to make sure that his clients and his professional co-respondent knew next to nothing about each other.

The trouble was that she'd only used the name Gloria Blossom once, with Mr. Thorne, because she'd forgotten to pick a pseudonym in advance and had to scramble for one at the last minute. It was careless of her: the entire reason for choosing a false name was the very real possibility that she'd be mentioned in the papers as co-respondent.

And Mr. Thorne's case had not, as far as Fleurette knew, made it to court.

Hadn't Mr. Ward introduced her to Alice Martin as Miss Blossom? He'd come up with that on his own. There seemed to be no reason to use a phony name if Fleurette was only to do the photography, but she hadn't objected. She would've chosen a name other than Miss Blossom if she'd had the opportunity, but the moment had slipped by so quickly that she didn't bother.

But the Martin case hadn't resulted in any divorce charges being filed, either.

Whoever G. W. Ballard might be, Fleurette was fairly sure she'd never met him.

Norma had by this time moved past the divorce cases to the next item of interest. Fleurette heard Constance coming down the stairs, or was she going up?

"Well, the county road supervisor doesn't know what he's doing," said Norma, folding the paper back and preparing to read aloud.

Then she paused and looked up at

Fleurette, who was staring at the wall. "Whatever happened to those cookies?"

21

"But why would you use a name your sister would recognize?" Mr. Ward asked, quite reasonably, after Fleurette explained the situation. She'd rushed right over after breakfast, too nervous to stay in the house another minute with that incriminating newspaper sitting around.

"I never meant to," Fleurette protested. "It was that awful night with Mr. Thorne. I'd been so busy doing myself up — because you asked me to — that I forgot to choose a name. Gloria Blossom just slipped out."

"Well, it stuck in my mind as well. G. W. Ballard's case is an old one only just now making its way to court. The paperwork came through a week ago. I suppose I might've put that Blossom name down without realizing where I'd heard it. You're right, you never met him. Be grateful for that. He was an old sourpuss. I sent a girl over for pictures and he lectured her on morality. Can you imagine that? A man looking for a divorce and he's quoting scripture to my girl?"

"Well, don't use it again," Fleurette said.

"It's already forgotten," said Mr. Ward. "Do you have film for me?"

"I don't," said Fleurette. "Arthur Martin goes to the theater at night, but he isn't having an affair. He's a vocal instructor. Did you know that?"

"I only know what Mrs. Martin told us. Do you mean to say that vocal instructors don't have affairs with their students? What an odd profession."

"Well, this one doesn't," said Fleurette, "or if he does, I saw no evidence of it. But here's the strange part. When I went back to ask Mrs. Martin —"

"Why'd you go to see her?" said Mr. Ward. "The client's my business."

"I thought there'd been some mistake," said Fleurette. "I just wanted to get the pictures. That's what Mrs. Martin paid us to do."

"That's a fine impulse," said Mr. Ward, "but you've already been paid. If she sent us on a wild-goose chase, that's for her to come and straighten out with me."

"Well, if you can straighten it out, good luck to you," said Fleurette. "She was furious with me for failing to take a picture of something that didn't exist. She seemed to have had the idea that we'd take it upon ourselves to put a girl in the picture if we had to."

"We might have, but that's another conversation entirely," Mr. Ward said.

"I wanted to tell her that, but I wasn't sure just how to put it," Fleurette said. "I also didn't want to explain to her that the gentleman is usually in on the entire operation."

"Don't bother," Mr. Ward said. "If she wants something along those lines from us, she's going to have to put it into words. Or if she wants to pay us to follow her husband around day and night until we catch him with this particular girl, we can do that too. But I don't think she knows what she wants, except to waste our time. Do you mind going over to Hoboken on Thursday? The fellow owns a steakhouse. I'd put on a dress myself, for one of his steaks."

Fleurette was still thinking about Alice Martin. "There's something odd about her. I had the impression that she was holding something back. What do you suppose it could be?"

Mr. Ward shrugged. "I'm not going to wonder about Mrs. Martin until she starts paying me to wonder about her."

"But couldn't we —" Before she could finish, she heard a familiar set of heavy footsteps in the hall. For one irrational moment she looked around for a place to hide. Could she dive under Mr. Ward's desk?

But there was no time for that. The doorknob rattled. With a stone in her heart, she turned around to face her sister.

Even in the more ladylike attire they made her wear at Schoonmaker's, Constance was formidable. She was also sweating and red-faced. Fleurette could just picture her racing downtown, mowing down everyone else on the sidewalk.

"Are you working for him?" she shouted.

Mr. Ward scrambled to his feet, his freshly lit pipe dropping into his chair and sending sparks and burnt tobacco across the leather. He glanced down at it but evidently decided that such a small fire posed less of a hazard than the woman standing before him.

"What a pleasure, Miss Kopp. My condolences about your brother."

"Stop that nonsense. Of all the girls you could've involved in your little schemes, you picked this one?" Constance pointed at Fleurette but did not look at her. Mr. Ward raised an eyebrow in Fleurette's direction and then turned his attention to his chair, swatting at the embers with a handkerchief.

Fleurette had been shrinking back into the corner of the room but thought she ought to do something to defend herself. She made a half-hearted attempt to rally some indignation and said, "You have no idea what I've —"

Constance put up a hand to stop her. "Gloria Blossom? Don't patronize me. Did you think I wouldn't find out?"

"Seems to me you'd like to have a sister in the legal profession," Mr. Ward said. "It's sort of the family business. Can I offer anyone a drink?" He swept a hand toward a cabinet under the window. Fleurette looked at the cabinet with just a drop of longing, but Constance ignored him.

"Submitting fraudulent evidence to the courts is not the family business," Constance said. "It's illegal and it's dangerous. Look at her. Have you really been putting a girl like this alone in a room with a strange man?"

Mr. Ward loosened his tie a little. It had grown uncommonly hot. "Exactly what sort of firm do you think we run here, Miss Kopp? As for your sister —"

"I know exactly what sort of firm you run," said Constance. "Either you've roped my sister into one of your phony divorce schemes —"

"Oh, there's nothing phony about these divorces, I can assure you of that," said Mr. Ward.

"Or you've somehow learned a name that she's used only once before, in connection with a case that had nothing to do with you, and you're throwing it around town without her consent. Which is it?"

Fleurette had, by now, had enough of Constance's haranguing and Mr. Ward's banter. How often, over the years, had she been expected to sit still while someone else argued over her? She stepped in between the two of them, her back against the edge of Mr. Ward's desk.

"You've no right to come in here and scold him. I don't go into your place of employment and shout at your boss over what he has you do all day."

Constance looked down at her in a cold fury. "Then you have been working for him."

"What if I have?" shouted Fleurette. "What business is it of yours? You wanted me to go out and find work and I did."

Constance looked around the room, sputtering. Fleurette couldn't remember the last time she'd seen her sister so angry. "But not this kind of work! If you can even call it work! What do you do, put on a pretty dress and . . ."

She couldn't go on, the idea was so repulsive to her.

Fleurette made herself as tall as she could. "You don't get to decide what I do! I'm bringing in more money than you are, and I've been going all over town paying down Francis's debts, which is more than you've done."

Constance took a step back. "What do you mean, all over town?"

Fleurette wasn't about to explain it in front of Mr. Ward. "You see? You don't even know. He left a mess behind, and who's cleaning it up? I am, and you don't get to say a word about it." She was walking toward the door now.

"Oh, I'll say more than a word about it," Constance shouted, chasing after her. "As long as we're living under the same roof —"

There it was. That was the truth of the matter.

Constance would never stop criticizing her. Anything Fleurette wanted to do required Constance's approval, or it had to be hidden and lied about. Was she expected to live like that forever?

She spun around and faced Constance. "Then we won't live under one roof. I'll be gone tonight."

She looked back at Mr. Ward, who was leaning against his desk with the air of a man watching a train derailment out of a window. "And I'll see you on Tuesday," she told him.

Constance turned around, too. "Don't you dare see my sister on Tuesday, or any other day, for that matter."

Some sort of response seemed to be required, so Mr. Ward offered a half-hearted wave. "If you insist. Good day, ladies."

22

Constance followed her down to the street, still shouting. "Tell me you have not gone into a room with a man and had your picture taken, so that picture could be —"

"Will you stop?" Fleurette hissed. Already they were attracting attention on the sidewalk.

"If it's too scandalous to mention on the street, then why were you doing it?"

"You've done secretive work, too," Fleurette said.

Constance snorted. "I was fighting the Germans. You're helping John Ward's playboys to get out of their marriage vows. And I never kept anything a secret from you."

"But why would you ever need to? I don't have a say in what you do. You're free to run your life as you see fit, and I'm only a spectator. But if you don't like what I'm doing, you come tearing after me like I'm a runaway child."

Fleurette was storming down the sidewalk now, but she couldn't outrun Constance.

"You're ashamed of what you're doing, or you would've told us about it," Constance said.

"Aren't you late to work?" Fleurette snapped. "You'll never make inventory manager if you don't show up on time."

Constance slowed and took a breath. "We'll talk about this tonight."

Fleurette stopped, mid-stride, and turned to look at her sister, all six feet of her, broad-shouldered and indefatigable. How it exhausted her to fight with Constance!

But it would never end. Constance would never stop interfering. They could keep arguing tonight, and the next night, and every night after that. It would carry on as long as Fleurette did anything at all that gave Constance reason to disapprove.

And Constance wasn't just a sister. She was a cop. She would always be a cop. She would track Fleurette down. She would barge in where she wasn't invited. She would give orders and make demands.

And it would go on for years. Fleurette could just see herself at forty, and Constance nearly sixty, still judging her and scolding her.

The only way to live with Constance was

to live on Constance's terms — always and forever.

Fleurette was still staring at her sister. Constance had a look about her like she'd brought the matter to a satisfactory conclusion. It was just like her to be so infuriatingly certain of herself.

"There's nothing to talk about," Fleurette said. "Whatever arrangement I had with Mr. Ward is over, thanks to you. He obviously wants nothing more to do with either of us."

Fleurette thought back to Francis's funeral. What a catastrophe it had seemed at the time — her brother gone, Bessie and the children devastated, a shadow cast over their lives.

But she'd had such hope then! The key to that little room at Mrs. Doyle's boardinghouse was still in her pocket. The contract with Freeman Bernstein had only to be revived with a single clear note from Fleurette's lips, and then she and Laura could take to the stage. All of her old dreams, all of her wild notions of a free and independent life, all of her ambitions — so confidently held, so sure she had been of herself! — all of that still lived and breathed within her back then.

That had only been two months ago, but

already her world had fallen apart. And everything she'd done to keep it together — the pleas to Freeman Bernstein for any kind of work, the failed efforts to resurrect her voice, her secretive employment with John Ward, her stealth payments of Francis's debts — what difference had any of it made?

They were sunk. Bessie might well lose the house. Whether Norma could sell the farm remained an open question. (Would they all be forced to decamp for the farmhouse after all, to dig turnips and raise chickens? It was starting to seem a likely prospect.)

And Fleurette's role in all of this would be to do whatever Constance approved of, and nothing more.

There was quite a bit Fleurette was willing to do, and would do, to keep body and soul together, and to help Bessie. But she wouldn't do it with Constance standing over her. Not any longer.

She hastened over to the train station and rode down to Rutherford, not with a feeling of independence or jubilance, but with the odd, dizzying sensation that the ground had been ripped out from under her feet and she no longer knew how to keep herself upright.

Her only plan, formulated in an instant

on the sidewalk, was to return to Mrs. Doyle, from whom she had intended to rent a room all along. Mrs. Doyle, who wouldn't mind her singing and offered the use of the piano in the parlor. Mrs. Doyle, who thought she might like the company of a parrot.

Of course, Mrs. Doyle had only two rooms to rent. What were the chances that one of them might still be available, now that Fleurette had returned the key and expressed her regrets?

She practically ran over from the train station, down Rutherford's quiet main avenue, with its three or four blocks of small shops, and hastened into the quiet leafy neighborhood beyond, all the while under the influence of the strange idea that another girl might be only steps ahead of her, about to take the last room Mrs. Doyle had available.

The very sight of the woman's wide, generous front porch cheered her. There were geraniums out already, which struck Fleurette as overly optimistic for a March day, but she could use a dose of optimism. Mrs. Doyle's was a comfortable old house, one in which daughters had grown up and moved on, one in which a husband had been looked after until the day he died, a house that still needed (in the words of Mrs. Doyle) girls and laughter under its roof.

Fleurette could have a good life here. She'd thought so before, and she knew so now.

It was her misfortune that Mrs. Doyle didn't have a room to offer her. "You poor dear, I would've held a place for you if I had any reason to think you'd be back," she said, once she'd brought Fleurette inside and settled her down in the boarders' parlor. "But when you told me it was a family emergency calling you back home . . . well, I know all about those, and they don't sort themselves out so easily."

"No, they don't," said Fleurette. "Only I'm just . . ." She turned to the window and blinked. She intended to say that there wasn't room for her at her sisters' house, but as the words came out, she found herself suddenly on the verge of tears. "I'm just in the way at home."

Now she turned away entirely from Mrs. Doyle, before her face crumpled. She was crushed all at once by the weight of everything that had gone wrong.

Where else could she go? Her friend Helen would take her for a night or two, but she didn't have a spare room. She could go to Freeman Bernstein and ask if he knew any actresses looking for a roommate. She could throw herself on Mr. Ward's mercy — but why would he want anything to do with her, after the way Constance had threatened him?

Mrs. Doyle must've recognized a girl with nowhere to go when she saw one. "I know what let's do," she said, brightly, which caused Fleurette to sniff and look up with some hope. "Let's put you in the attic. My girls used to love to sleep up there, but we'd only allow it once in a while, as a special treat. We had a pair of camping beds under the eaves at one time. I'm sure they're full of dust now, but —"

"But I can shake them out in the back garden, if you'll let me," Fleurette said. She found the idea of a cleaning project unexpectedly cheering. Here was a mess she could put right. "I'll have it all straightened up by supper-time. Is there room for a parrot up there?"

There was room for a parrot, and for all of Fleurette's things, once an old wardrobe was cleared out and its contents (old playclothes belonging to girls who were now grown women, and Mr. Doyle's long wool coats, brittle and moth-eaten) carefully packed away. Mrs. Doyle fretted over the lack of modern conveniences — there was no heating nor electrical lighting, and the bathroom, shared with the other girls, was on the second floor — but in compensation she reduced the rent and offered weekly, rather than monthly, terms.

Fleurette accepted without hesitation. For an absurdly modest sum, she had landed in a place where her sisters could not harangue her, and where she would not be obliged to pretend to run a seamstressing business if she didn't wish to. (Although Mrs. Doyle did offer the use of her sewing room in the basement, and a further reduction in rent if Fleurette could make herself useful along those lines.) With great relief she spent the afternoon dusting, sorting, and straightening, while Mrs. Doyle huffed up and down the stairs with what contributions she could gather from the rest of the house: a lace curtain for the attic window, a pile of mismatched linens, an old gas parlor-lamp with a soot-stained glass globe, and a collection of dusty pictures in frames of the sort Fleurette might've once had in her own room as a girl. Fleurette blew the dust off the glass and saw magazine illustrations that Mrs. Doyle's own daughters had cut out and hung on their walls to admire: ladies in fancy dresses and scenes of Paris at night.

Fleurette smiled down at those pictures.

Neither Constance nor Norma would've ever thought to give her something pretty and frivolous to decorate her walls.

She and Mrs. Doyle beamed at one another. Fleurette was so desperately in need of looking after, and Mrs. Doyle equally eager to have another girl in the house to do for. They felt a great sympathy for one another in that moment.

"They're just perfect," Fleurette said. "I'll put them next to my bed and see them every morning when I wake up."

Now there was nothing left to do but to return home to collect her things — and to say good-bye to her sisters.

23

A taxicab brought her back to Hawthorne.
The man agreed to return shortly to collect
her and her possessions. She would only
need a few minutes, she explained, to gather
her things and have a word with her family.
The driver gave an uninterested nod. It was
surely not the first time he'd idled around
the block while a woman packed her bags
and left.

It was by then early evening. Fleurette
expected to find Constance and Norma at
Bessie's house, around the table, having dinner with Bessie and the children. But as the
taxi drew near, she saw no light on at
Bessie's and an automobile in front of the
Wilkinsons'.

It wasn't until she stepped out and made
her arrangements with the driver that she
noticed the insignia. It was a Paterson Police
Department vehicle.

Constance had brought Officer Heath into this.

Sure enough, she opened the door to a room filled with solemn faces: Norma in her customary armchair; Bessie sprawled in the other chair, a hand over her belly; and Constance and Officer Heath sitting stiffly on the divan.

All but Bessie leapt to their feet when she walked in.

"You've obviously all been told," said Fleurette. "I'm in no mood for an inquest. I've only come to collect my things."

"Collect your things?" said Bessie. "But where would you go?"

"You're not leaving this house," said Constance. "I said we'd talk about this tonight. Officer Heath and I —"

"Stop right there." Fleurette glared at the two of them, Constance and Officer Heath, standing together so rigidly on the side of all that was right and just. It infuriated her to think of Constance running to him, as if he had any reason to be involved in their affairs, and the two of them deciding on a sensible and sound course of action that would be issued to Fleurette as an edict.

"You had no business barging into Mr. Ward's office," Fleurette said, "and you certainly had no business running to Officer

Heath about this. Unless I'm under arrest, I don't know why he's here. This is a family dispute. We might have a shortage of men to tell us what to do, but we're not looking to replace the one we've lost."

In spite of her rage, Officer Heath looked at her tenderly. He'd only known her for a few years, but there had always been something fatherly about his treatment of her. She couldn't help but remember a night, back in 1915, when a man fired shots at her, down by the creek behind their farmhouse. Officer Heath (he was sheriff at the time) had handled her so gently, as if she were a wounded bird, but there was a directness about him, too, that won her over.

He never lied to her. He never tried to keep frightful news from her. He neither exaggerated nor minimized the threats against them in those days.

Surely she could stand to hear what he had to say.

"I don't intend to get involved in your family affairs, miss," he said, "and you're a grown woman who doesn't have to be told what could happen in the kinds of situations you might find yourself in under the employment of Mr. Ward."

"I can look after myself," said Fleurette. "Constance should know that."

"She does," said Officer Heath, shooting a glance at Constance, perhaps to keep her quiet. "And it's admirable that you'd want to go into the legal profession. The Kopps are obviously a civic-minded family. You come by it naturally."

"My profession isn't your concern," said Fleurette.

"What we mean to say," put in Constance, unable to contain herself any longer, "is that an association with Mr. Ward might not always keep you on the right side of the law, much less the right side of decency. But Officer Heath had a fine idea today. If you're drawn to the legal profession, a secretarial course —"

"Secretarial course!" Fleurette was practically shouting now. "Did you bring him all the way over here to tell me to train as a secretary?"

"I brought him here," said Constance, "to impress upon you the danger you've been in, because you won't listen to me. We can't have you putting yourself at risk like that."

Fleurette stared back and forth at the two of them. "At risk? At risk? Are you telling me I can't take a job that has an element of danger to it?"

Officer Heath, trying again in his calmly authoritative way to settle them down, said,

"Your sister naturally wants to see you in a line of work that doesn't pose a threat to your . . . ah, to your well-being. You can understand that."

"I don't know that I can," said Fleurette. "As I recall, my sister took a job with you as deputy sheriff and carried a gun and worked every day around crooks and ne'er-do-wells, and I don't recall any of us telling her that she couldn't."

Officer Heath glanced over at Constance: he was obviously getting into the weeds.

"And then I believe she worked for the Bureau of Investigation, chasing after German spies determined to conquer this nation of ours or destroy it in the process, and not once did you or I or anyone tell her that the work was too dangerous. I don't believe a word was said about her well-being."

"But I've had training!" said Constance. "I was brought into this line of work in an official capacity."

Fleurette snorted. "Training! Yes, please tell me all about the school for policewomen you attended before you went to work for the sheriff."

"Ladies, I don't know if this is quite the point," said Officer Heath.

"You're right," said Fleurette. "That's not the point. The point is that Constance wants to decide what I do, and where I go, but has she ever 'had to answer to anyone? Whose permission did she need to accept a job as a deputy sheriff? Or to carry a gun? I don't recall being consulted about that."

She turned to Constance, who was by then quite red-faced. "I don't recall you having to explain to us how you came by the experience and the training to do what you're doing. You just went ahead and did it. Why? Because you're the eldest? The biggest? The strongest? Is it an accident of birth that gives you permission to do as you like and denies the rest of us?"

Constance furrowed her brow and tried to take Fleurette's hands, but she drew them away. "This isn't at all what we came here to say. It would be irresponsible of me not to point out the very real perils of the sort of work you've been pursuing, to say nothing of the scandal if it came out in the papers."

"The papers?" Fleurette barked. "Oh, now we're afraid of being in the papers! After Constance Kopp, Hackensack's Real Lady Cop, was in every paper in the country? After they dragged you through the mud during the election? Now we're afraid of a scandal!"

"But can't you see," said Constance,

pleading now, in the most unappealing manner, "that's exactly why I don't want the same for you."

"That's just it!" shouted Fleurette. Norma and Bessie were both flattened against their chairs, wide-eyed. "You don't get to want things for me anymore. If that's how it's going to work — if I can only live in this house if I follow your rules, and you don't have to follow mine — then you leave me no choice. I'm moving out. I've found my own place, and I'll send money home to Bessie every week. I'll pay my share."

She looked over at Bessie and was hit suddenly with a wave of tenderness. "And I'll do your sewing. Everything you need. This isn't your fault. I just can't live here."

Bessie was by now dabbing at her eyes with a handkerchief: it was a terrible idea to fight in front of a pregnant woman. "I can't stand to see what this has done to you girls. This is too much for all of us. I knew it would be."

"It's nothing to do with you," said Fleurette. "If none of this had happened . . . if the war hadn't happened, for that matter . . . the day still would've come when I had to be on my own. Constance is too accustomed to telling me how to live, that's all. This is the only way. I'm only sorry I didn't say so from the start."

Constance sighed. They were all quieter now. "I don't mean to tell you how to live. But that business with Mr. Ward was not just dangerous. It's morally reprehensible, and if you were caught —"

"If I was caught, I wouldn't have called you, so don't worry about it," snapped Fleurette. "I'm sure Bessie's told you by now what I did with my ill-gotten gains. Francis hadn't just hidden a mortgage from her. He'd run up accounts all over town. But I paid them, every last one of them. You're square with the butcher now, and the baker, and the druggist and everyone else."

Norma coughed and shifted in her chair. She'd been uncharacteristically silent until then. "How much, exactly, did you go around and pay on those accounts?"

Norma had an eyebrow raised and she was leaning forward, looking at Fleurette with more interest than contempt.

"I earned anywhere from twenty to a hundred dollars, depending on the job," said Fleurette, "and sometimes that came with a substantial gratuity from the client."

Constance snorted. "The client."

But Norma was still eyeing her thoughtfully. "And that was all for having your picture taken?"

"Or sometimes I was hired to take the picture," said Fleurette.

Constance said, "Norma, I can't believe you're even asking about this! It's illegal to present fraudulent evidence to the courts. There's nothing more you need to know."

"But Fleurette wasn't presenting any evidence," Norma said. "She was having her picture taken."

Constance stared at her, stunned. "Why are you taking her side?"

Norma sat back, her arms folded across her chest, her brow furrowed. Just then an automobile's horn sounded from the street.

"Well, you can work this out for yourselves," Fleurette said. "That's my car."

24

George Swan, leaning over his glass counter, looked up at Fleurette and squinted through the jeweler's glass wedged against his eye. "You say it was a gift from an admirer?"

"It was . . . no. It was someone connected to my work. Appreciation for a job well done."

"Mmmm." Mr. Swan bent over the piece again. "It's a beautiful setting, and of course that's entirely gold. But I'm afraid your emerald is made of glass, my dear."

Fleurette pressed her lips together and kept her chin high. That emerald — that glittering gift from Mr. Packard — had been her safety net, her hedge against disaster. Now disaster had struck. She intended to sell it to pay her rent and start over in seamstressing from Mrs. Doyle's basement.

The jeweler pushed his little tray across the counter. "It has some small value as a costume piece, but I couldn't offer it to my customers. If I have glass gems in and among the real ones, it tends to raise suspicion in the minds of gentlemen looking to make a wise investment. They begin to question whether anything is authentic. You'd be better off wearing it and enjoying it."

Fleurette lifted it from the tray and held it to the light. Already it had lost some of its luster. As an ornament it no longer appealed to her: she'd only enjoyed wearing it because she felt that if it had value, she had value, too. Now it was just a foolish bit of trickery, an artifact to which one might pin one's false hopes. She had no need of that.

She dropped it into her pocketbook, where it could collect lint along with the train tokens and stray buttons.

"I wish I had better news for you," Mr. Swan said.

"So do I," said Fleurette.

She went mournfully out of the jeweler's and stood on the street, wondering which way to go. There was nothing to do but to visit the dress shops again, looking for work, and leave cards with her new address at Mrs. Doyle's. She was nearly out of essentials: basting thread, hooks and eyes, seam binding, elastic, and ribbon. She tallied her remaining funds as she considered stopping for notions on the way home.

Just then she looked up and saw Alice Martin across the street, hurrying along the sidewalk.

Alice didn't look well. Her arms were wrapped tightly across her chest, her head was down, and she was walking as fast as one conceivably could without breaking into a run. It was almost as if she were being chased.

What a puzzle this woman was! She was hiding something, but what and to what end? It didn't matter anymore, but Fleurette couldn't help but wonder. Her curiosity was just strong enough to propel her to follow.

Fleurette slipped across the street, staying well behind Alice. There might've been the slightest thrill of a detective on the chase, but she would never admit it, having already been accused more than once of showing an inclination toward the family business.

Nonetheless, she pursued Alice, who didn't seem to know where she was going. She turned right, then right again, and came eventually almost to the spot where she'd started. She stopped more than once to consult a little scrap of paper. Finally she pushed open a door at one end of an enormous old stone office building and slipped inside.

LOUIS HERMAN, read the sign on the door. ATTORNEY-AT-LAW.

Fleurette almost stopped right there. Obviously Alice had decided to consult another lawyer about her husband's so-called affair. That was no business of Fleurette's.

But it was foolish to engage another attorney when Mr. Ward had already collected a fee. If Alice had any sense at all, she'd go back to him and demand that he finish the job. If she could hardly afford one lawyer, why would she engage two?

Fleurette hesitated on the sidewalk. It was a street of similarly tall stone buildings, soot-stained and imposing. All around her, people were rushing to work: salesgirls in their good hats, businessmen in dark suits, delivery boys pushing carts. It looked in every sense to be an ordinary day, but for just a second, Fleurette had a feeling that something very much out of the ordinary was going on.

It was nothing but a prickle at the back of her neck that convinced her to push open the door and slip inside.

The reception room was tiny and dark-paneled, the secretary's desk vacant, with no other furnishings save two chairs and an ashtray on a stand. There was absolutely

252

nowhere to hide.

Fleurette could hear all too plainly the discussion taking place within Mr. Herman's office. She didn't have to lean against the door with a water glass, as Norma liked to do, but she did inch closer anyway, hoping she'd catch the scrape of a chair leg or a light step across the floor to suggest that Alice was on her way out. She could flee if she had only a few seconds' warning.

The lawyer was speaking as Fleurette leaned close. "Of course there's still the transfer fee, which has to be paid in advance."

"Another fee! How much is that?" said Alice, obviously in a state of agitation.

"Let me see . . ." Here Fleurette heard the shuffling of papers. She'd noticed that lawyers liked to make a show of digging through papers when they had bad news to deliver, as if the papers made them less culpable personally. "Three hundred and twenty-seven dollars."

"But I don't have anything like that kind of money anymore!"

"Ah, but you will," the lawyer said. "Remember, the house is worth a fortune! And there's a pile of money in a bank account, too. You'll be made whole as soon as the paperwork goes through, and you'll be rich, besides."

"I told you that all I had left was the jewelry I brought today. Most of it comes from Arthur's mother. He'll want it back, you know he will. I can't sell it."

"No, you mustn't sell it, Mrs. Martin. I would never advise that, not with a divorce proceeding under way. If you'll let me take it over to Mr. Talbot, I'm sure he'll give you a fair offer. He'll only hold it as collateral. As soon as the fee is paid, the entire estate is yours, and you'll get it all back."

Alice sniffed. "Oh, what would Arthur say if he knew I was pawning his mother's things?"

"It's nothing so vile as a pawn shop. Mr. Talbot is a lender of the highest caliber. He won't work with anyone but an attorney like myself who brings him a solid proposition. He's quite choosy — and it's precisely because he doesn't want to end up with your mother-in-law's jewelry. He wants his money back, that's all."

"Plus a small percentage," said Alice bitterly.

"He's a respectable businessman who works with wealthy clients, as you are soon to be. I'm not sending you to a charity, because you have no need of charity. Look, I'll put it right here in my safe, and I'll write out a receipt. Did you bring absolutely everything with you?"

"Even the spoons," muttered Alice.

"Never forget the spoons," said Mr. Herman breezily. "They're easily overlooked, but they bring in a nice bundle."

"We don't use them anyway."

"No one does," he said, "but they'll be put to good use now."

Fleurette could hear the clinking of metal and the jingling of a chain. Then the lawyer said, "This all looks in order. Watch me as I write out your receipt, and make sure I don't miss anything. I'll get this over to Mr. Talbot this afternoon, and we will take care of that transfer fee without delay. Then it's just a matter of making sure back taxes due on the property —"

"Back taxes? This is the first I've heard about another tax!"

"That's because it hardly ever comes up. I'm sure it's all paid, considering how much your uncle had in the bank. I'm obligated to let you know that all back taxes are due at transfer, that's all. It's just something we lawyers have to say."

"Then I won't worry about it?" asked Alice, timidly.

"You oughtn't to worry about anything anymore, Mrs. Martin. Look at what you

255

stand to inherit! But it wouldn't hurt for you to think about what else you might have of value, just in case. Is there anything else in the way of silver? Or a fur you wouldn't mind parting with for a few weeks?"

Now Fleurette heard the tell-tale scrape of the chair leg against the floor. She also heard the unmistakable sound of Alice crying.

Mr. Herman must have rushed over to her side, because Fleurette didn't hear a footstep toward the door, but only muffled sobs from Alice.

"There, Mrs. Martin. It's been a terrible strain for you, I know. They don't make it easy to inherit, we can say that for our government officials. But I'm here to look after it all. That's what you pay me for, remember? I worry about it so you don't have to. Now, go off and enjoy your afternoon. Don't give any of this another thought. Didn't you have a coat when you came in? Here, let me . . ."

Fleurette was out the door and across the street before Alice Martin emerged.

25

If Alice had seemed harried and determined going in, she was utterly dejected going out. She practically dragged herself down the sidewalk toward home.

It wouldn't have been a long walk — the Martins didn't live far from downtown — but Alice hopped a street-car nonetheless, and Fleurette took a chance and jumped on behind her. Alice took a seat in the front and kept her head down. Fleurette, watching from a safe distance, saw her muttering to herself, wringing her hands, and pulling at her gloves. A lady seated across from her noticed and moved two rows away. Alice was coming unraveled.

It was only at that moment that Fleurette stopped to ask herself what, exactly, she believed her role to be in this little drama. Was she going to confront Alice and demand to know all? Was she going to follow her, and then report to Mr. Ward on what she'd seen?

There was no point in going back to Mr. Ward. He'd already made it clear that he would worry about what he was paid to worry about and nothing more. In fact, Alice's new lawyer had just said something along those very lines. Fleurette supposed the two of them might have a great deal in common. For all she knew, Mr. Ward and Mr. Herman were thoroughly acquainted and sat together at their club in the evening, commiserating over Alice Martin with whiskey sodas in hand.

No, Mr. Ward would be of no use. But Alice was mixed up in something that caused her a great deal of distress. She had already run to one lawyer with a tale of divorce and to another with a tale of an inheritance. What did any of it mean?

The street-car came to a stop near Alice's street. Out of curiosity, if nothing else, Fleurette decided to intervene.

"Mrs. Martin," she called, coming up behind her on the sidewalk.

Alice jumped and turned, a look of absolute terror on her face, but — to Fleurette's surprise — that soon melted to relief.

"Oh, Miss . . . Blossom, was it?" said Alice.

Would she ever get away from that name? "That's only my professional name," Fleurette said. "Mr. Ward insists on it. Please call me Fleurette. Fleurette Kopp."

"Fleurette," said Alice. "Were you coming to see me? Is this about the pictures?"

"No, but I do want to talk to you." It wouldn't do to say all of this on the sidewalk. Fleurette started walking, and Alice went along. "Is your husband at home?"

"I expect not. He said he'd be in the city all day," said Alice.

"Good, then we can go to your house. I hope you won't be offended, but I overheard you at your lawyer's office just now. I had gone into the reception room just behind you, and I stopped to listen. You looked awfully worried when you came out of there. It seemed to me that something wasn't quite right. I'm in no position to advise you, but I do have some experience in the legal profession."

That was an exaggeration, but Fleurette hoped Alice would find it reassuring.

"Have you any experience with inheritance? Because it sounds so wonderful, but it's been such a mess."

"It isn't so wonderful to lose a family member," said Fleurette. "Am I to understand that it was an uncle who died?"

259

"Oh, but I never knew him," Alice said. "He'd been estranged from our family for years."

"But it sounds as though he left you quite a bundle," said Fleurette.

"He did, and he did so precisely because I'm also estranged from the family. We are the two outcasts. Apparently he'd been keeping an eye on me all these years. I only wish I'd known!"

"What a peculiar situation," Fleurette said. "Why were you both cast out — do you mind my asking?"

"Oh, what does it matter?" said Alice. They'd reached her house by then. Alice fumbled with her keys and, once inside, they settled into the same front room Fleurette had seen before — the upright piano, the theater programs on the wall. "My family was terribly strict. They didn't approve of music or dancing or anything about Arthur's way of life. They hated him and blamed him when I broke off another engagement to marry him instead."

"Your family preferred the other fellow?" asked Fleurette. She didn't seem, to Fleurette's eye, to be the sort of girl who would have two suitors competing for her. She was terribly plain and tended toward a nervous and fretful disposition.

Alice nodded and twisted the handkerchief in her hand. "I was to marry a friend of the family. A doctor. I worked summers in his office. He wanted me to take a nursing course and work alongside him every day. I thought I wanted that, too. But I liked the idea of it more than the reality."

"The idea of nursing or of the man?"

"Both," said Alice. "I found that I hated tending the sick and couldn't stand the sight of blood. But medicine was all my husband-to-be cared about, and all he could talk about. He wanted to serve a mission over-seas with the church. The very idea of it ter-rified me. I tried to tell him that we didn't have any interests in common, but my interests didn't seem to matter to him. He never asked me what I wanted. To tell you the truth, I wasn't sure myself. I just knew that I didn't want . . ."

"Any of that," said Fleurette.

"Right," said Alice. "And then who do you suppose hobbled into his surgery one day? Arthur, fresh off the train, with a broken toe. He'd hooked it on a strap, climbing down from the upper berth. It was so comi-cal, the way he told the story. He had me laughing the entire time Cecil — that was my fiancé, Cecil — splinted his toe. I'm not sure I'd ever laughed so hard. You should've seen how Cecil scowled at me for making merry with a patient!"

"Cecil must've known he had some competition."

"He might have," said Alice musingly. "We hadn't any small plasters, so I walked with Arthur to the druggist to make sure he had what he needed before he boarded the next train. We weren't together for more than an hour in all, but by then I couldn't bear to let him out of my sight. He was such a breath of fresh air. So we exchanged addresses, and before long we were writing almost every day. I had to take a letter box at the post office so my parents wouldn't know. It was all so daring and exciting."

"I'm surprised you could keep it from them," Fleurette said. "My sisters would've found out about a private letter box within an hour."

"Well, it took my father a few weeks, but he did find out. Then he wanted Arthur charged with some sort of crime. I told him that it wasn't a crime to write to an unmarried woman, and he said it was. So I told him I could remedy that. I ran off on the next train and married Arthur."

"You were awfully certain of yourself, after a few letters," Fleurette said.

"Oh, Arthur was so sweet and funny and

charming. He didn't expect me to be his help-mate. He seemed to just like me for my own sake."

Like her? It didn't sound like a basis for a marriage, but Fleurette said, "Well, that's what matters. It's a shame your family didn't see it that way."

Alice rolled her eyes. "He's not a Baptist, so that disqualified him with my parents. They're horrified that he makes his living in the theater. They think I'm tainted from living within spitting distance of a vile city like New York. None of them have ever been out of South Carolina, but they pass judgment on the entire world from down there. It's all right, I don't want them back."

"And was it the same for this uncle of yours?" asked Fleurette.

"Apparently it was. I never heard about him, but that's just like my family not to tell. What I have learned is that my grandfather had another woman on the side, and they had a child together. That child was this uncle, really my half-uncle, I suppose. At some point my grandmother found out about it and insisted that he cut off all ties. My grandfather was a preacher, you understand, and I suppose my grandmother didn't want the parishioners knowing."

"And didn't want the rest of the family

knowing, if you're only just finding out," said Fleurette.

"That's right. So Everett — that's my uncle — grew up without any family at all. It was just him and his mother. When his mother passed away, about ten years ago, he found a few letters and things that she had kept. He went back down to South Carolina and tried to talk to my relations, but they didn't want anything to do with him. Somehow he found out about me — I don't know who told him — but he never did approach me. He only . . . Well, according to his will, he only kept an eye on me. Like a fairy godmother."

"Hmm," said Fleurette. She'd found the story plausible until that last bit, and then it started to sound too good to be true. "He must've died a wealthy man."

"Oh, he did!" said Alice. "He worked hard all his life, but he was given a very fortunate opportunity, too. When he and his mother were in Virginia — he was about ten, I believe — he saved a little boy from drowning. The boy was the son of a railroad tycoon."

"And to show his gratitude . . ." Fleurette said, feeling as though she was reading a Sunday serial.

Alice didn't seem to notice. "Yes, to show

his gratitude, the boy's father put my uncle Everett to work. Everett stayed with it and made good money in railroads, and always owned stock."

"And he's left you a nice little country house he bought with that railroad stock, is that it?" said Fleurette.

Alice laughed. "Oh, it's quite a bit more than that. He rented in Manhattan, and that apartment's gone already. But he owned a lovely summer home on Long Island, with eight bedrooms, a ballroom for dancing, an enormous lawn with a bandstand, a garage with an automobile, and a chauffeur in a little apartment above. It's in Sands Point, on the North Shore."

"Have you been to see it?" asked Fleurette, quite reasonably. It wasn't a long trip.

"Only the pictures. My lawyer warns me that it's nothing like what the Vanderbilts and the Guggenheims are building out there. He says it's practically a carriage house by their standards, but comfortable for the summer. I wouldn't want anything too high-flown anyway. I'd never be able to keep it up."

"Neither would I," said Fleurette, just to sound agreeable. "What does Arthur have to say?" She had almost forgotten about the divorce. What an unfortunate time for Arthur to run off with another woman, just when his wife stood to inherit!

But that was when she saw through Alice's ruse.

Alice must've realized she'd been caught in a lie. "If you've never been married, you can't understand," she said, tentatively. "But when I learned all that I was to inherit, and how my life would be changed by it, I knew in an instant that I didn't want Arthur to be any part of it. I could see a future for myself again — and he wasn't in it."

"You didn't want him to have half the estate," said Fleurette.

"It isn't just the money," Alice insisted. "I didn't want him in the picture. I wanted something else. I didn't want this — my life with Arthur — to be how it all turned out. I realized all at once that I had only settled for Arthur. He had been a way out of a difficulty, but that was never enough to make a marriage. Can't you understand?"

"You've explained it well enough," said Fleurette briskly. "But why involve Mr. Ward in all this when you already had an attorney?"

"The first time I met Mr. Herman, he was quite insistent that if I had a husband, I had to bring him in, and he would have to sign papers, too, like I did. I told him that we were already in the middle of divorcing. He said that I couldn't take ownership of the property on my own unless I was an unmarried woman, and he warned me not to mention any of this to Arthur, or I'd never get that divorce."

"But Mr. Herman wouldn't help you with the divorce himself?"

"He told me that he wasn't that sort of attorney. I'd heard about Ward & McGinnis and the kinds of tricks they get up to. I thought that with Arthur in and out of the theater so much, it would be easy to get a picture of him with a girl. I suppose I didn't know exactly how to ask for what I wanted."

"No, you didn't," said Fleurette, "and it sounds like you're running out of time. When exactly are you to receive this inheritance?"

Alice pulled a pillow into her lap and picked at the tassel. "Oh, it's taking forever. There always seems to be another paper to sign and another fee to pay. Mr. Herman's been so kind about it, and he always takes the time to explain everything, but I've spent every penny I have, and now the jewelry's gone, and I don't know what's next."

Fleurette sat up at the mention of the

jewelry. "What exactly did you give him today?"

"Oh, everything. A few bracelets, a comb and pin set, a nice long string of pearls, the silver spoons, and a good ruby ring in a big gold setting. It was enormous. I never wore it."

"And you paid him some fees before that?" asked Fleurette.

"Oh yes, there have been all sorts of fees. Twenty dollars here, fifty dollars there, all for notaries and assessors and who knows what. Two hundred for a probate tax."

"So . . . three or four hundred in all, plus the jewelry . . ."

She was quiet just long enough for Alice to look over at her sharply. "What are you suggesting?"

Fleurette had already guessed at the truth. But she wanted Alice to see it for herself. "How did you first learn of your uncle's death and of your inheritance?"

"I had a letter from Mr. Herman telling me all that I've told you."

"And you'd never heard of this attorney before? Never spoken to anyone about your . . . well, your personal situation? A chance encounter with a stranger, perhaps, before the letter arrived?"

"No, I've told no one! Who would I talk to?"

Fleurette crossed her arms and paced around the room. If there really had been an uncle, he wouldn't have died alone and unnoticed. She thought of all the mourners at her brother's funeral, acquaintances and neighbors and club men. "Haven't you heard from anyone else connected to this uncle? Friends or associates of his?"

"No, it all comes through Mr. Herman. He had everything: the will, the pictures of the house, all of it."

"Was there an obituary? Did you attend the funeral?"

"I . . . There was no mention of that."

"And where have your uncle's personal effects gone? His letters and pictures and things of that sort? People leave papers behind. Usually the heir would get everything."

Alice stared open-mouthed at Fleurette. "If you're looking for proof that my uncle Everett even existed, I don't have any beyond what Mr. Herman has shown me."

Fleurette stood up and patted down her skirt. "I think I might like to go have a word with Mr. Herman."

26

Alice insisted on going along. On the way back to Mr. Herman's office, she didn't say a word: she was pale and tight-lipped and once again wrung her gloves into knots as they rode back downtown. Fleurette saw her tugging at the finger where her ring was missing and wanted to reach a hand out to calm her, but thought better of it.

Back on Market Street, at the end of that long soot-stained building where Alice had only just left Mr. Herman an hour or two previously, Fleurette's suspicions were confirmed.

Mr. Herman was gone. The brass plate bearing his name was gone, too. Only two black holes remained where the screws had held it in place.

Alice stood stricken in the doorway. "Oh, but surely he's only stepped out. In fact, he was going to take my jewelry over to Mr. . . . . Mr. . . . ."

"The name was Talbot, but it doesn't matter," said Fleurette. "I believe he's gone, Alice."

Fleurette, although the shorter and slighter of the two, had to take Alice's arm to stop her from dropping.

"Steady," Fleurette muttered. Alice would only attract attention if she fell into a near-swoon in front of an empty doorway. "Take a breath. Calm yourself."

Alice leaned against the door and dabbed a handkerchief at her forehead. "You can't mean that he's just run off," she whispered, "and all my jewelry . . . and the fees and taxes and things I've paid him . . . but what about that house, and my uncle . . . You don't mean . . ."

She looked at Fleurette with such distress that Fleurette now felt the weight of what she'd done. Before that afternoon, Alice Martin's troubles had belonged entirely to Alice. Whatever happened next to her — whether Mr. Herman appeared again or didn't, whether he kept his promises or not — wouldn't have mattered a bit to Fleurette, because she wouldn't have known about it.

But Fleurette was the one who'd raised all these questions. She was the one who had seen through Alice's stories all along, starting with the pointless investigation into her

271

husband's nonexistent affair, and now the very real possibility that Alice had been swindled over a phony inheritance.

This was a mess entirely of Alice's own making, but now here was Fleurette, squarely in the middle of it. And Alice was staring desperately at her, as if there were anything in the world she could do about it.

"I suspect that when you started to cry, Mr. Herman realized that he wasn't going to get any more money out of you," Fleurette said. "Now he's gone."

"But where? Couldn't we . . . Oh, isn't there a way to find him?"

"You ought to go to the police," Fleurette said. "Have them look into this Mr. Herman. They'll know how to go about it."

"But we don't know that there's anything to look into," Alice said. "What if it's all a misunderstanding? Mr. Herman could be back in an hour. The name-plate could've fallen off. Besides, I can't have Arthur finding out. All I've wanted was to get through this without him knowing, and to have my house on Long Island and my chauffeur . . ." Her voice gave out. The house, and the garage with the apartment above it, and the man who was to have brought around the auto when she called for it had all seemed so solid only just that morning, but now shimmered and faded under Fleurette's scrutiny.

It was a good deal too much pressure for Fleurette. She wondered, fleetingly, how Constance had ever learned to handle having the fate of some unfortunate girl in her hands. Fleurette had hardly managed to run her own life lately. What was she supposed to do for Alice?

What came to mind just then was not what Constance would've done — Constance, the detective, Constance the lady cop — but what Norma would've done.

"You don't have to go to the police just yet," she told Alice. "I'll look into it."

"But how?"

"I'll go to the library."

The library! Repository of newspapers and directories, cataloger of obituaries, painstaking indexer of names and dates and events both significant and trivial, employer of persnickety women for whom no fact was too elusive, no detail too obscure. Norma had always been a habitué of libraries, consulting them on subjects as varied as bird-keeping, fence-building, and parties of interest to the Kopps of whom she particularly disapproved (candidates for sheriff, vaudeville managers, bankers).

At the library Fleurette could answer the two most pressing questions at hand: the circumstances surrounding the life and death of Alice's putative uncle Everett, and the validity of Mr. Herman's law practice.

Alice made a half-hearted offer to go along, but in the same breath mentioned that Arthur would be home soon and would want his dinner, and that she'd need some time to compose herself before she saw him, or she might break down in tears and tell all.

Fleurette suspected that a tearful confession lay in Alice's future regardless, but she didn't say that. Instead she said, "Go on home and let me see what I can find. If you hear from Mr. Herman, tell me about it right away." She wrote down Mrs. Doyle's address in Rutherford and her telephone number as if she'd lived there all her life. Had she really only just yesterday stormed out of her sisters' house and taken up a new life under a widow's eaves in Rutherford?

Alice took the little scrap of paper but said, "Miss Kopp, don't you think we might've worked ourselves into a state over nothing? Won't we laugh about it when Mr. Herman returns, and the papers are signed, and you and I can go out to Long Island together, and see for ourselves that everything he promised is true?"

"I suppose we would laugh about it," said Fleurette, "but just now I think you ought to go home and carry on as if nothing's happened. I'll come to you as soon as I know something. It might be a few days. Will you be all right until then?"

It was a strange sensation for Fleurette to be inquiring after the welfare of this older, married woman. Fleurette was the one who was accustomed to being looked after. Of the two of them, who could say that Alice was even in the worse position? All she'd lost was some money and jewelry, along with her good sense. Fleurette, on the other hand, had buried a brother, walked out on her sisters, lost her voice, and gotten herself tangled up in a lawyer's dubious schemes. Which one of them was most in need of reassurance?

"I'll be fine," said Alice. "I'll hold my breath, and I won't sleep, and I won't be able to look Arthur in the eye, but I'll be fine."

"Go on home, then."

It was by then so late in the afternoon that Fleurette had only an hour at the library, but that was all she needed. A Mrs. Peabody was dispatched to scour the obituaries and found no record of an Everett Seabury (that was the uncle's surname, Seabury) in the New York or New Jersey index. The eager and efficient Miss Parr paged through probate notices filed in all the major papers, and likewise found no mention of either Everett Seabury or his attorney, Mr. Herman.

Of Mr. Herman there was likewise no trace found. The state bar directories showed no such man among the membership in either New Jersey or New York. The Paterson city directory showed an attorney's office at his address, but it didn't belong to him. An attorney named William Griswold occupied that address.

"Of course, the directories are out of date the minute they're printed," said Mrs. Peabody. "Perhaps Mr. Griswold has vacated the premises and this Mr. Herman has moved in."

"But we've no suggestion of a Louis Herman practicing law here in Paterson," said Fleurette, "and William Griswold is registered with the state bar, and has a home address in Paterson, and in every other way looks legitimate."

"It would seem so," said the librarian.

"Then the only question is whether Mr. Herman is occupying William Griswold's office without his knowledge," Fleurette said.

Miss Parr went back to her daily papers (How the entire operation reminded Fleurette of Norma! Why hadn't Norma trained as a librarian? Couldn't she now?) and soon had an answer. "Mr. Griswold was in the social pages just a few weeks ago," she said. "He took a winter cruise to Cuba. He's expected back this week."

"Then his office has been empty, and anyone who reads the papers would've known about it," said Fleurette.

"That's exactly why I never talk to the papers," sniffed Miss Parr, sounding for all the world like Norma's long-lost twin. What a pair they would make! Fleurette found herself wondering if librarians all roomed together in some meticulous and well-ordered boarding-house, and if a place could be found for Norma in such an establishment. She came very close to asking about it when the bells chimed, signaling the library's closing hours.

"You've given me more than I could've hoped for," said Fleurette, gathering up her notes.

"Well, that's the business we're in," said Mrs. Peabody.

27

Mr. Ward jumped when he saw her the next morning. "Did your sister follow you? I can't have her in here issuing threats. I have a weak chest, you know. The doctor says I mustn't go within a hundred yards of an angry woman."

"Constance doesn't know where I am anymore," said Fleurette. "I've taken a room of my own, down in Rutherford."

"I've never understood the attraction of Rutherford."

Fleurette shrugged. "It's just a hop into Manhattan, and I don't run into my sisters on the street."

"That's reason enough. But you know I can't put you back to work. You Kopps are bad for business. I'm hiring another girl."

"Yes, I worked that one out for myself," Fleurette said, although it stung to hear him say it. She wasn't about to beg him for another chance, though. He wasn't the sort of man who went in for begging. The way to handle Mr. Ward, she thought, was to meet him as an equal, to keep up the banter, and to never look desperate.

"I only stopped in to tell you about Alice," she said, as offhandedly as she could.

"Alice? You're going to have to narrow it down."

"Alice Martin. Your client with the husband who isn't actually having an affair."

"Ah, Mrs. Martin! What a rich imagination on that one. She must get it from novels. They can ruin a girl."

"I believe Mrs. Martin's being swindled. She only wanted a divorce to get her husband out of the way so she could claim an inheritance."

"Now, that does sound like a novel or a stage play. You should write it, Miss Kopp."

Fleurette forgot her troubles long enough to consider that briefly. Who did write stage plays and song lyrics? Was there money in it?

Mr. Ward was a master of distractions, but Fleurette wasn't going to allow it. "The inheritance is a con. A lawyer going by the name of Louis Herman has her paying all sorts of fees and taxes for the estate she's due to inherit. But I don't believe there's any estate at all."

"Who's the deceased?" asked Mr. Ward.

"An uncle she never knew. I can't find any evidence of him, either."

"And how did this Mr. Herman get his hooks into her?"

"No idea. Alice doesn't know, either. His letter came out of the blue."

Mr. Ward leaned back in his chair, his hands behind his head. "You've been playing detective. Did Mrs. Martin hire you behind my back?"

"No one's hired me," said Fleurette. "Only I saw her yesterday going into Mr. Herman's office and I listened at the door. I was just curious. It bothered me, with all the inconsistencies in her story. I thought she might be in trouble, and she is."

Mr. Ward grinned at her and scratched his chin. "I said I didn't want your sister in here, but you sound just like her. She can't resist a girl in trouble."

Fleurette wasn't about to get drawn into an argument about Constance. What would it take to get out from under her shadow?

"I only came to ask if you know the attorney whose office was being used by this shady lawyer fellow. Apparently the office belongs to a man named William Griswold. He's been away in Cuba for a few weeks. Is there any chance he would've allowed his office to be used by someone else while he was away?"

"Griswold? Not him. He's a real stuffed shirt. Wouldn't let another man borrow a pencil, much less his desk."

"I suppose I could go ask him regardless."

Mr. Ward shrugged. "Go ahead. You're not working for me on this one."

"I know. You're not going to worry about Alice Martin because she's not paying you to worry. But . . . what would you do, if she were paying you?"

"You aren't thinking of hiring yourself out, are you?"

"No," Fleurette snapped, "I'm thinking of doing something for a woman who's gotten herself mixed up in some sort of scheme. But I don't know what to do, apart from telling her to go to the police."

"And she refuses."

"She does."

"Because she doesn't want her husband to know."

"Exactly."

"Well, that's the trouble," said Mr. Ward. "The police won't take her complaint unless Mr. Martin comes in as well. If she went to them by herself, the first thing they'd do is go around and talk to the husband and make sure the missus isn't just hysterical.

They're not going to go running off to chase after an imaginary swindler on her word alone."

And how, exactly, does one chase after an imaginary swindler? Fleurette knew better than to ask.

"Then I'll just find out what this William Griswold has to say, and that'll be the end of it," she said. She rose to leave and picked up her hat.

"Or you could let Alice worry about all that and get back to business," Mr. Ward called as she left.

Fleurette did not, at that moment, have any other business, but she saw no reason to tell Mr. Ward that.

Besides having no other business, Fleurette had very little to look forward to. Whatever satisfaction it might've given her to go storming out of the Wilkinsons' and refusing to live under her sisters' supervision any longer, she did find herself awfully bored at her new lodgings. Although Mrs. Doyle was everything one might hope for in a landlady — quiet, unobtrusive, timely with meals, and a decent cook — she was no conversationalist. She did not, as far as Fleurette could tell, possess any interests of her own, and as such was inept at talking to anyone else about their interests. Beyond the weather and the price of eggs, she had little to say on any subject at all.

Likewise were the two other girls in the house placid and dull. One of them, Emily, worked for a doctor. Fleurette thought she might at least bring home a gruesome story about a man impaling himself at a rail-yard, or perhaps she might complain about a demanding patient, an intrusive mother, or a spoiled child. But there was never anything of the sort on offer. Whenever Fleurette asked her about her day, she would only give a little half-laugh and say, "Oh, about what you'd expect."

"I'd expect quite a lot," Fleurette said at first, offering a few hopeful suggestions of her own. "Children swallowing pennies and unexplained rashes and tropical diseases picked up abroad."

"Oh goodness!" was all Emily would say. "What an imagination. Can you believe these lilies of the valley, up so early this year? And I thought it was a rather cold spring."

Mrs. Doyle went to great effort to keep fresh flowers in the parlor. Even when there was nothing to cut, she would bring in an arrangement of branches and moss, having instructed herself in the Japanese art of flower-arranging from a magazine article. Each new arrangement offered both Emily and Mrs. Doyle another opportunity to remark upon the weather.

The other girl, who insisted upon being called Pinky although that couldn't possibly have been her given name, was in training to work as a telephone operator. Surely, thought Fleurette, that would be an intriguing profession. Listening in on calls all day, patching together desperate lovers, facilitating the conduct of important business, relaying urgent medical emergencies (a situation Emily might know something about and have a shocking story to share as well). Telephone operator was a lively enough job, wasn't it?

But Pinky was, quite possibly, the least curious person Fleurette had ever met. "You must hear all sorts of things when they think you're not listening" was one conversational gambit Fleurette attempted.

"Oh, they go on and on," said Pinky.

"About what? Today, for instance. What was the strangest thing you heard?"

Pinky laughed a little, as if she and Fleurette were in on a joke. "Oh, it's just a lot of chatter. You know how people are."

"I don't, really," said Fleurette. "Not all of them, anyway."

"Oh goodness!" said Pinky. "Who would want to?"

Emily and Pinky were equally uninterested in anything Fleurette got up to. Once or twice, when they happened to dawdle around the table after dinner, she would offer up some tidbit from her time on the stage.

"In Philadelphia we were booked into a theater that had a little secret club in the basement," she began, only to be interrupted by Emily.

"I heard it snowed in Philadelphia this week. Isn't that awfully late?"

"You never can tell," said Pinky. "Just when you think spring is here for good, and you put away your long coat —"

"Oh, that's always the sign that it's going to snow, when I put away my winter coat!" said Emily. "You can count on it."

"Well, you'd better warn me before you do, and I'll know to keep mine out," said Pinky, and they both laughed at that.

After enough of those conversations, Fleurette kept to herself. Although she was happy to be away from her sisters, and thought every day about what a relief it was to be free of their oversight, it did occur to her that Constance and Norma were, at the very least, interested in something. They held opinions, which they expressed forthrightly and argued over. Nothing of the sort happened at Mrs. Doyle's. Fleurette came to feel that she merely existed there, but that she didn't really live.

When the house was empty, she and Laura practiced their singing. She worked through Mr. Martin's exercises diligently: *wa, wo, we,* up and down the scale, with her larynx relaxed, or as relaxed as she could make it.

Laura sang along flawlessly. If anything, her imitation was too good: Laura picked up on the imperfections in Fleurette's voice, going thin and breathless on the high notes and skipping a bit when she should've held steady. Once or twice Fleurette dissolved into a coughing fit as she used to when she was ill, and Laura coughed alongside her, even dropping her head down the way Fleurette did.

"You need a Victrola to sing along to," Fleurette told her. "I don't want you learning my ways."

"Sing along," answered Laura.

Lacking any other occupation, Fleurette resumed, half-heartedly, her seamstressing business. She spent a day going around with new cards for the shop windows, this time printed with Mrs. Doyle's telephone number, and she picked up temporary work at a dress shop when the demand for alterations was more than the regular seamstress could handle. She also accepted Mrs. Doyle's offer for the use of her sewing room and took on the household mending in exchange for a reduction in rent.

And every day, without fail, she went by Market Street to see if William Griswold had returned from his cruise to Cuba.

28

Finally she saw a handwritten name-plate affixed to his door. Mr. Griswold had returned. She walked into the reception room and found the tiny desk occupied by a secretary who was at that moment telephoning the engraver about a replacement name-plate.

"Stole it right off our door," the secretary was shouting into the receiver. "I can't imagine what use anyone would have for it, unless the thief happens to be named William Griswold."

When she was finished with that business, Fleurette said, "You've had a robbery."

"Oh, if you could call it that," said the secretary, a no-nonsense silver-haired woman. "Boys playing a prank, most likely."

"Is Mr. Griswold in? I'm afraid I don't have an appointment."

"No one does, yet. He took a few weeks off and gave me the time away, too. What's this about?"

"A legal matter," said Fleurette.

"Well, I'd guessed that much," said the secretary. "Never mind, go on in and tell him about it yourself."

Fleurette found Mr. Griswold to be just as John Ward had described him: a stuffed shirt. He wore an immaculate suit with a perfectly folded handkerchief, a starched collar, and a watch with a chain hooked around his vest button. He carried his chin at a very particular angle. His hair bore the marks of his comb and would all day. His desk was immaculate: there would be no shuffling of papers.

"We're only just this morning opened for business again," he said when he saw her.

"I know. I've been waiting for you. I've come to tell you that someone used your office while you were away."

He looked up at her sharply. "What makes you say that?"

"Because I was here, and I heard him. He removed your name-plate and replaced it with his own."

"Then you know who he was?"

"The plate said Louis Herman, but I doubt that's his real name."

"And why do you know so much about it, Miss . . ."

"Kopp. I only happened to see a friend come in here, and I followed her. I never saw the man, but I heard him through the door."

Mr. Griswold seemed to disapprove of that. "Then you were spying."

"I believe my friend's been the victim of some sort of fraud. I was hoping you could tell me about the man who was here."

"I can't, and I think you must've been mistaken. There's no sign of a robbery. The lock wasn't forced. Are you sure you went to the right door? There are a few dozen attorneys in this building."

"But only one missing his name-plate. Would your secretary know anything about this?"

The secretary was called in, and in fact she did know something. She had stayed in the office for a few days after Mr. Griswold sailed for Cuba, and in that time a man had come in to ask when Mr. Griswold would return, and whether she could get word to him.

"I told him you couldn't be reached," she said, "and that I'd be away to visit my mother anyway, after I finished up some paperwork."

"Then he knew the office would be empty," said Mr. Griswold, sounding put out about it.

"Anyone would know," said Fleurette. "There was a notice in the paper."

"That's the last time I'll do anything of that sort. But we still don't know how he got inside."

Fleurette went over to the door and peered through the keyhole. In her stage days, she'd toured with a girl who could get into any trunk, locked drawer, or hotel room she liked. All it took was a hairpin and a good ear.

"That would've been the easy part," she said. "The brass plate was the giveaway. I'm surprised your neighbors didn't notice, or any of your clients who happened to pass by."

"Even if they had, there was no way to reach either of us," said Mr. Griswold, "and it would've been too small a matter to take to the police. Anyone might assume I'd simply moved offices."

"And you found nothing unusual when you returned?" asked Fleurette. "An unfamiliar brand of cigarette in the ash-tray, a note in the wastebasket, nothing at all?"

This was too much for Mr. Griswold. "If I wanted the police here looking for evidence, I'd call them. I'm sorry, Miss . . ."

"Kopp."

"Miss Kopp, but I don't see how this has anything more to do with you. Please express our regrets to your friend. I trust she's come to no harm. You've told us what you know, and I'll handle it from here."

Fleurette was peering under his desk while he spoke. "Is that a café you frequent?" she asked, reaching for a match-book.

"Didn't I just tell you we'd sort this out on our own?"

"The Black Cat," Fleurette said, turning the match-book over. "It's just over on Pearl Street. Doesn't sound familiar?"

"No," Mr. Griswold admitted.

Fleurette glanced over at the secretary, who likewise shook her head. She tossed the match-book on his desk. "This man who stopped in — what do you remember about him?"

Before Mr. Griswold could stop her, the secretary answered. "He was perfectly ordinary. Medium height, brown hair, light complexion, a black coat with perhaps a dark blue suit underneath."

"Nothing to distinguish him at all?" asked Fleurette. "A beaky nose, a lazy eye, an unfortunate mole with a whisker sprouting from it?"

"I'm afraid not."

Fleurette had not, of course, seen the man

in question, and Alice's description had been equally useless. It occurred to her that it must be a good quality in a con man to look like everyone and no one at all.

Mr. Griswold had had enough of Fleurette's questions. "It's been a delight, Miss Kopp, but our visit is at an end." He said it so officiously that Fleurette thought it best not to press her luck.

"Put a new lock on that door," she said, and then she was gone.

The match-book was but a slim lead, but she thought she ought to take an excursion over to Pearl Street anyway. The Black Cat, Fleurette realized, had been there for years, under a different name. It had formerly stood as Miss Emeline's Tea House, and had been, as Fleurette recalled, a dull and musty place even as far back as when tea houses were popular. Either Miss Emeline had come to her senses, or she'd sold the place to a more savvy operator, because the Black Cat was as thoroughly modern a place as one might hope to find in Paterson, with checked tablecloths in the French style, a polished black counter, and paintings (as one might expect) of black cats in Parisian settings. All was designed to appeal to the returning soldier. It must've worked, because men and women equally partook of the omelets, *poulet en casserole Parisienne,* and the potato soufflés.

With only a vague description of an ordinary-looking man and a name that was most likely false, Fleurette's inquiries led nowhere. "That sounds like half the men who come in here," said the waitress. "Look around. Would you remember a fellow like that?"

"Of course not," said Fleurette, and wandered out, entirely at a loss.

She stood across from the Black Cat and scrutinized it, as if she might read in the brickwork a story about a man pretending to be an attorney peddling false stories about inheritances. But no new information emerged from the squat little building.

Under its striped awning the lights from inside had begun to glow as the sky above it darkened. It seemed a cheerful place, optimistic about the coming decade, free of the worries brought on by war and want. On either side of it loomed hulking old brick buildings that housed decrepit apartments upstairs and a hodge-podge of tiny businesses on the ground floor: a watch repair shop, an upholsterer, a fortune-teller, and a Japanese novelty shop. From upstairs came the stench of something vinegary brought to a boil and a baby's wail.

If Louis Herman had been there, he hadn't left a trace.

29

Just as Fleurette pursued Louis Herman, Constance pursued the bank manager, with better results.

She stopped by in the morning, on her way to work, and surveyed the place. It was a small bank, employing only three tellers, with Mr. Tichborne, the bank manager, tucked away in a corner office behind an elaborately carved door that looked as impenetrable as the door to the vault itself.

Seated outside the office was his secretary, a woman of middle years who seemed to manage everything that went on in the building. She answered the telephone, fielded questions from the tellers, managed an appointment diary, and juggled towering stacks of files and ledger books.

MRS. WALLACE, her name-plate read. Constance suspected that nothing went on at the bank that escaped Mrs. Wallace's attention.

She further guessed that Mr. Tichborne took a long and leisurely lunch every afternoon, as a bank manager would, but that Mrs. Wallace ate a sandwich at her desk and never stopped working.

Her guesswork was proven correct when she returned at lunch to find Mr. Tichborne away and Mrs. Wallace polishing an apple.

"He'll be back by two because he has an appointment then," said Mrs. Wallace, "but after that he hasn't so much as ten minutes to spare for the rest of the day." She pointed to her notes in the appointment diary, an efficient and neatly printed list of names and times.

"I don't suppose he'll have an answer for me anyway," said Constance. "What I need would require a great deal of digging around in files, but he told my sister that the files were a mess and nothing could be found in them if he tried."

Mrs. Wallace slammed her apple down on the desk as a judge would a gavel and rose to her feet. "He wouldn't dare! I keep these files in perfect order. He never touches them."

"I found it hard to believe myself," said Constance. "We're only trying to reconcile the bank statements since my brother died.

His widow's in no condition to do it herself."

"I'm sure she's not," said Mrs. Wallace. "After my husband died, I could hardly put one foot in front of the other."

"Then you know," Constance said.

"Oh, of course I know. Mr. Tichborne only hired me because he and my husband were old friends. But if it wasn't for that, he would've fired me in the first week. It took so long for me to even be able to think clearly."

"Our Bessie's going through the same, only she's expecting their third child, too."

"Poor dear. I remember that name. She was here recently, wasn't she? With another of your sisters?"

"She was," said Constance. "I wish she'd spoken to you instead of Mr. Tichborne."

Mrs. Wallace was already reaching for her ledgers. "What's the name?"

"Francis Kopp. We're only looking for a list of debits and credits. I believe it's July we're missing, or August."

After a few minutes the ledger was found, and Constance and Mrs. Wallace leaned over it together. "Tell me what you need and I'll copy it down for you," Mrs. Wallace said.

Constance ran her finger down the column

of figures. The number jumped out plainly enough.

Fifteen hundred dollars, paid to Mr. Griggs, Francis's employer.

"Oh yes, I remember this," said Mrs. Wallace. "That was when your brother bought a share of his employer's business. They signed the papers in Mr. Tichborne's office. It must've been quite a celebration at home."

"It certainly was," said Constance, "and that solves the riddle. I can make the books balance now."

"There, you see? Nothing to it. I don't know why Mr. Tichborne has to make everything more complicated than it really is."

"It's only complicated for him," said Constance, smiling down at her. "You have it all perfectly in hand."

"Indeed, I do."

A share of his employer's business! Mr. Griggs had been to pay his condolences, but hadn't said a word about it.

"Not that we gave him much of an opportunity," said Bessie, ever the peacemaker.

Norma insisted on going over to confront Mr. Griggs the very next day. She was as strategic about it as a war general, announcing that they would arrive early enough to ambush him first thing in the morning. "We want to catch him unawares, before he barricades himself in some back office. Francis was at his desk by seven-thirty. We'll go at seven."

Bessie, sensing the possibility of a lengthy siege, packed sandwiches. She was no longer so sick in the morning and instead preferred not to be more than about three feet away from her next meal.

Their strategy was rewarded: just after eight, as they waited under an awning over the loading dock, Mr. Griggs arrived in his automobile.

"It's about time you turned up," Norma called as he was stepping out. "Isn't the boss supposed to be the first man in?"

Mr. Griggs turned around, a bit startled to have a woman telling him his business at that hour. "Miss Kopp. Ah, and Mrs. Kopp. I want you to know once again that on behalf of the entire firm —"

"That's all well and good," said Norma, "but we've been to the bank, and they had quite a surprise for us. You must've wondered why it took us so long to come and see about our interest in this affair."

Mr. Griggs looked as though they'd just handed him a rotten fish. They were still

300

outside, in the gravel lot where the delivery trucks came and went, back when there were deliveries to be made. The business was situated in a district of similar operations, all red brick and low-slung and a bit dismal. It was a chilly morning, with a little wind and a few splatters of rain. Bessie kept tugging at the scarf she wore over her head.

"Ladies," he said, seeing no alternative, "please don't stand out here in the wet. Come inside, and tell me what I can do for you."

"I intend to tell you exactly what you can do," said Norma, who was all too happy to step inside and get to her business. The two of them followed Mr. Griggs and found themselves in the administrative end of an enormous warehouse.

Norma had never in her life run any sort of packing and shipping facility, but she could see at once that this was not the way to do it. Although there were enormous old wooden shelves lining the walls of the warehouse, and a few more in rows near the back, there was nothing on them but dust. What remained of the business's stock — brittle, yellowed old baskets in a motley assortment of styles that had once been popular but were no longer — was simply tossed about on the floor, neither stacked nor grouped according to any system that might, to Norma's methodical mind, have made any kind of sense: not by height nor width nor purpose nor color nor style of decoration. Some were broken or frayed at the handles. The damaged inventory was simply mixed in with what little was in salable condition.

A dozen or so work-tables, of standing height, were buried under precisely the sort of clutter Norma could not abide: the kind that had no discernible pattern or reason to it. Bits of fabric, used for lining baskets, were mixed indiscriminately with unopened mail, half-typed invoices, dried glue-pots, shipping twine, and — most horribly — empty boxes of a particular type of salted soda cracker that Francis had loved. Bessie gave a little start at the familiar green and white packages, remembering the way he'd left those boxes tossed around at home.

The place was so dimly lit as to make it nearly impossible to do any sort of work, the only light coming in from the high and distant windows and a few electrical bulbs strung not across any area where a person might work, but seemingly at random, perhaps illuminating work-benches that had once stood there but had since been moved or (Norma suspected) simply allowed to crumble and be swept up in the detritus.

There were but two people working in the enormous, shambling operation, both of whom had attended Francis's funeral: an elderly clerk named Mr. Hastings, and a young man named Thomas Wells, whose duties consisted, as far as Norma knew, of driving the delivery truck, sorting the merchandise and handling the packages, and any sort of heavy lifting that Francis didn't wish to do himself. Francis had been in charge of most other operations: sales, purchasing, negotiations with vendors, and so on.

Bessie went to speak to Mr. Hastings and then to Thomas Wells, both long-time acquaintances, but Norma stood back, her arms folded across her chest.

"It isn't much of an operation," she said to Mr. Griggs.

"Well, it's a bit quiet now, but if you'd been here before the war —"

"What it used to be is of no interest. We own a portion of what we see before us. It's half, as I recall." In fact, Norma had no idea what sort of interest Francis owned, but thought she'd start high and let Mr. Griggs correct her.

"One-quarter," said Mr. Griggs, and then hesitated to say more.

"Do you keep an office here, or do you merely take a seat amid the piles of rubble?"

Bessie returned to them just then, wearing a strained and worried expression.

"This way, ladies," said Mr. Griggs, escorting them to a little room in the corner knocked together with wood panels.

Inside there was at last some sense of order: two leather chairs, worn but serviceable, a desk under the window with pigeonholes labeled in a manner that at least made sense for an operation of this sort (BILLS OF LADING, CUSTOMS, PAYABLES, RECEIVABLES, and the always-overflowing MISCELLANY), and a bookshelf stacked with a decade's worth of ledgers, catalogs, and merchant directories.

"We were surprised to hear from the bank," Norma said, before any of them had taken a seat. "The mortgage came as quite a shock, but we were relieved to hear that we owned an interest in a business to make up for it. A quarter interest," she said, raising an eyebrow at Bessie who nodded grimly and dropped into the nearest chair.

"Then Francis never told you," said Mr. Griggs.

"I'm afraid not," said Bessie, "but we are here today to learn all that we can."

"That's the right spirit," said Mr. Griggs.

304

"Now, as to the prospects going forward, we feel certain that with the war over and business operations returning to normal —"

"Why don't we save the future prospects for the future, and have you tell us what, exactly, led Francis to mortgage his family's home? What sort of business opportunity presented itself last summer, while the fighting in France was at its worst, that proved irresistible to my brother?" Norma asked.

Mr. Griggs looked helplessly between the two of them. "It wasn't so much the opportunity as the lack of it," he said. "We weren't the only business to find itself in an impossible position. We could hold on, with the certainty that better days would return, or close our doors forever and let some other competitor take the lead when things turned around."

"Then you asked Francis to put in money to keep the doors open," said Bessie. Her hand rested absently on her belly. Mr. Griggs tried not to look.

"It was only temporary," he said, "until the war came to an end, as you suggested."

"And was he being paid according to any schedule?" asked Norma.

"Paid? Surely you know he received his salary."

"No, paid something for his interest in the

operation."

"Well, that's just it," said Mr. Griggs. "There was so little coming in, and only expenses going out."

"Expenses," said Norma. "Purchasing new baskets and so forth."

"Well! There was nothing to purchase, don't you see? We had no ships coming from China, not during the war."

"Then by expenses, you refer to salaries," said Norma.

"Yes, exactly," said Mr. Griggs, relieved to have made his point at last.

Now it was Bessie who leaned forward to drive home the final point. "Are you asking us to believe," she said, "that my husband mortgaged his house, handed the proceeds over to you, and that you then handed the money back to him in the form of his own salary?"

Mr. Griggs, abashed and flustered, attempted to dig himself out of that particular hole. "I wouldn't put it quite like that. There was his quarter interest, too. I handed over a sizable portion of the operation to him. It was worth quite a bit more than that, in better times."

"But it isn't now," said Norma.

"Well," said Mr. Griggs. There was no advantage in him offering any more information than what Norma was able to deduce for herself.

"I suppose we could inspect the books," said Norma, "considering we own a quarter interest."

"Oh, it's an awful lot to explain," said Mr. Griggs, unwisely, having no idea who he was up against. "Just columns and columns of figures. If you wanted to know anything in particular, I'd be happy to answer —"

"I believe we will have a look at the books," said Norma, "but there is also the matter of the warehouse. It must be worth something. It sits on such a good plot of land." Norma had already cast her appraiser's eye over the boundaries of the property and calculated what it might fetch, as compared to the acreage out in Wyckoff she was parceling out.

"Well, then it's a pity that we rent," said Mr. Griggs, earning an astonished expression from both women.

"Rent?" said Bessie. "After all these years?"

Mr. Griggs could only shrug at that. "I put my capital in the baskets," he sniffed, pridefully.

"Yes," Norma muttered, "because baskets are forever, whereas land . . ."

"We'll have a look at those ledgers now,"

307

Bessie put in. "There's no need to take up any more of your time. We'll just clear ourselves a space in the warehouse."

Mr. Griggs rose to pull the topmost books off the shelf. "Take all the time you like," he said. "And while you're going over the figures, there's one more possibility you might consider."

"What's that?" asked Bessie, eager for any possibility.

Mr. Griggs hesitated and cleared his throat. "Becoming half owners."

Here Norma saw an opportunity. It had, over the last several weeks, become clear to her that the Kopps would be better served by some sort of enterprise that they could own and manage themselves, rather than depending on the largesse of, say, a department store in need of a detective. If Constance were to take charge of Schoonmaker's inventory, the situation would only be worse: the store would grow more profitable through Constance's efforts, and the Kopps would see nothing of it beyond a weekly salary. Mr. Schoonmaker was a shrewd businessman. He'd pay his people only what was necessary and pocket the profits.

To support a growing family, one needed a stake in something that could grow, too.

Norma settled back into her chair and considered what a half interest might mean. "You would give us a larger share, and we would come and run it with you. I suppose that's what you came around to talk about that morning just after the funeral."

The idea animated Bessie considerably. "I don't see why we couldn't. If Constance could be persuaded, and even Fleurette . . ."

Mr. Griggs's chin wobbled as he tried to form the words. "Oh, my dears. I only meant to suggest that it might make a good investment."

Norma stood again and seized the ledger. "Then you're only asking us to put more money in."

"Well, I —"

"After Francis mortgaged the house and left us with the payments, and no money with which to pay it."

"I wouldn't —"

"And I suppose these books are going to show us that we shouldn't expect anything in the way of profits to be attributed to our share any time soon."

"Oh, I don't know if I'd go so far as to say —"

"And now you're telling us that we couldn't, even if we wanted to, come in and work to put the business on a more profitable footing. I suppose you've never hired a woman and don't intend to start now."

"Miss Kopp, it's hardly a place for ladies. Why, you've had a look at the warehouse."

"You do understand that I've just returned from France. I'm quite accustomed to plain living and hard work. Constance practically lived at the Hackensack jail when she was deputy. Is it worse than a jail around here?"

"Now, Miss Kopp and Mrs. Kopp, I don't think you understand. I only wished to offer another opportunity."

"You'll take our money, but you won't have us working here. I understand perfectly. Bessie and I will have a look at the books, and we'll be on our way. Oh, and I don't suppose you have a copy of the partnership agreement you signed with Francis?"

"Partnership agreement?"

"Yes, some sort of paper confirming that what you've told us is true. Or did Francis just hand over every penny he had in the world on the strength of your good word?"

"If you understood a bit more about how businesses like ours are conducted, you might see that such formalities are rarely necessary."

"Yes, rarely," said Norma. "Bessie, have we anything more to say to Mr. Griggs?"

"Nothing that I dare utter with a child present," sighed Bessie, one hand on her belly and the other reaching for a sandwich.

30

"Well, it's good news and bad news," Norma said later that evening, when Constance returned home from work. "The good news is that Francis owned a quarter interest in Griggs Basketry and Trimmings. The bad news is that the business is worthless."

"But it must not have been worthless when Francis bought his share," said Constance, "and that wasn't so terribly long ago."

"Apparently it was worthless then," said Norma. "Mr. Griggs persuaded our brother to put money into the business to keep it alive. Otherwise the company was on the verge of insolvency."

"I wondered why anyone was buying baskets when we could hardly get butter and eggs," said Bessie.

"Well, they weren't," said Norma. "No one needs a darling little Chinese basket in war-time. Also, the ships weren't coming from China because there was no trade going back the other way. Everything we had to sell or trade or give went straight to Europe."

"But he could afford to pay Francis," Constance said. "His salary never stopped, did it?"

Bessie shook her head. "He was always paid. But now we know why."

Constance slumped back in her chair, dumbfounded. "Do you mean to say that Francis mortgaged the house, gave the money to Mr. Griggs, and then Mr. Griggs used that money to pay Francis a salary?"

"I put the question to Mr. Griggs in exactly those terms," said Norma. "He wouldn't admit to it at first, but there's no arguing with the figures. Whether Mr. Griggs intended it that way, that was the result."

Constance said, "I can't understand why Francis went along with it. He must've seen what would happen. If the business was losing money because of the war, it wouldn't recover until the war ended. There was no point in throwing good money after bad. I only wish he'd talked to one of us about it. I was here most every Sunday for dinner over the summer. He must've been sitting right there thinking about it, but he never once said a word."

"He didn't have any use for our opinions and you know it," said Norma.

"He had his pride," Bessie said. "It wasn't just that he was the only boy in the family. He was the eldest, too. He thought it his responsibility to look after you girls. He wouldn't have wanted to worry you."

"Well, we worried him to no end," said Constance. "He could've returned the favor."

"The point is," said Norma, who didn't like to waste time on *might-have-beens*, "the money's gone. Or so Mr. Griggs claims. He spent every penny Francis put in, and now he's asked us for another investment. He wants an infusion of capital to balance the books and get him back on a pre-war footing."

Constance groaned. "I can't believe he had the nerve to ask you for money."

"He means well," said Bessie. "He wants to protect us all. We do own a quarter of the business."

"It isn't much of a business," said Norma. "We spent an hour looking over the figures, and I could see at once that he'd been paying himself handsomely for years and running at a small loss. I doubt he'd want to give that up, but he'd have to, if we were to recoup any of our investment. No, he only asked because he thought we were too gullible to see right through him."

"He must be hoping to bring it back to what it was before the war," said Bessie.

"That's just the trouble," said Norma. "Francis did everything. He ran the shipments, he handled the sales, he oversaw the delivery drivers. The place is falling apart without him. He was their key man."

"You told Mr. Griggs right after the funeral that he ought to hire one of us or all of us," said Constance.

"Well, he won't," said Norma. "He's old-fashioned that way. Anyway, he's weeks away from closing. Even if we had the money to invest, we'd be doing just what Francis did. We'd put the money in and take it out as salary. What's the point in that?"

"Then the money's gone," said Constance. "What, exactly, do we own a quarter of?"

Bessie sighed. "There are still a few piles of dusty old baskets, all the sort of things people liked before the war. You remember those Chinese baskets trimmed in tassels and ribbons? Sometimes Francis would bring one home filled with chocolate. They had those Chinese coins stitched on, or beads. Lorraine might still have one. All those little ornaments were meant to sym-

315

bolize something: charm, dignity, beauty, stability."

"He gave Fleurette one with a strand of beads around it, symbolizing virtue," said Norma grimly. At the mention of Fleurette, Constance flinched but didn't answer.

"It was all that sort of thing," said Bessie. "Some of them were lacquered with a mahogany finish, like you might want for a lined sewing basket. There were still a few of the sort people used to use for flower arrangements or fruit."

"I can't imagine much demand for that right now," said Constance. "At Schoonmaker's people are mostly buying needful things — a pair of shoes or a practical hat. Nobody yet has money for luxuries."

"And I told him so," said Norma. "Before we left I told him that if any of us wanted to open a basket-importing business — and none of us do — we could do it ourselves, for the same investment, and own all of it, not just a quarter or half. But we're not interested in sinking our fortune into baskets, and anyway we won't have a dime until the lots sell. Fortunately the surveyor's been out and the land's been divided. Now that it's spring, I think we can put the lots up for sale and hope to have the money by the end of summer. But I'm not giving any of it to Mr. Griggs."

"What about the warehouse?" asked Constance, sitting up suddenly. "That's property. Do we own a quarter of that?"

"Norma asked, of course," said Bessie. "But no, Mr. Griggs rents the place. He doesn't own anything but the dregs of his basket inventory, a few desks and chairs, and that old delivery truck Francis used to drive. It's worthless, all of it."

"I still think we ought to go see a lawyer about it," said Norma.

Bessie sighed. "I just don't want to put Mr. Griggs through it, or us, for that matter. He's an old man and he's about to be out of business. Francis wouldn't have wanted us dragging him through court."

"Hmph," said Norma, which was her way of keeping her arguments to herself.

"Then we start making the mortgage payments in three months," said Constance.

"I'm going back to the bank to insist on six," Norma said.

"It only kicks the can down the road," said Constance.

"That's exactly what I intend to do," said Norma.

"I suppose someone ought to tell Fleurette," said Bessie.

Both Bessie and Norma looked over at

Constance, who tucked her chin down and refused to meet their eyes.

"You're trying to get me to apologize, and I won't," she said. "It was wrong of her to go behind our backs, and now she's thrown a fit and stormed off, just when she's needed at home. She's the one who should apologize."

Bessie sighed. "She was only trying to help."

"Which she did," Norma said. "She paid all the accounts and never said a word about it. This is the girl who used to expect a round of applause for making her bed in the morning. I'd say she's grown up."

"She didn't have to ask for applause, but she could've been honest about what she was doing," Constance said.

"She was covering for Francis," Norma said. "He couldn't keep up with his bills because he had that mortgage to pay, but she didn't know that. All she knew was that he'd been in some kind of trouble and she could put it to rest. It was an entirely selfless act. We haven't seen many of those from Fleurette."

"And we won't again, now that she's skipped out on us. Wouldn't you call that selfish?"

Norma snorted. "It's not as if we need

her here to manage the household. We're overrun with women and children as it is."

Bessie leaned over and patted Constance's knee. "There was no harm done. She's a grown woman now and she'll do what she likes. Do we really want to be the kind of family where everyone walks around in fear of each other's disapproval and disappointment?"

"She was in fear because she knew better," Constance grumbled.

"Constance, I beg you to think about this," Bessie said. "Francis didn't tell me the truth, because he couldn't bear to disappoint me. He would've rather mortgaged the house than walk in the door and tell me he'd lost his job. And look at what that drove him to do. Lying to me and running up debts all over town."

"I suppose," Constance said, reluctantly. "But Francis should've known you'd love him anyway."

"He should have," said Bessie, "and I will ask myself why he didn't every day for the rest of my life. But there's only one way to prove that we will not turn our backs or scold or reprimand when things go horribly wrong. And that's not to do it."

"She turned her back, too," said Constance. "She's the one who left."

"And imagine how terrified she must've been," said Bessie. "Imagine how frightful it would be to run from your family, just because you couldn't stand their judgment."

It was the closest Bessie had ever come to acknowledging the truth, a secret that Francis must've told her years ago. Constance had fled her own family when she was younger than Fleurette, fearing their fury when they learned she was pregnant. It had taken Norma — stalwart, persistent Norma, even as a teenage girl — to track Constance down and bring her back, and to convince their mother to forgive and accept the child.

That child, of course, was Fleurette, who was never told the truth. She grew up believing that the three of them were sisters, and Constance never saw a reason to tell her otherwise. What had happened back in 1897 was best left there.

Did Constance know what it meant to live in terror of her family's wrath? To know that they would reject her if they knew the truth?

She knew it better than any of them.

31

The seamstressing work was dull when she had to do it all day. Fleurette found that she didn't mind making over a dress or cuffing a pair of pants when it was something extra, to be fitted in around the edges of an otherwise interesting and engaging life, but when she woke up with nothing else to look forward to but a day behind the sewing machine and a few limp dollars to show for it, her enthusiasm flagged.

Was this to be her life now, tucked in the attic of a boarding-house, living with women who didn't know how to talk, repairing other people's terrible choices in clothing, scrimping to save the odd dollar to send home to her brother's widow?

She had only her parrot for companionship, and for one terrible moment she even considered giving Laura away. She had been working in Mrs. Doyle's basement sewing room, which had recently been improved upon by the addition of an ancient Victrola, one that had been gathering dust in the parlor because no one else had the wit or imagination to put on music and dance.

Now as she sewed she played songs from Mrs. Doyle's collection, and Laura from atop her cage shrieked and whistled along. (Fleurette tried to join in but still could not, and from a sitting position it was worse, as the breath simply would not come. She gave up any attempt at a duet and let Laura enjoy her solos.)

It being a basement room, the windows were high, and Fleurette kept them open to drive the musty odor out. Laura liked to turn toward the stream of fresh air and sing directly out the open window, as if calling to her avian counterparts in the trees.

Once a pair of brown leather shoes stopped along the sidewalk. Fleurette watched as a toe tapped in time to the music. Then the legs bent, and a hand came to rest on the pavement, and a man's face peered in the window. "I thought you had a parrot down there!" he called. "I used to train them myself."

Fleurette stood up. She was eye-to-eye with him, except that his face was nearly upside-down. "What'd you train them to do?" she asked.

"I had an uncle who raised them," he said. "Used to sell them to traveling acts. Magicians, circuses, that sort of thing. I stayed with him in the summertime and helped with the training. Well, mostly I cleaned cages."

"There is quite a bit of that to do," Fleurette said.

The man glanced over at Laura. "My cousin runs the place now. You should see what he can do with these birds. Has some of them singing opera. Some of them tell jokes. The whole joke, not just a word or two at the end. Can you imagine that?"

"Laura's learning new words every day," Fleurette said.

The man settled down cross-legged on the sidewalk, having grown tired of looking in upside-down. "Would you ever consider parting with her? She could have a good long life on the stage, if she was given the chance."

"Couldn't we all," said Fleurette, mournfully.

"What's that?" said the man.

"Never mind. She probably would like to travel and be admired. But she's staying with me for now."

He cast another appreciative look at Laura, who unabashedly preened and lengthened her neck, and even extended a leg as if showing off a pretty ankle. Poor Laura, stuffed away in a basement, when the world was waiting for her!

"If you change your mind," the man said, "it's Dietz & Sons, over in Trenton. Can you remember that?"

"I'll write it down," said Fleurette, but she knew she wouldn't. It might be selfish to deny Laura a chance to realize her full potential, but without her, who did Fleurette have to bestow her affections upon?

She tried not to dwell upon her sisters, and Bessie and the children, and fought the temptation to wonder how they were faring or what they might be saying about her, in her absence, when they sat around the dinner table at night.

She did intend to return at some point, perhaps for Sunday dinner, or to drop by for a visit now and then. But the trouble was that she didn't know how to be a visitor in her own family's home.

Was she to wait for an invitation, or to just turn up on the doorstep? Was she expected to knock first, or could she just walk in? And how was she to talk about her life to people who were no longer in it from day to day? There would be so much explaining that had never been necessary before, and so much tiptoeing around sore subjects.

If she did turn up, unannounced and uninvited, how would she be received? Would Constance be standing there, tapping her foot, demanding an apology? Because she wasn't about to apologize.

Every time she thought about expressing any remorse at all, it resurrected in her mind those old arguments between them, and she found herself, to her everlasting irritation, bickering with Constance all over again — but this time the argument lived only in her mind and ran around in circles, endlessly.

In fact, all of her relations lived in her mind. Even when she tried not to think of them, she couldn't push them away. Everything she saw, everything she heard, everything she did, was anchored somehow to her family.

She'd hear a new song coming out of one of the music shops and think how annoyed Norma would be if she played that song at home.

She'd see a pair of kid slippers in a window and wonder if Lorraine would wear them.

She'd find a set of patterns for a layette and put it aside for Bessie's baby.

She'd read a story about a lady officer in

San Diego who'd been hired to police women's swimming costumes at the beach, and she'd think about how Constance would laugh at the foolishness of that.

It was impossible to escape her family. They were her point of reference. They were the star by which she navigated, whether she liked it or not.

Perhaps she kept after the Alice Martin case to distract herself from those thoughts, and to break up the monotony of Mrs. Doyle's sewing room. Perhaps she wanted the company — not just of another person, but of another person's problems.

Whatever the reason, she kept after Louis Herman. She returned to the jeweler who'd given her the bad news about her emerald and asked him how a thief would go about selling stolen jewelry.

"I hope you're not getting into the business," said Mr. Swan, clearly amused.

"A friend has been robbed, but she's afraid to go to the police owing to . . . well, difficult circumstances," said Fleurette. "I only wondered if a man who had bracelets and pins and things to sell would come to you, or where he would go."

"If he was smart about it, he'd wait," said Mr. Swan. "A professional's going to give his goods a few months to cool off. And he'd take them out of town, or even out of state."

"Does that make such a difference?"

"Well, it's like this. If I suspected a man was offering me stolen jewelry for sale, I might speak to the Paterson police about it. But if the robbery had taken place in Pittsburgh or Chicago, what are the police here going to know about it?"

"And you've seen nothing lately that might've been stolen?" Fleurette asked. "There was a heavy ruby ring, I believe, and a long string of pearls."

"Well, everyone has pearls to sell," said Mr. Swan, "but no, there's been nothing out of the ordinary. Tell your friend to go to the police regardless. They ought to have a report on file in case this fellow does turn up."

"I'll tell her," said Fleurette dispiritedly.

For a few days Fleurette made the rounds of the jewelry shops, although she agreed with Mr. Swan that any jewel thief who knew his business would take his goods out of town. She went around to hotels and other places of temporary lodging for men, posing as a cousin, requesting only a forwarding address, but found no one admitting to a lodger of Mr. Herman's name. This

327

didn't surprise her: he probably operated under several names at once.

He was gone — of course he was. And where did that leave Fleurette?

The fact that he'd broken into William Griswold's office and used it to carry out his schemes seemed to be a matter that only Mr. Griswold could pursue, and if the man intended to do so, he certainly didn't seem inclined to involve Fleurette.

The match-book had yielded nothing, which was probably why it had been so carelessly left behind. The Black Cat was simply swimming in customers: everyone in Paterson stopped in at one time or another.

There really was nothing left but for Alice to go to the police. Fleurette appeared at her doorstep on a Wednesday evening, when Arthur was away, to tell her so.

Alice seemed glad to see her in spite of the fact that they had only this sordid mess in common. She invited her in and poured each of them a thimbleful of sherry, as if they had cause for celebration. But once Fleurette told all that she knew, and explained that the police were the only option remaining, Alice sunk into her chair, discouraged.

"You know I can't do that. Arthur would never forgive me."

"But you're divorcing him, aren't you? Do you really need his forgiveness?"

Alice groaned. "Divorcing him? How could I? I don't have a penny to live on. I only ever thought of leaving him when I believed I was to inherit. Where would I go now? What would I do?"

"But won't he notice that the jewelry and things are gone? And what about the money you spent? Won't he ask?"

"Oh, he might, eventually. He doesn't often question my spending."

"But the jewelry? Wasn't some of it his mother's?"

"Well, it isn't as if he snoops around in my jewelry box. I suppose if he does ask, I could just tell him that I don't know where those things have gone."

"And if he suspects they were stolen? What if he wants to go to the police?"

She shrugged. "Let him. I'm tired of thinking about it. It's been exhausting, this business. I should've listened to that fortune-teller the first time."

Fleurette nearly fell out of her chair. "You never told me about a fortune-teller."

"Oh, didn't I? I went to see her a few months ago. I was just miserable and out of sorts. A boy was handing out cards at the train station, and I took one. 'Discover the

Truth About Your Past, Present, and Future,' it said. 'Find Your Heart's Journey.' Well, I liked the sound of all that, so I went."

"And what did she have to say? What was her name?"

"Madame Zella, I believe. Oh, she told me so much! She looked at my palm and saw right away that there had been a break with my family. She couldn't have been more right about that. Did I tell you that when my father died, nobody even got word to me so that I might attend the funeral? Not that I would, after the way they treated me. The last time I spoke to my mother, she had the nerve to blame Arthur for us not having children. And she didn't suggest it was because of — well, the usual reasons! It was because he'd lured me to the wicked city, and the city had ruined me."

"I don't think it works like that," said Fleurette. "People do have babies in the city."

"Well, of course they do. Madame Zella said that I must love Arthur a great deal to give up my family for him, but like I told her, he ignores me and runs off to the theater! I sit around this lonely old house, and what am I to do? He's out day and night, and when he is home, he's so tired he never wants to go anywhere. I thought my life would have some adventure to it, do you know what I mean? I imagined that someday I'd get out of this dull little bungalow, and live in a grand house with an enormous lawn and a view to the sea, and go to dances and parties, but nothing like that has happened, has it? Let me tell you something, Miss Kopp. Don't ever dream of a grand life, because when you don't get it, you just have to go on living anyway, and it's awful."

Fleurette couldn't help but shudder. Is that what she was to do, just go on living?

"Did you say all this to Madame Zella?"

"Oh, yes. Once she understood, she insisted on reading my cards at no extra charge. Everything the cards said was exactly right — that I'd lost my way, that I was destined for something greater but had been pulled away from it and couldn't find a path back. She said that I had only to wait for a sign, that one was coming, and I would know it and would know what to do. She was right that something was coming, but it was only an enormous mess! I should go back and demand a refund."

Fleurette leaned forward, trying not to appear too eager.

"Madame Zella," she said. "Where exactly

was her shop? Her parlor, whatever it's called?"

"She did call it a parlor," Alice said. "It was right here in Paterson, on Pearl Street."

32

And so it was! Madame Zella's Card-Reading and Palmistry Parlor sat at 617 Pearl Street. Just three doors down was the Black Cat. (Alice, having always come from the other direction, had never noticed the café and didn't recall the name when Fleurette mentioned the match-book.)

Fleurette stood across the street for the better part of an afternoon and watched the comings and goings at Madame Zella's parlor. The clientele were all women, during the hours that Fleurette observed the place, mostly young and desperate-looking, some middle-aged and downtrodden, and a few older women, grim and stalwart, paying their visits as one might attend a church service.

What happened when they arrived was always the same. They would ring a little bell next to the door, a red curtain in the bay window would part, and Madame

Zella's face would briefly appear then dis-appear. The door would open, revealing a dark and shadowy interior. Only a glimpse of Madame Zella herself could be seen as each woman was admitted, but from what Fleurette could gather, the fortune-teller was as short as Fleurette herself, only rounder. She was stiff and slow-moving, and fond of enormous scarves and dark, dra-matic velvets.

Once her parlor was occupied, Madame turned around a little hand-lettered sign in the window, which Fleurette scurried across and read when she was sure she wouldn't be seen. VISITORS ADMITTED, it read on one side. SESSION IN PROGRESS, PLEASE DO NOT RING, read the other.

Not a single man was seen coming or leav-ing, and no one matching Louis Herman's description walked by the parlor or the Black Cat.

Nonetheless, Madame Zella had to be the connection to Louis Herman. She had to be listening to these women's stories and slipping word of the most likely prospects to him.

Now it was up to Fleurette to be the most likely of prospects. She stood across the street, her heart in her mouth, rehearsing her story. She couldn't pretend to be destitute — these were swindlers, and they'd be looking for a woman of means — but she also couldn't make it seem as if she were surrounded by sensible, intelligent people who would be suspicious of a letter from an unknown attorney. There could be no Norma in her story, nor anyone remotely resembling Constance. Imagine how quickly Madame Zella would bundle her up and send her back out on the street with the promise of love and babies in her future if she said that she had a sister who opened all the mail and scrutinized it for irregularities, and another who'd worked at the Bureau of Investigation!

No, today Fleurette would be a war widow, with her husband's insurance payment having just arrived, and her entire family back in Chicago, leaving her with no reason to stay in Paterson. The problem she would pose was this one: What was a young widow in her position to do with herself and her modest income, and perhaps (Fleurette added this, as an extra enticement) a small inheritance? Madame Zella would have the answer.

When fifteen minutes had passed with no new visitors, Fleurette dashed across the street and rang the bell. She tried not to turn to the window in expectation of the fortune-teller yanking aside the curtain and scrutinizing her, but saw her out of the corner of her eye and knew at once that she would be admitted inside. If Madame Zella had any powers at all, it was the power to recognize a young, vulnerable, and not entirely destitute woman seeking guidance.

The card in the window turned around and Madame Zella opened the door. "Come in quickly," she said. "Don't tell your business out on the street."

Fleurette rushed inside and found herself almost smothered by curtains: dark velvet curtains partitioning the foyer from the parlor, red and purple gauze curtains draped against the walls, and every window hung in layer upon layer of tasseled and beaded fabric. She calculated that she could've outfitted an entire chorus on Broadway, including several changes of costume, with the material strewn around the place.

Madame Zella herself was, in fact, exactly Fleurette's diminutive height, so that the two of them peered at one another eye-to-eye. It was impossible, in the dim light, to decide exactly how old the fortune-teller might be, nor was Fleurette able to gain any idea of her nationality, as she spoke in an ever-shifting accent that might be Spanish, Italian, Russian, or Brooklyn.

"Dear girl," Madame Zella said, clutching Fleurette's hands in hers. "There is sorrow in your eyes, but I see hope, too. Come in and let Madame have a look at your palm. Put your dollar in the tin there, sign the guest book, and let me get you settled and then we shall see all."

Fleurette did as she was told, putting down a false name and Mrs. Doyle's address in the book (she wondered if Alice Martin's name was on those pages, but didn't dare to look), and allowed herself to be led into a tiny room — again, formed by curtains draped from the ceiling, giving no idea of the walls or other rooms within — where she was offered a high and deep armchair, cushioned with tasseled pillows so enormous that Fleurette felt like a child nestled within it.

She'd crafted such a fine story that she was eager to deliver it. "The reason I've come to you, Madame, is that my —"

But the fortune-teller reached across the little table (adorned, just as Fleurette might've imagined it, with a candle inside a saucer and a globe of bubbled glass held aloft by a little footed stand) and put her finger to Fleurette's lips. Fleurette smelled burnt tobacco and backed away at once.

"Not a word, dear. Not even your name.

337

Let Madame read the truth in your palm."

Fleurette turned over her hand and let the woman run her fingers across it. As a child Fleurette had been fascinated by palmistry but wasn't allowed to have a book about it, as her mother considered it heresy and her sisters thought it nonsense. Nonetheless she once cut out a diagram of the palm from a magazine, with the lines and mounds indicated, and kept that scrap of paper hidden away for years, consulting it from time to time when she wondered what on earth was to become of her life.

She was, in other words, familiar enough with the general methods and principles. She was not therefore surprised when Madame Zella said, "Your heart line is like a chain, which suggests a flirtatious and capricious nature. No man has ever entirely satisfied you."

Fleurette, forgetting for the moment that she was meant to play a part, said, "I suppose you're right, although I wonder if it doesn't also mean that my heart is weak. My brother —"

Madame Zella glanced up sharply. "Nothing about your family just yet!" she hissed. "Your fate line shows a break coming soon. Have your palms itched lately?"

They did just then, when the fortune-teller

suggested it. "I do believe something's about to change," admitted Fleurette, "or I hope it will, now that . . . Well, I suppose you don't want me to say. My prospects have improved, that's all."

The fortune-teller looked up brightly. "Then we must consult the cards. This time, though, it is different. You must put your hands on the deck, so" — and she pressed a deck of cards, wrapped in yet another scarf, into Fleurette's hands — "and you must speak aloud your question. The cards will answer the questions put to them, nothing more."

Fleurette closed her eyes and smiled slightly. What a delicious role it was, that of the naïve young widow about to be duped by an unscrupulous fortune-teller! She could put every bit of this scene on stage just as it was.

"I never thought I'd be widowed so young, but I never expected to be a bride in wartime, either. Now, with my husband gone and buried in France, I've nothing to keep me in Paterson. With only a small inheritance and of course the widow's pension, I feel certain I'm meant to go somewhere else and start again. But where? And what am I to pursue?"

She opened one eye hopefully and found

Madame Zella nodding vigorously, her face fixed in an expression of powerful concentration. "The cards have their answer!" she cried, and pulled them away from Fleurette. She began to slap them down on the table, not bothering to exclaim over what was revealed or explain the mystical symbols.

"Opportunity!" she called triumphantly, tapping on one. "But not in the way of love or family. It suggests business, or some means of profiting from one's experience. Have you any sort of training, or a past line of work, perhaps in a family enterprise?"

"The theater," Fleurette said, taking the first idea that came to mind. "I was on the stage once, but had to give it up when . . ."

She was getting too close to the truth, wasn't she?

"When you were married," Madame Zella muttered. "Of course. It could be something to do with that. But this card suggests property, something tangible that could be sold or leased. Is there anything of that sort?"

Fleurette almost mentioned the farm, but remembered that she was to play a part and answered, "Nothing at all. We'd only just moved to Paterson before my husband left for France. We — well, I — rent a little apartment. That's all."

Madame tapped the card again before moving on. "It could mean war bonds, something along those lines."

"Well, yes, there are a few of those, of course," Fleurette said. It was effortless, conjuring up war bonds out of thin air.

"That's it, then," she said, and shuffled the deck again. "Here I see a suggestion of a relative trying to reach you. Have you lost touch with anyone significant? Anyone who might be eager to find you but doesn't know how?"

There it was! The long-lost relative with an inheritance to pass along, or a business opportunity, or an investment that couldn't fail. Fleurette decided to make it easy for Madame Zella and her co-conspirator. "I've a much older sister from whom I'm estranged," she said, "but I can't imagine that she'd want to find me."

"Where is she now?" asked Madame Zella.

Just down the road in Hawthorne, Fleurette wanted to say, but instead answered, "She moved out to Colorado when she married and has quite a large family of her own, I believe."

Another card revealed itself. "Ah, yes, I see something buried, but it doesn't have to mean a funeral. It could be . . . something to do with mining, perhaps?"

"I suppose that's the sort of business her husband is in," Fleurette said carelessly, as if she hadn't thought about this long-departed sister for years. "I wouldn't know anymore."

"And this sister . . . it is a name from the beginning of the alphabet . . . a B or a D . . ."

"Dora," supplied Fleurette, happy to give Madame a victory.

"Yes, Dora, a short name, I see that. Do not ignore any sort of communication from her."

"Well, I'm not going to Colorado, if that's what you mean," said Fleurette, pouting a little. "What about me, and my difficulties? Where am I to go, and what am I to do with myself? I expected my husband home by now, and children on the way, and my life settled. I'm at quite a loss, and you've given me nothing to go on. How am I to decide whether to stay or to go, and what sort of life to pursue? I'm so lonely here. I had friends in the theater, but they've all moved on. They were my only family and now what do I have?"

Madame Zella kept shuffling the cards. "I do see you finding your people again, but not as you expect."

"Then am I to just wait for another

husband to come along? Because I don't think I could love again, but perhaps I'm meant to. I thought you would tell me that, at least."

This little tirade gave her a great deal of satisfaction. Why *couldn't* anyone tell her where to go, or what to do? Fleurette hadn't done a very good job of working out her own life for herself. Why couldn't there be a Madame Zella who had all the answers?

Madame knew her business and promptly turned over a few more cards. "You have only to ask, and the cards will answer," she murmured. "You are to stay here for now. Another month at least. There is another husband in your future, but he is years away. Do not take seriously the next man who claims to love you. He is not the right one. You are destined for quite an active life, in a place far from here. You won't have to wonder where to go. You'll be summoned. Patience is your watchword."

Fleurette sighed, disappointed for herself and for the character she'd invented. A little clock from somewhere within the curtained rooms chimed just then, and Madame put away her cards and stood. "Our time is at an end," she said. "Come to me again, but not for a month, at least. Your future will have started to take shape by then, and the cards might hold fresh answers for you."

"I certainly hope they will," Fleurette said. She handed Madame Zella a few coins, to better impress upon her that her latest customer was free with her money and an easy mark.

It was dark by the time she left the parlor. She walked past the Black Cat on the way home, but did not bother to look within. She didn't have to search for Louis Herman anymore. She had only to wait for him to come to her.

33

"I'm still not convinced they could've known enough about me to concoct a story I'd so readily believe." Alice frowned to herself as she set down a tray of little ham sandwiches and sliced cucumbers.

"Madame Zella wouldn't have needed you to tell her much," Fleurette answered. She lifted a sandwich from the tray and looked around for the little pot of mustard Alice usually put out. Alice, seeing that it was missing, jumped up to retrieve it. "Didn't you sign the guest book when you walked in, and supply your name and address?"

"I suppose so," Alice called from the kitchen. "I don't really remember that part."

"That's why she has you do it at the beginning," Fleurette said. "Everything that comes after is so distracting that you don't ever think of it again."

"Still, Mr. Herman knew so much about my family, and my grandfather . . ." Alice picked at the cucumbers with the only dainty silver fork she hadn't already handed over to Louis Herman.

"I'm sure you said enough during the reading with Madame Zella to get him started. And I wouldn't be surprised if you told Mr. Herman even more during your first meeting, and he used that, too," Fleurette said.

"I just don't remember," Alice mused.

"That's why it works," said Fleurette. "I'd like to get my hands on that guest book. I suspect it's full of the names of women who've been swindled and never thought to mention that they'd seen a fortune-teller a few weeks before."

Fleurette and Alice were by then striking up an odd sort of friendship. Alice was home during the day and often bored, and Fleurette found that she couldn't stand to spend eight hours a day at her sewing machine. She took to dropping by Alice's around lunch-time, and would happily eat any sort of sandwich and speculate about their case in progress.

"What sort of letter do you suppose he'll send you?" Alice said. "Do you think it's always a deceased uncle, or is it a different sort of con every time?"

"He had to be clever about it, if he doesn't

346

want to be caught," Fleurette said. "I let slip that I have a much older sister from whom I'm estranged. I expect it'll have something to do with that."

"Then you simply told the truth, like I did," said Alice.

"No, I didn't. I invented a sister in Colorado, whose husband is in the gold mines. It's nothing to do with me."

"But didn't you tell me that you have a much older sister from whom you're estranged?" said Alice. "It doesn't matter if she's in Colorado or right here in Paterson if you don't speak to her or see her."

Fleurette put the sandwich down. She lost her appetite all of a sudden. "We aren't estranged," she said. "We just — she owes me an apology, that's all. It won't last forever."

"Sometimes it does," said Alice mildly. "I didn't plan never to see my family again. But they won't apologize because they're not sorry, and neither am I. We have nothing in common. I don't even know what we'd say, if we did see each other again. I suppose that's how it is for you and your sister. Or is it both sisters? You have two of them, is that right?"

"Two, plus a sister-in-law, and a niece and nephew and another on the way," said

Fleurette dispiritedly. Exactly how many relations had she tossed overboard in an effort to put some distance between her and Constance?

"Well, but if they want to control you, and tell you how to live your life, you've no choice but to go as far away as you can. Are you really thinking of moving away?"

"Why would I do that?" asked Fleurette.

"You said as much to the fortune-teller," said Alice. "Or didn't you mean it?"

"That was only the story I invented," said Fleurette. "Of course, if my voice was better . . ." She stopped there. She didn't even like to speculate about returning to the stage, and she hadn't told Alice about the difficulties with her voice.

But Alice pounced on it. "You have a fine voice. What does your voice have to do with it?"

There was no getting out of it now, unless Fleurette simply refused to answer. "Oh," she said weakly, "I used to sing. But I was ill last fall and now it seems I can't quite get my breath back."

Alice said, "You should be talking to Arthur, not to me."

"If I'd met him under different circumstances, I might have," said Fleurette.

"What sort of illness was it?"

"Streptococci turned to scarlet fever. My throat was absolutely ruined. I couldn't speak a word. I coughed for months. I still do sometimes."

"Oh."

Alice sounded so solemn that Fleurette looked over quickly. "What do you mean, *oh*?"

"Just — how long has it been, exactly?"

"I was sick around the beginning of November, so about six months."

"Oh," she said again. "Well, you never know."

Fleurette knew Alice well enough by now to detect a false note. "You're thinking something, but you're not saying it. You might as well tell me."

Alice looked at her with pity. Fleurette found herself panicking. The wife of a vocal expressionist might just know a thing or two about cases like hers. It was a wonder she hadn't thought to ask sooner.

"Arthur would say that it's too late. He'd say that you have a scar in your throat and it makes your breath catch. It turns your voice rough in places and weak in others. You can learn to speak around it, as you have, but you can't sing around it. You'll never make full use of your range again, and there are plenty of other girls who can."

349

The truth of it hit Fleurette hard enough to make her shudder. "That's exactly what it feels like," she muttered. "That I'm trying to sing around it."

Alice nodded. "He sees it all the time. You can ask him yourself if you like. Come over sometime and I'll pretend not to know you. You could disguise yourself a little."

Fleurette groaned. "I don't think I could bear to hear any more bad news right now."

"At least you had a talent for it," said Alice, which was generous of her, as she'd never heard Fleurette sing. "I just don't feel as if I have a talent for anything. I just — well, I just sit here all day."

"But you could do anything you like," said Fleurette. "Just because nursing didn't work out for you doesn't mean the next thing won't."

"Yes, let's say that, why don't we?" Alice said, a little bitterly. "But don't you see? It was supposed to be nursing, and then it was supposed to be marriage and children, and when the children didn't come, I found myself at a fortune-teller and next thing I knew, I'd handed over every penny I had in the world, and now I'm supposed to decide what's next?"

Fleurette kept quiet. What was next, for either of them?

34

The letter arrived at last. Over three weeks had passed. Fleurette thought it clever of Louis Herman to wait a while, so that the announcement of an unexpected windfall would not follow too closely after the visit to the fortune-teller.

He did not, of course, call himself Louis Herman this time. He was Mr. Van Der Meer, Attorney-at-Law, from Philadelphia but arriving to Paterson on business. Lacking an office in Paterson, he proposed a meeting at a hotel with which Fleurette had some familiarity — the Metropolitan, where many of her assignations with Ward & McGinnis's clients had taken place. He could promise a quiet corner in the back of the restaurant where her privacy would be assured.

Fleurette took the letter to Alice at once so that they might compare it with the one she'd received. Both letters were typewritten, with a slight skip near the top of the capital S. The signatures (two florid scrawls) looked nothing alike, but were both done in the same bold ink. Both letters were written in a kind of baroque language that did not seem, to Alice and Fleurette, to be the way an attorney would ordinarily conduct business.

Alice's letter began:

"I write with tidings of a benediction quite unexpected but not, I trust, unwelcome. It is my somber duty but also my legal obligation to inform you . . ."

Fleurette's, nearly identical, began:

"Please allow me to convey tidings of the most fortunate variety, which I trust you will find unexpected but not in the least unwelcome. As the attorney of record representing certain mining interests in Western states, it is my legal obligation to notify you . . ."

"He ought to find someone else to write his letters," Fleurette said, feeling very much like Norma with that pronouncement. It was a job poorly done and she felt it necessary to say so. "Anyone can see that they're nearly identical. And I don't know why he doesn't change typewriters. That broken S is a giveaway."

"It's a wonder the police have never spot-

352

ted the similarities," Alice said.

"They couldn't, if they've never seen the letters," said Fleurette. "Most women would be ashamed to tell, just like you've been. Besides, he probably moves from one city to another as soon as there's any sign of trouble."

"Do you suppose Madame Zella goes with him, or does he find a new fortune-teller in each town?"

Fleurette considered that. "It would be easy enough to find out how long Madame Zella's been there. I might pop in and ask those ladies at the library. If I had to guess, I'd say he travels alone. It's twice the risk and twice the expense to go everywhere together. The two of them as a pair would be more easily recognized. Besides, he might not use a fortune-teller every time. Who knows how many schemes he's tried over the years?"

It gave Fleurette a great deal of satisfaction to imagine her adversary as a seasoned criminal, expert in all manner of confidence tricks and swindles. What a thrill it would be to bring down a man like that! Wouldn't it just show Constance if she put him behind bars while Constance lingered around the perfume counter at Schoonmaker's?

She shrugged off that idea before it took hold. Constance had a way of creeping around the corners of her mind uninvited. They weren't even on speaking terms at the moment, but Constance popped into her thoughts anyway, like an old habit she couldn't shake.

There was nothing of Constance's investigations in this matter anyway. She wasn't working in any official capacity, now that Mr. Ward had been scared off of hiring her. This was only a way to keep herself amused and to help a friend — and Alice had become a friend, of sorts.

"I don't particularly like the scheme he's come up with for you," Alice said. "It isn't nearly as attractive as mine."

"That's because he invented it just for me," Fleurette said. "Or not for me, exactly, but for the character I was playing. I said that I longed for the theater, and for a great big group of friends around me. I practically begged Madame Zella for a playhouse."

The proposition outlined in the letter involved a theatrical playhouse that had been put up as loan collateral for a stake in a mining operation out in Colorado. The husband of Dora, the long-vanished older sister, found himself in possession of the playhouse when the owner defaulted on his obligations and fled. Now Dora wished to offer the playhouse to Fleurette — or, rather, to the character Fleurette was playing — as a sort of compensation for her years of estrangement.

"I hardly knew you as a child, and now you are grown," read Dora's letter, forwarded on by Mr. Van Der Meer, "and now I understand through our attorney that you are a widow. I should've done more for you years ago and I hope you'll allow me to do so now. A nice respectable playhouse down in Florida, with rooms above for an apartment and (so I've been told) a few extra rooms to let, would offer you a life in the theater but also the comforts of a true home. I enclose my address if you wish to write to me yourself, but please know that you may trust Mr. Van Der Meer to make all the arrangements directly. He has handled our legal matters for years and we have full faith in him."

Fleurette was touched by the way Alice took the matter seriously and gave the opportunity careful consideration. "But would you really take ownership of a theatrical playhouse, and a company of actors, and all the entanglements it involves? Ticket sales and rehearsals and leaky roofs and . . . Oh,

I don't know, it all sounds like a bit much."

"But for a woman who's been so bored and lonely, it might be just the thing," Fleurette said. "And it was awfully clever of Mr. Van Der Meer to include an address in Colorado where I might write to this Dora. Of course, it's only a postal box in Denver."

"I wonder who would answer if you did write," said Alice.

"Probably no one at all. I expect he's only chosen a box-number at random, and hopes to take as much money from me as he can before the letters come back and I realize it's all a hoax. I'm sure he'll make every effort to hurry me along before that happens."

"Oh yes, that's how he was with me," Alice said. "Everything had to happen in such a rush. Past-due fees and back taxes and the like."

Fleurette nodded and turned the letter over. "I'm going to need something of value to hand over to him," she said.

Alice laughed. "I couldn't help you with that. I haven't any jewelry left to give!"

"Well, neither have I. My most valuable possessions are my sewing machine and my parrot, and neither of them would matter to a crook looking to make a quick profit."

It was then that Fleurette remembered the emerald — that cheap flashy thing that was meant to come to her rescue but only disappointed her. She'd tossed it in a box of notions and forgotten about it.

"Then again, perhaps I do have a piece of costume jewelry I could offer him," Fleurette said. "Did he seem to you to know anything about jewelry? Did he eye anything of yours as if he was an expert in gems and the like?"

"Not at all," said Alice. "He hardly glanced at my things. He just wrapped them in a handkerchief and put them in his pocket."

"Then I have everything I need," said Fleurette.

35

Fleurette sailed into the Metropolitan looking every inch the grieving widow with a
modest (but not too paltry) inheritance to
spend. She hadn't said when, exactly, her
husband had died — neither Madame Zella
nor Mr. Van Der Meer seemed at all interested in the husband, except to be assured
that he was well and truly dead, and had
left her provided for in some way. Fleurette
had decided for herself that the husband
had perished early in the war, so that she
might be through her period of formal
mourning and into somber dark blue dresses
rather than black.

In fact, she wore the very same dress she'd
worn on that first night, when Petey snuck
her in through the hotel kitchen and up to
the room of Mr. Lyman, that kind and ami-
able man who'd treated her tenderly and
doubled her pay. What a promising start that
had been! She couldn't have imagined that

a couple of months later, she'd be living on her own, not speaking to her sisters, and steeling herself to take down a notorious swindler, all for . . . well, for no pay at all.

It was a thrill to do it, but that was all it would be. This night, she realized, represented her last tie to her old job at Ward & McGinnis, and to Alice Martin. After tonight, her role in this little drama would come to an end. It would be seamstressing at Mrs. Doyle's from now on, until the next thing came along, whatever that might be.

All the more reason to make as much of the moment as she could. The Metropolitan was bright and gleaming and welcoming, and she felt that she belonged there entirely. She nodded at the doorman as she breezed past him, swept through the lobby, and glanced appreciatively up at those glorious chandeliers and down at a red and gold carpet in a French pattern of fleur-de-lis.

At the entrance to the restaurant, she issued a word to the maître d' and was at once ushered into one of those quiet little rooms tucked in the back, behind a curtain.

There sat her criminal.

Mr. Van Der Meer — or Louis Herman, or whatever else he called himself — looked exactly as Alice had described. He was a nondescript man of medium height, medium coloring, brown eyes, with absolutely no distinguishing marks or features. It seemed a convenient appearance for a swindler. In any crowd, half the men would match his description.

"I hope I haven't kept you waiting," Fleurette said as she handed over her coat and hat. "I was so nervous about our meeting that I thought I might be here an hour early, but somehow the time got away from me and now here I am . . ."

She thought it best to appear flustered, unsure of herself, and unaware of how to behave in a first meeting with a strange man. Mr. Van Der Meer played along perfectly, rising to pull out Fleurette's chair, giving a nod to the waiter to fill her glass, and assuring her that she was just in time.

"I'm only sorry we had to choose such an unlikely meeting place," he said. "As I mentioned, my offices are in Philadelphia, not here. But I thought you might prefer to talk things over in person, and I didn't want you to have to make such a long trip."

"You're very kind. I can see why Dora puts her trust in you."

"I understand it might've come as something of a surprise to hear from her," he said.

"We hardly know each other. She's been

gone so long, and I was quite young when she left. She must only remember me as a child."

"Nevertheless she wishes to do something for you now. I warned her that I couldn't be at all certain how a gift like this might be received. She'd heard that you were widowed — I suppose someone in the family must have written to her?"

"Perhaps a cousin, I wouldn't know," muttered Fleurette, as if no one in the family meant a thing to her. She saw what he was doing. He was making sure that she wouldn't confide in a relation who would then mention this unexpected gift to the real Dora. Fleurette was happy to reassure him on that matter.

"Well, she knew you'd been widowed — my condolences, by the way —"

"Thank you," Fleurette said.

"And she remembered your love of the theater and thought you might like to take on the running of this little playhouse. Naturally, it's not a decision to make lightly . . ." Here he paused, gauging Fleurette's response.

"Naturally," she said. She thought it best to hesitate a bit. He should have to persuade her. "It's kind of her, but I'm surprised her husband doesn't want it sold. As a building alone it must have some value."

"You're entirely right to wonder," Mr. Van Der Meer said. "It's just a terrible time to sell, right after the war. A theater is always a tricky sort of property. It can't easily be made into a storefront, for instance, or an office building. A buyer would have to be found who specifically wanted a theater in St. Petersburg. And to be honest, enough little playhouses of this sort closed during the war that there are already plenty of them out there, to be had for very little money."

"St. Petersburg," said Fleurette. "Isn't that rather out of the way?"

"Yes, but they enjoy a busy winter season down there. As I understand it, the theater keeps up some rehearsals over the summer, but then closes entirely for the month of August. You'd have your home there, of course, if you chose to live upstairs, but you might want some time away, too. Any number of wealthy patrons of the arts might have summer homes on offer. I expect you'd be invited to the Cape or Long Island if you liked that sort of thing. These wealthy types like to keep an artist around to make their dinner parties interesting."

Fleurette couldn't help but smile at that. What a life he offered! She might've liked to take him up on it, if only it were real.

"I can't promise I'll make a dinner party interesting, but it sounds awfully nice. I wouldn't mind getting away from these New Jersey winters."

"Yes, that Florida sunshine! You'll want to see the pictures, of course."

The waiter brought a plate of clams in butter sauce just then. Fleurette took one happily. She intended to have a good dinner at Mr. Van Der Meer's expense. He passed the pictures across to her, and she perused them as one might look at a brochure from a cruise ship. The theater was a lovely little white building in the Spanish style, with a nice marquee and a ticket booth in front, flanked by two gleaming double doors. Another picture showed the lobby, with its sweeping curved staircase up to the balcony, and a third showed the stage itself and a modest orchestra pit, perhaps large enough for a five-piece band. The seats (Fleurette was already taking a proprietary interest) were of the old-fashioned folding wooden variety and would require upholstery.

She told Mr. Van Der Meer as much, just as two plates of thin-sliced veal arrived.

"Naturally, you'll want to make it your own," he said, "but you'll have the capital to do so. While the building's owner has vanished, the theatrical company has not.

They've been operating as usual, what with the winter season under way. There's a director, but you might take that role yourself and the salary along with it. And you'll have those rooms to let upstairs."

"Not to mention my widow's pension," Fleurette said.

Mr. Van Der Meer sounded a bit eager when he said, "Yes, I understand you have your own resources. You'll be very well situated."

"I will now," Fleurette said. "I'll write to Dora at once and thank her. Is there anything left to do, besides packing a trunk for Florida?"

"Not at all," said Mr. Van Der Meer, and continued on smoothly, as if the rest was only an afterthought. "I'll put the papers together for the transfer of ownership. Florida real estate law's a bit tricky, but I know a fellow down there who will take care of it all for you. I don't expect his fee to go over three hundred dollars, plus whatever transfer fees the county might charge, and of course I don't charge a dime for my own services. Your sister's seen to that."

"Isn't she generous," said Fleurette, just as smoothly, "only I don't have quite that much on hand at the moment. Rent was due, and I'm afraid I splurged on a few spring dresses. We all went without during the war, you know."

"I do," said Mr. Van Der Meer, sympathetically.

"Then perhaps your man in Florida can wait a month. The building's not going anywhere."

"I wish that were the case," he said, "but in fact, the notice must be filed by Monday for the new owner to take possession. I won't bother you with the legalities, but in Florida we have only ninety days to transfer ownership in a case of loan default such as this one, and it took most of those ninety days to find you."

"Oh goodness!" said Fleurette, in mock surprise, but also in genuine surprise, over the flimsiness of his excuse. Did other women actually fall for this sort of thing?

"Isn't there someone who might loan you the money, until the end of the month?"

Now was the moment for Fleurette to show a bit of worry. She teared up beautifully: she always could cry on command. "There isn't a soul I could ask," she whispered. "That's the trouble with this town. I don't know anyone, not even my neighbors. We only just moved here before my dear husband shipped off to France. Everyone I met seemed to have their own friends and their own lives. As much as I tried, I just never got to know the people here. That's why I thought it might be all right for me to go somewhere else and try again. There's just no one keeping me here."

It was quite a speech, but Fleurette thought it best if she went on a bit and seemed rattled. Mr. Van Der Meer listened sympathetically. She looked up at him again, her eyes still wet with tears.

"Isn't there anything you could do?" she implored.

What sorrow and regret passed across his face! It occurred to Fleurette that he was quite a good actor, and that if she really was to take ownership of a little playhouse down in Florida, she would certainly put him on the stage.

"I would advance the funds myself if I could, but lawyers are not allowed to do anything of the sort. It has to do with the commingling of funds and conflicts of financial interest. I'm so sorry, but it's strictly forbidden."

"But what about the man down in Florida? He's not my lawyer, is he? Couldn't he file the paperwork on my behalf and pay the fees, and I'd get the cheque down to him the very minute I could?"

"I'm afraid not," Mr. Van Der Meer said.

"But this is only one small hurdle. We mustn't let it get in our way. I wouldn't like to go back to your sister and her husband and tell them that we lost our chance. No, I wouldn't like to tell them that at all."

"It puts you in an awkward position, too," said Fleurette sympathetically.

He made an expression of relief. "I'm glad you understand. It would look like I bungled the whole business. I shouldn't have taken so long to find you. I left the job to my secretary, and I'm afraid she's let any number of important matters slip lately."

"Oh, I wouldn't want your secretary to be blamed," said Fleurette. "There must be something we can do."

Mr. Van Der Meer looked down at the table for a minute. He was sliding a spoon back and forth across the tablecloth, like a pendulum swinging.

At last he took a deep breath and said, "I suppose . . ."

"Yes?" said Fleurette eagerly.

He seemed to reconsider. "You would have to promise me that no one would know."

Fleurette gave a little laugh and said, "Whom would I tell?"

He smiled at that. "Of course. You wouldn't want to put this at risk any more than I would. What I propose is this: If you have something of value that could be held until the end of the month, I could take it to a man I know who lends money privately. That way, you see, it isn't my money I'm putting in, but someone else's. Only I would arrange it and put my good name behind it. Is there anything you'd consider parting with? It's only for a short time."

Fleurette's hand went to her throat, but she pretended to be quite unaware of the gesture. Around her neck hung Mr. Packard's perfectly convincing glass emerald.

36

That last bit of business conducted, Fleurette walked out of the hotel and waited across the street for Mr. Van Der Meer to leave. She intended to follow him home, where she was sure the evidence of his wrongdoing could be found.

Once she'd pinned down his lodgings definitively, she would summon the police and tell all. From the fraud he'd perpetrated against her, there would be evidence enough to arrest him. She very much hoped that he was still in possession of Alice Martin's jewelry or any trinkets of value from his other victims. The guest book at Madame Zella's would be of interest, too. Put together like that, she would have enough evidence for the police to launch a proper investigation.

Mr. Van Der Meer had told her that he was staying at the Metropolitan, but she knew better: no crook lives where he commits his crimes and, besides, she had telephoned earlier in the day and asked for him under both his new name and his previous name, Louis Herman. No such man was registered.

If he was clever about it, he would've rented a room privately, perhaps from someone who posted a notice in a market or put a sign in the window. He would've paid his rent early, kept respectable hours, assumed a featureless name like Brown or Smith, and pretended to work at a dull and forgettable trade: stationery sales or life insurance.

That way, if he had to flee town quickly, he could merely tell his landlady that his assignment in Paterson had concluded, or that he'd taken a more permanent sort of lodging across town. She would think nothing of it. Even if the police began a search for Mr. Van Der Meer, they probably wouldn't stop at a place like hers. They would go around to the hotels and the better-known boarding-houses, but they wouldn't have any way of tracking down every rented room in the city.

Fleurette, lurking undetected in the doorway of a closed shop, waited for Mr. Van Der Meer to exit the hotel and prove her correct.

By the illuminated clock in the little tower above the bank, twenty minutes passed before he appeared. She almost missed him when he walked out because he was far more encumbered by luggage than she'd expected him to be and, in his coat and hat, under cover of darkness, even more closely resembled every other man walking in and out.

He carried a briefcase in one hand, an enormous leather bag over that shoulder, and in the other hand lugged a large, cheap suitcase. Efforts by the doorman to call a porter for him were rebuffed: Mr. Van Der Meer shuffled off as if the load he carried were nothing at all.

From her vantage point, Fleurette watched him walk down the block. He wasn't in a hurry — to run with so much luggage would attract attention — but he moved along purposefully.

Where was he going? Had he left his little rented room that afternoon (already she could picture the kind of place it was, not entirely different from Mrs. Doyle's, owned by a widow who liked to have a man on the premises) and moved to a quiet hotel? But why wouldn't he have deposited the luggage there before meeting Fleurette at the Metropolitan? And if he was in fact carrying all of

371

his possessions, did that mean that whatever evidence he possessed was in his hands at that moment?

She followed him through the lamplit streets of Paterson, past the shuttered shops and darkened office buildings, staying always half a block behind, with her hat pulled down low. She, too, had to walk with purpose, as any decent man watching a slender young woman pass by unaccompanied was bound to offer his assistance or summon a taxicab. Just as Mr. Van Der Meer had waved away the porter, so Fleurette had to wave away her eager protectors.

They passed one promising hotel after another without stopping. Where was he going? Small apartment buildings, sitting discreetly down the side streets, went unnoticed. He paused near a street-car stop and Fleurette feared he might jump aboard the next car, but he was only pausing to hitch his bag over his shoulder again.

By the time they'd passed the courthouse and City Hall, Fleurette was forced to reckon with the possibility that Mr. Van Der Meer was walking to the train station, and that she might have very little opportunity to summon a police officer and make her explanations.

Her quarry turned the corner and the train station came into sight. He was by now moving at a swifter pace, presumably to catch his train, and Fleurette had to hurry to keep up. Now she was looking back and forth, frantically, for a police officer. The police were always standing around train stations, idling with their coffee and rolls, looking officious but only taking advantage of the shelter and the hot refreshments. An officer could almost always be seen with the station agent, the two of them preening in their uniforms and observing the ordinary comings and goings around them.

But tonight there was no such officer at the station. She didn't like to admit such thoughts into her head, but the words *What would Constance do?* might've flitted briefly past. Constance would tackle the man, of course. She'd bring him down in a great rib-cracking commotion, and shout for the police, and put forth her accusations in a booming voice imbued with absolute certainty, and she would refuse to release the man until he was in custody.

A crowd would gather — amused, horrified — and she would take no notice of them. She wouldn't even remember them later. She would have her man hauled off to jail in an absolute triumph of brute force and indomitable will. Later, at home, Fleurette would bring her an ice-pack (she always bruised something in these tussles), and Norma would speculate, tartly, on what the papers would say about it the next day.

But could Fleurette possibly do all of that? He had the advantage in size and strength: he could easily shrug her off and board the train.

She watched as Mr. Van Der Meer purchased his ticket and went to the platform to wait. The train to New York was only five minutes away. Already the platform was crowded.

What choice did she have but to confront him, in such a manner that a crowd would gather, and in the commotion prevent him from boarding the train?

She couldn't imagine doing it. She wasn't prepared to do it. She'd only expected to take down his address and to deliver it to the police. What did she know about apprehending a criminal in a public place like this one?

Then she realized that she did know one thing: she knew how to play to a crowd. This was a performance. She had only to gather an audience and to hold their attention. The crowd would do the rest.

With only three minutes before the train's

arrival, and already the whistle sounding in the distance, Fleurette backed out of the station, so as to give herself a good head of steam, and ran back in, shouting, "Thief! He's a thief! Don't let him on the train!"

This naturally brought every eye in the station to her. Mr. Van Der Meer, ever the professional, looked lazily to one side and then another as if some distant commotion were taking place that had nothing to do with him.

But Fleurette had her sights on him. She was flying toward him, pointing as she ran. "That man stole my jewelry, and now he's leaving town! Stop him!"

Mr. Van Der Meer only shifted slightly and picked up the suitcase that he'd left standing alongside him. He looked around as if amused but untroubled by the scene being played out on the platform.

A path had cleared between the two of them. Fleurette felt a hand on her shoulder, and then one at her elbow, perhaps to offer assistance, but she shrugged them off and hurled herself at him.

There was a bit of her oldest sister in the move. She rushed at him with all the force she could muster, and slammed a palm squarely in the middle of his chest. He did stumble around and drop his suitcase, but he did not fall and in fact regained both his footing and his composure much faster than he might have if a woman of Constance's size and fury had thrown herself at him. He merely took a startled step back, gave a small and embarrassed laugh, and said, "I'm sorry, miss, I believe you've mistaken me for someone else. Are you quite sure the man you're looking for is on this platform?"

Fleurette knew she had but a moment to hold her audience's attention. As soon as the train rolled into the platform, she'd have to contend with passengers disembarking and boarding all at once.

"Hand it over!" she sounded, loud enough to be heard in the cheap seats. "You're not getting on this train until I have my necklace back. You put it right in that pocket there."

Here she poked him in the chest again. "Go ahead, then! Turn out your pockets!"

She began to rifle through his pockets herself, a move calculated to force him to respond — and he did. He took hold of her wrist, roughly, and yanked her arm up and away from him.

He was stronger than he looked. One foot left the ground entirely.

"Let go of me!" she screamed.

He dropped his bag and took hold of her with both hands. Fleurette could hear the bag fall open and wondered what sort of evidence, exactly, might be falling out onto the platform.

It was turning into a brawl, which was exactly what she wanted. As the two of them wrestled, the onlookers crowded in. Once or twice a man clamped his hand on Mr. Van Der Meer's shoulder and mumbled something like, "There now, old fellow," and a woman called out, "Let the girl go!" But the skirmish had not yet reached the crisis that the situation demanded.

With Mr. Van Der Meer's hands wrapped around both of her wrists, Fleurette had but one trick left to play, and it was a risky one, being so close to the edge of the platform. They must be on the ground and in complete chaos by the time the train — bearing down now, its whistle louder — pulled in.

She had no time to waste. She kicked a leg behind his knee — his left knee, the one farthest from the platform — and down he tumbled, with her on top of him. Her elbow went right into his chest, and he coughed and gasped for air.

Fleurette's audience was, by this time, substantial. Old men in their dark coats regarded her disapprovingly, women eyed Mr. Van Der Meer suspiciously, and a few handsome and well-dressed young men were preparing to play the part of the gentleman rescuer. But what Fleurette needed was to attract the attention of someone in a position of authority, and now she had accomplished that.

With a piercing whistle, the station agent pushed through the crowd. The train was now squealing as it shuddered to a halt. "If you're not boarding the 9:02, clear the platform!" he shouted. When he came to Fleurette and Mr. Van Der Meer — both of them still on the ground, Fleurette's skirt in disarray, the contents of Mr. Van Der Meer's bags tossed around in exactly the sort of disorder a station agent despises — he looked down at both of them with contempt.

"I don't know which one of you started it" — a lady at his elbow tried to offer an answer, but he waved her away — "but I won't have this nonsense in my station."

Fleurette scrambled to her feet. "He's a thief. He was about to board the train with my valuables."

Mr. Van Der Meer sat up, rubbing a shoulder. "I've no doubt the lady's been wronged, but I'm afraid she's mistaken. I've never seen her before. If you don't mind, I'll gather up my things and clear your platform myself."

Passengers were by now disembarking from the train and glancing over at the scene in confusion. Among the items that had spilled from Mr. Van Der Meer's bag in the commotion were a sort of desk diary or calendar, a cardboard folio of papers, a pair of socks rolled in a ball (they could've had any sort of valuable secreted within them, Fleurette thought), and a spare necktie, undone and trampled upon. He gathered these possessions up and stuffed them back into the bag as the people in Fleurette's audience began to look nervously over their shoulders, not wanting to miss the train.

"He's a criminal," Fleurette said, with some urgency, to the station agent. "He goes by any number of aliases. I'm sure there's stolen property in those bags."

Mr. Van Der Meer, having risen unsteadily to his feet, tried one more dignified smile. "You've been reading too many detective stories, young lady. I hope you find the man you're looking for. If you'll excuse me, my train's arrived."

"You're not boarding that train," said the station agent. "I already put a call in to the police. You can both wait here and explain it to them."

37

The Paterson jail was nothing like the Hackensack jail, where Constance had once worked and where Fleurette had, one eventful night back in 1916, sung a concert for the inmates. Hackensack's jail had been new when then sheriff Heath took possession of it. Like any new building, it was riddled with faults: some of the drains didn't clear, a few doors were crooked and didn't close properly (fortunately, those were not the doors behind which inmates were locked), and the electrical lighting was unreliable.

But at least the Hackensack jail was a modern building, equipped with the essentials. It was scrubbed mercilessly every day, cleaning being a regular duty of the inmates, and it was served by an enormous boiler that kept it warm throughout the darkest and coldest months of the year.

Paterson's old jail had nothing like that on offer. It was a frigid, Gothic structure, bereft of windows, and lacking in any sort of modern convenience. The old stone walls had been erected half a century before Fleurette was born and exuded both a permanent chill and a kind of malodorous air born of mildew, encroaching moss, and the sweat and tears of one generation of inmates after another.

Into such a forbidding institution both Fleurette and Mr. Van Der Meer had been confined, after a querulous and chaotic dust-up with the police at the train station. Mr. Van Der Meer had been taken away without fanfare, to be booked into a cell until morning, when he would be questioned and either charged or released.

Fleurette, however, posed a problem, as she knew all too well: a female inmate required special handling by a lady deputy, and the sheriff at this particular jail didn't employ one.

She'd been placed instead in the custody of Deputy Bagby, surely the most elderly of the jail's deputies, and perhaps, by default, the least intimidating to female inmates. He took a grandfatherly interest in her and went to great lengths to reassure her that she would be kept comfortable while the situation was sorted out.

"Sometimes the sheriff's wife comes to sit

381

with the ladies," said Deputy Bagby, handing her a cup of lukewarm tea, "but she's in the family way and confined to her bed. Then there's a lady officer at the police department —"

Fleurette had heard of her, a policeman's widow named Belle Headison, who saw herself more as a mother hen to wayward girls than any sort of crime-fighter.

"But we've sent someone over to her house and she isn't in. Next they'll try a nurse from the county hospital."

Fleurette was waiting in a windowless room furnished with nothing but a wooden chair bolted to the ground on iron plates. It was damp and cold, and utterly dark, save for a little light coming from the hall, where Deputy Bagby stood.

"And if a nurse can't be found?" asked Fleurette.

"Then you might have to stay here tonight. We can't take you up to a cell, you see, until . . . well, ah . . ."

Fleurette knew already what he was trying to say. "Until I've been de-loused."

"Are you familiar with it, miss?" asked Deputy Bagby, perhaps worried that he'd misjudged her criminal history, or lack of one.

"I've only heard of it," said Fleurette,

"from reading the papers. I've never been arrested if that's what you'd like to know. I'm the victim in this case, and I'd like to give my statement so the police can go to work. The man you arrested with me is a notorious swindler. I'm not the only woman he's cheated."

"I'm sure you're not, miss," said Deputy Bagby, in that disinterested voice that deputies use when they are merely marking time with an inmate. "But you weren't brought in as a victim. You were arrested for brawling on a train platform. That's why we need a lady officer."

"But I am a victim, and you'll need my statement before you decide what to do with Mr. Van Der Meer. You can't very well turn him loose before someone talks to me. He assumes a false identity everywhere he goes. If you release him, we'll never catch him again."

None of this aroused in Deputy Bagby any sense of urgency. "It'll all look different by morning," he said distractedly, watching someone come and go at the end of the corridor out of Fleurette's view. "It always does."

Morning could be too late. There was a way out of this and Fleurette knew it. She had only to decide which was worse: a night in this horrid dark room, followed by the risk of Mr. Van Der Meer's escape, or her sister's wrath.

Another hour passed in which Deputy Bagby attended to other duties while she remained locked in the little holding room, with only a glimpse of light through a few narrow bars cut into an otherwise imposing steel door. From time to time he would return and open the door, allowing a little more light in and something like fresh air, although it only came from the corridor.

"Haven't heard a word, miss," he would say. "It can take a few hours for a nurse to get here. It all depends on how busy they are."

Later, when he came back, he said, "You might be waiting until morning. I'll ask again but it doesn't look like anyone's turned up."

Then, after another interminable wait, he returned and said, "I'm off duty in a few minutes, miss. There will be a guard at the end of the hall, and he'll hear you if you shout for him. I'm going to bring you another blanket so you can make yourself comfortable. By morning —"

But Fleurette couldn't bear to think about morning. "My family doesn't know where I am," she said, having previously refused to answer any questions about whether she had any family who should be notified or questioned. "They'll call the police themselves if I don't turn up. Can't you get word to them?"

"Not at this hour, miss. You should've said so earlier. They'll take care of all that in the morning. Try to rest now."

He turned to leave. She was running out of chances. If he wouldn't telephone her family, there was still one person he might be willing to summon.

She put her face between the bars and only hoped she looked as forlorn as she felt. "Couldn't you get word to a Paterson police officer I know? He's an old family friend. Officer Heath? Do you know him?"

That stopped him. He turned around, opened the door again, and looked more closely at Fleurette. "I still want to call him Sheriff Heath," he said.

"So do I," said Fleurette. She didn't dare to say another word, for fear of ruining her last chance.

"He's a good man. Wasn't too proud to come and walk a beat again. He just wants to do the job."

Fleurette had never bothered to consider what Officer Heath wanted or didn't want, but now she did. She supposed he was like

Constance in that way: devoted to crime-fighting, as if he'd been born to it.

Perhaps that would appeal to Deputy Bagby. "He was born to law enforcement. That's what I've always thought."

He leaned in the doorway, settling in for a conversation. "How did a girl like you become acquainted with the sheriff?"

Now she faced a quandary. Would it hurt or help her cause to invoke Constance's name? Having no other, more convincing story close at hand, she resorted, out of desperation, to the truth. "My older sister worked for him. She was his deputy."

Now he straightened up and leaned in to examine her more closely. "You're one of *those* Kopps? Constance Kopp is your sister? You don't look nothing like her."

"Then you know her!"

"I know her, all right," Deputy Bagby said. "Everybody knows her. She cost your friend Heath that election, but he wouldn't stand for a word against her. He'd be in Congress right now, if only he hadn't brought in a lady deputy."

Had it been as bad as all that? Constance had her share of critics, but Fleurette had always assumed that Heath lost the election for — well, any number of reasons. There were as many reasons as there were voters.

Had it really all come down to Constance? No wonder she took to her bed all that miserable winter.

But it was no time to rehash the election. She thought to appeal to his lawman's instincts. There was such fraternity among officers, she knew that. "He's better off in a policeman's uniform, wouldn't you say? He would've been wasting his time down in Washington."

Deputy Bagby snorted. "I never understood why he wanted to be a congressman."

"I think it was his wife's idea." Fleurette didn't like to cast blame on Cordelia Heath — she hardly knew the woman — but she had to keep him talking.

"Could be. Now, what would he say, if I told him you were locked up here?"

"I'd be in for quite a lecture," Fleurette said, mournfully, because it was the truth. "But he would want to be told about it. Couldn't you telephone him?"

The deputy squinted down the hall, perhaps reading a clock, and said, "It's just after midnight."

"Wouldn't you want to be called?" Fleurette implored. "If a girl who was almost like family to you landed in jail, wouldn't you want to know?"

Deputy Bagby leaned against the doorway

again, his eyes up at the ceiling, calculating. "His missus won't like it," he said.

"No, she doesn't like anything to do with police work. There's no pleasing her."

He gave a little shrug that seemed to say, *In that case* . . .

"I'll put the call through," he said at last, "but then I'm off duty for the night. What Officer Heath does after that is his business."

"I'll tell him you were good to me," she said, a little too eagerly.

"Don't bother telling him about me," he said, as he locked the door, leaving her once again in darkness. He looked through the narrow bars at her. "The only person he's going to want an explanation about is you."

38

Fleurette couldn't be sure how much time passed after Deputy Bagby left. She didn't sleep — how could she, with only a hard wooden chair or a cold cement floor to choose between? Instead she sat on that awful chair, her knees tucked under her chin, the blanket wrapped snugly around her to keep what little heat she could generate within, and tried to work up a palatable explanation for Officer Heath — and for Constance, whom Officer Heath would no doubt bring along.

It would help, she had to admit, if she and Constance had spoken even a word before now. Fleurette could've relented already and turned up for Sunday dinner to make amends. She could've tried to tolerate Constance's overbearing ways: after all, hadn't she proven to her own satisfaction that Constance had no real power over her? Fleurette was now free to live her life as she pleased, and Constance could only remark upon it from a safe distance.

Although she wasn't really living exactly as she pleased, was she, or she wouldn't be spending the night in the Paterson jail. Still, setting her present circumstances aside, look what she had accomplished, now that she was free from her sisters!

She had established herself at Mrs. Doyle's and built a small but growing clientele of ladies in need of mending and alterations. She would design dresses for them, too, once they came to appreciate her work a bit more. Why, she could outfit a woman from head to toe, winter and summer. Mrs. Doyle might even be persuaded to let her hold fittings in the basement. A fitting would be an occasion of sorts, a reason to put on the coffee-pot, and Mrs. Doyle liked that.

Was any of that really such an accomplishment, though, if her true aim was to get back on the stage? She'd hardly had time to think about what Alice had said about her voice. What if her singing ability really was truly and irreparably gone?

She couldn't bear the thought. The possibility that she could damage her throat and that the damage would nestle in deep, and find permanent quarters, was simply not in keeping with her experience of her own body thus far. She had not yet reached the age when injuries became permanent, when an unreliable knee or a stiff shoulder could be expected to stay on as a long-term tenant, not a visitor who stops briefly on the front porch and moves on.

But what if Alice was right and her voice was ruined for good? What, in that case, was left for her? On what grounds had she marched out of her sisters' house, and out of their lives, if not to follow her own grand ambitions? What were those ambitions now — a line of dresses she could sell to Paterson ladies?

There seemed, at that moment, no real point to her rift with Constance. Yes, Constance had patronized her and badgered her over her work for John Ward, but she never intended to work for him forever. She only saw it as a temporary measure, to bring in money while she waited for her voice to recover.

It wasn't a career. It wasn't a livelihood. It was a lark, that was all. One that had been lucrative for a while, but was never meant to last.

And what was she to say about Alice Martin, and her own involvement in Alice's predicament? This was, of course, her more immediate concern. The man who had swindled Alice might well walk out of jail in the morning, if Officer Heath didn't intervene.

She would have to tell all. Nothing but the entire, implausible truth would do when the moment came to state her case. Constance would be furious that she'd once again put herself in danger and tried to interfere with a known criminal when she could've come to either of them — Constance or Heath — for help. It had been a disservice to Alice, Constance would say, to leave her in the hands of an amateur. Alice deserved better.

Fleurette could already hear her sister saying it. And perhaps she was right.

At last those familiar footsteps sounded down the corridor. Fleurette would know the particular strike of Constance's boots anywhere. She always took long strides, but now the pace was even quicker, the strides even longer, the ringing of her boots on the floor even louder, fueled by some mixture of worry and rage, the exact proportions of which Fleurette could not yet divine. The steps alongside her were almost certainly Officer Heath's, and mingled in between them was the now-familiar footfall of the guard who had been pacing back and forth.

Then came the rattling of keys, and all at once a burst of light from the corridor, and three figures silhouetted against it.

Fleurette raised her hand against the glare and thought of how disheveled she must look.

"We don't hear from you for weeks and now I'm called out of my bed in the middle of the night to visit you in jail," said Constance.

Between worry and rage, Fleurette saw that rage had the upper hand. "I didn't ask for you," she said, churlish and defensive again. "I asked for Officer Heath."

"But you knew he wouldn't come without me. Go ahead and tell us whatever it is that couldn't wait until morning."

Fleurette felt herself suddenly very tired: what time was it, exactly? She peered up at Officer Heath with a pleading look in her eyes, although what she was pleading for, exactly, she could not say. Forgiveness? Sympathy? Leniency?

"I wonder if we might borrow another chair," said Officer Heath to the guard, who lingered nearby.

"It ain't supposed to be a sitting-room," the guard mumbled, but then came a whisper from Officer Heath, and he took a step back, then returned in a few minutes with another wooden chair of the sort Fleurette perched upon.

Constance took a seat and waited, her arms crossed. "Go ahead. They wouldn't tell us anything."

"That's because they don't know anything," said Fleurette. "They won't take a statement without a lady officer present, only there's a man they're keeping upstairs and I need to tell them what happened before they release him. They think this is all about a fight on a train platform. But that isn't it at all."

Constance sighed. "I'm sure we could've sorted all this out in the morning before they let him go, but you might as well tell us."

Officer Heath was standing off to himself, in the corner, leaning against the wall with a judicial air about him. It was Heath she needed to convince. Constance had no authority here.

"I believe he's been swindling women all over Paterson," Fleurette said. "I caught up with him at the train station and tried to stop him. That's when the police came."

Constance was interested now: she leaned forward in her chair and said, "What do you mean, you caught up with him? How on earth did you get involved with a man like that?"

"He cheated a woman I know," Fleurette said. "Alice Martin. She was one of . . . well, one of John Ward's clients. One of his divorce cases."

There was no way to leave John Ward out of it, although any mention of the man would only provoke Constance. It didn't matter. She wanted only to tell all, and to turn the mess over to the two of them.

Officer Heath seemed to have the same idea. From his spot in the corner, he said, "Miss Kopp, would you be able to tell us everything, from the beginning, starting the day you met Alice Martin?"

Fleurette did. She recounted every moment of it, from Alice's first appearance at Mr. Ward's office, to Fleurette's attempt to capture Mr. Martin in the arms of another woman (Constance flinched at this, and Fleurette was quick to remind her of the hundred dollars she was paid, and how she spent it to rectify Francis's unpaid debts all over town), to the realization that Mr. Martin had not, by all appearances, violated his marriage vows at all, followed by Alice Martin's suspicious behavior when confronted with this obvious fact.

She was struck by how adventurous it

sounded in the retelling: how she eaves-dropped on Alice's heated conversation with Louis Herman (or Mr. Van Der Meer, or whatever name he'd given the police), how she'd tracked down the occupant of the office he was using, the discovery of the match-book from the Black Cat, the trip to the fortune-teller, the dinner at the Metropolitan . . . It all made for quite a riveting tale, one she could easily imagine setting to music and putting on the stage. The Black Cat itself would have to assume a larger role, with the diners transformed into a large chorus who could sing about what they'd seen on the nights when the swindler and the fortune-teller met to talk over their latest victim. It really was a delicious premise, far more exciting than she'd realized.

By the end, Constance was not so much sitting as sprawling back in her chair, glancing over occasionally to Officer Heath, with whom she exchanged inscrutable expressions.

"I believe," Fleurette said grandly, finishing her tale, "that Mr. Van Der Meer was carrying some of those valuables with him tonight. He might still have Alice Martin's jewelry, or some other woman's. You should certainly find my emerald among his possessions, although as I've said it's only glass."

"You never told me how you came by the glass emerald," said Constance.

"From a friend," said Fleurette, hoping to imply a female friend. "It was just a little trinket."

"And you did all this on your own?" Constance said. "You never thought to come to me?"

Fleurette only looked at her, silently. How could she ask a question like that?

From his corner, Officer Heath said, "It was a matter for the police."

"It was," said Fleurette, "but Alice wouldn't go to the police. I couldn't force her. And remember, I intended to run straight to the police as soon as I had his address. I didn't expect him to leave the Metropolitan and go to the train station."

"So you ran your own investigation." It was still dim within the room, even with the door open, but Fleurette thought she detected a smile from Officer Heath.

"I wanted to," Fleurette admitted. "After a while I was caught up in it. The thought of going to the fortune-teller and pretending to be a widow in distress . . ."

"It was play-acting to you," said Constance. She still spoke sharply, as if she hadn't yet taken a position on the matter.

"No, it was an investigation, just like Officer Heath said. I wanted it done right. I wanted to know for myself what he was up to. And I intended to see it through. I was the one who uncovered the crime. I wasn't about to hand it off until I'd wrapped it up to my satisfaction."

At this Constance softened a little. "I've felt the same way."

The guard was coming back down the corridor. Officer Heath turned at the sound of his footsteps. "We can't take you home tonight. Even I can't walk out of the Paterson jail with an inmate. But you'll be let go first thing in the morning. I'll see to it. Constance will be here to take you home."

Fleurette bristled at that. "I can get back on my own. I have to feed Laura. She's been without me all night."

"Won't you come back to Hawthorne and let Bessie look after you?" said Constance.

"I don't need looking after," said Fleurette. "What I need is for Mr. Van Der Meer to be investigated. And someone should go around to Madame Zella's and have a look at that guest book, and of course she should be interrogated, too. From that you might have a whole list of victims to go around and question. There's only one thing

I'd like you to do for me."

"You're not in any position to give orders," said Constance, prickly again, "but go ahead."

"The police will want to talk to Alice Martin. I don't want anyone going over to the Martins and blurting all this out in front of Mr. Martin. It'll be just awful for Alice. At least let me go and tell her first, so that she can find the right way to tell him. This all started because she was planning to divorce him. I don't believe she intends to anymore. But I also don't think they're entirely happy together. It's a delicate situation, that's all."

"I can't make any promises," said Officer Heath, "but I also can't stop you from going over on your own, if you decide to. I believe our time is at an end" — here he glanced over at the guard and nodded — "but you'll be out in a few hours. Will you be all right until then?"

Fleurette said yes, but all at once she thought she might cry. She would rather bicker with Constance all night than sit in that dark cell for another minute. Constance must've guessed at that, because she bent down and kissed her.

"You'll be fine on your own," she whispered. "You always are."

39

Fleurette wasn't released first thing in the morning. It was nearly noon before they let her go. There were endless procedural matters, including recording her arrest properly and making a picture of her for their records, of which Fleurette was deeply ashamed. Having no mirror, she could only imagine how horrible she looked, but even worse was the idea of the Kopp name in an inmate's record book at the Paterson jail. The only possible greater affront would've been to get booked into the Hackensack jail, where Constance had once worked: this would've proven once and for all that the Kopps had fallen and could fall no further.

She had been allowed to give her statement, with Officer Heath standing in the corner, just as he had done only hours previously in her wretched little room. He nodded encouragingly at her and spoke a few quiet words to the detectives from time to time, and went to great pains to remind them that in her so-called investigative work she was not, in fact, employed by Ward & McGinnis nor acting under the direction of anyone associated with the firm. (Fleurette remembered dimly that Officer Heath and John Ward were friends, unlikely as it seemed, and thought that Heath might've wanted to keep him out of trouble.) He pointed out several times that Fleurette had, in fact, been acting only out of friendship to Alice Martin.

The detectives took her story seriously, or they at least pretended to in Officer Heath's presence, perhaps as a professional courtesy. They assured her that Mr. Van Der Meer would not be released until a thorough inquiry could be made.

Beyond that, she was told nothing, because she had no standing. She wasn't a victim in this case (save for the glass emerald, which she did want returned and went to great pains to remind the detectives of that), nor was she, in any official capacity, an investigator.

The best way to describe her, in the eyes of the detectives now closing their notebooks and walking away, was as a bystander, a spectator, even. She was of no use to them anymore.

Fleurette walked out of the interview exhausted, having slept not at all. Her last meal had been those clams the evening before at the Metropolitan. Had it really only been yesterday when she and Mr. Van Der Meer had dined together in that fine restaurant, she playing her part so perfectly, just as he played his?

At any rate, she'd been given nothing but weak coffee and a stale dinner roll for breakfast. Now she couldn't decide which she'd rather do: collapse face-down on her own bed, in a clean nightgown, with good crisp sheets against her skin, or raid Mrs. Doyle's kitchen and eat absolutely everything in sight.

But she could do none of that until she'd seen to Alice Martin.

While she completed a few more formalities and had her belongings returned to her, Officer Heath waited nearby, chatting with the guards and deputies. He walked outside with her.

"I shouldn't say too much about what we've learned this morning, but I trust you won't tell anyone, particularly the Martin woman," he said.

"Have the police been to see her yet?"

"Not until you and I speak to her. She'll have to give a statement to the detectives, but I told them they'd have an easier time of it if we went first."

"But what are we to tell her? Have they found her things?"

"There was a considerable amount of jewelry and small valuables hidden away in those bags," Officer Heath said. "We believe we've also connected Mr. Van Der Meer to an address in New York. We'll have that place searched today. And then there's the matter of Madame Zella's guest book. The police have already seized it and arrested her."

They were nearly outside now. He paused before the great metal doors.

"Yes?" Fleurette asked, a little breathless. She was revived now, bolstered by the momentum of the case, even as it was being taken away from her.

"At least four of the women in that book had gone to the police with some kind of story about a lawyer and a windfall. Nothing was ever done about it. I expect we'll find more in that guest book."

"I knew it!" said Fleurette triumphantly. "I mean — it's terrible, of course, but if we've caught the man and put a stop to it, that's . . ."

Fleurette had run out of superlatives, but Officer Heath supplied one.

"That's fine detective work, that's what it is."

Constance was waiting outside. Fleurette's heart sank a little: they hadn't parted on the best of terms, and a day without another argument with Constance sounded particularly welcome at that moment. But Constance and Officer Heath had obviously made some arrangement to accompany Fleurette out of the jail together. That was their plan, and she felt she had little choice but to surrender to it.

"I've already been to see Mrs. Doyle about feeding your parrot," Constance said briskly, as they walked away from the jail. "She's relieved to know you're safe. I didn't tell her that you'd been in jail."

"Thank you," Fleurette said meekly.

"And I'm sure you'd like to go and speak to Mrs. Martin alone, but it isn't your affair anymore, it's a matter for the police. You're lucky that Officer Heath will allow us to go along. After we finish with that business, I'm under orders to take you straight to Bessie. She's been cooking since she got up this morning."

If there was one way to entice Fleurette back to her family's bosom, it was through Bessie's cooking. "I wouldn't want to offend her," Fleurette said weakly.

"I thought not."

and her," Fleurette said weakly.

"I thought no."

40

Alice Martin was at home, as was her husband. Fleurette could hear him out in his study behind the house, running a student through her scales. From the shock in Alice's expression, Fleurette realized that it must have looked as though Officer Heath had arrested her, or was coming to arrest Alice.

"He's a friend," Fleurette said quickly, knowing that there was no time to waste. "And this is my sister, the one I told you about."

"I guessed that," said Alice. "She's just how you described."

Constance frowned at that. Before she could say anything, Fleurette hurried along with her explanations. "We caught Mr. Van Der Meer — Louis Herman, whatever his name might be — last night. He was trying to board a train, but I stopped him. The police found quite a bit of jewelry in his bags, but we don't yet know if he has yours. Either way, the police will want a statement. You'll have to tell Arthur something."

"Tell me what?" he called from the back of the house. Alice jumped. The student was still singing, but Mr. Martin had obviously left her there with the metronome ticking and come inside.

He strolled in, hands in his pockets, his spectacles perched on top of his head. "Alice, won't you invite these ladies in?" Then, seeing Officer Heath, he added, "Good afternoon, officer. I hope we aren't in any sort of trouble. Or are you collecting for the maimed and wounded fund? Always happy to make a donation."

Officer Heath started to answer, but Fleurette stepped in. Wasn't this her case?

"Mr. Martin, you might not remember me. We met one night at the theater."

He dropped his spectacles down on his nose and looked at her again. "The understudy, isn't that right? You were having some sort of trouble with your voice. Do I recall that you'd been ill?"

Constance looked down at her, puzzled. "There's nothing wrong with your voice."

"Oh, but there is," said Alice. "She can't find the notes anymore."

Mr. Martin crossed his arms and looked

at her with the air of a physician puzzling out a diagnosis. "How long has it been since your illness?"

Fleurette said, "We haven't come to talk about my voice. We do need to speak to you both regarding a matter —"

"Oh yes, I can hear it now," said Mr. Martin. "A constriction. Try a little of 'You Made Me Love You.' Just come over to the piano."

At least they'd been invited inside. Alice and Fleurette exchanged a worried glance, but Alice nodded toward the piano. Perhaps she wanted a minute to think about how she was going to explain the situation to her husband.

It was ridiculous to burst into song at a moment like this, but Fleurette hardly felt she could refuse.

"At full volume, please. Let them hear you in the mezzanine." Arthur played the first few notes. Fleurette gathered her breath and did what she could.

You made me love you
I didn't want to do it
I didn't want to do it
You made me want you,
And all the time you knew it
I guess you always knew it.

She sounded terrible. If anything, her voice was worse than before. It cracked, it scratched, it couldn't sustain the most comfortable notes. She was, of course, exhausted and parched at that particular moment, having spent the night in that cold and musty cell, but there was no hiding it. She couldn't sing.

Constance had dropped into the chair across from her and was quite simply gaping at her, open-mouthed. "What happened? You've sounded fine lately."

"But not to sing," said Mr. Martin. "I'm sorry, my dear. It's been a terrible winter, between the Spanish influenza and every other bug making the rounds. I've had a dozen girls that sound just like you lately."

"I've lost it, haven't I?" said Fleurette. She'd felt so triumphant only a moment ago, delivering the good news to Alice, but now a fresh wave of misery swept over her. "I won't go on the stage again."

He shook his head sorrowfully. "Not any time soon. If you were one of my girls and you were in a show, I'd have to tell you to call the understudy. You could practice, and learn to sing around it, and perhaps in a year's time —"

"Why didn't you tell me?" said Constance. "None of us had any idea."

Now Fleurette was truly wrung out. She sank into Alice's sofa and said, "Can we please just tell Mr. Martin why we're here?"

Alice said, a little nervously, "Why don't you start?"

For the third time in twenty-four hours, Fleurette told — this time with some help from Alice — the convoluted tale of the fortune-teller and the inheritance letter. She wisely skipped the bit about Alice going to John Ward for help in obtaining evidence against her husband for a divorce case, but she knew they'd circle back to that eventually.

Arthur, for his part, was an attentive if often perplexed listener. With some frequency he turned to his wife, incredulous, with expressions of shock and disbelief and — Fleurette noticed this particularly — a generous and perhaps undeserved amount of sympathy. "If only you'd told me!" he said, more than once, and "I should've noticed something was wrong." He seemed unconcerned about the sums of money Alice had put out (although she had been vague concerning the exact amounts, and Fleurette stayed silent on that subject), and took it as a given that the jewelry and the silver spoons would be recovered.

He did, however, come around eventually

to the part of the story Fleurette had been avoiding.

"What I still don't understand," he said, turning now to Fleurette, "is how you came to be involved. That is, how did the two of you meet?"

Fleurette wasn't about to tell. Alice's marriage was hers to ruin.

"Remember, darling, that she met you first, at the theater," Alice put in hastily. "She wasn't really an understudy, only a friend of one of the other girls, hoping to get hired on. Nonetheless she took your card — didn't you, Miss Kopp?"

Fleurette nodded hastily. This part of the story, at least, was true.

"Oh, I see," said Arthur. "She came to the house, and I wasn't here, and the two of you struck up a friendship. Yes, of course. But I still don't know what led you, Miss Kopp, to pursue this fellow. You went about it like a detective, and even put on a disguise and laid a trap to catch him in the act. Why would you do such a thing?"

Alice had by now assumed the role of answering for Fleurette and said, "It's the family business, Arthur. Her sister — this one, Constance — is a real policewoman, and her other sister went to war with the Army. Fleurette comes by it naturally."

41

On the subject of coming by things naturally, Fleurette had nothing to say. Constance's presence at the Martins' had been purely ceremonial: she watched over Fleurette as a chaperone might, and injected only the mildest comment or question here and there as the story unfolded, once again, for Arthur's benefit.

When they left, Constance had only this to say: "I hope that's the end of it, as far as we're concerned."

Fleurette, for her part, felt the sense of let-down that comes at the end of a holiday. The momentum that had carried her through these last few weeks — when she'd had something to puzzle over, someone to chase, and the next maneuver to plan — was over now.

Even the air felt heavy and oppressive as she walked alongside Constance and Officer Heath. When she thought about what she had waiting for her, back at Mrs. Doyle's — well, she didn't want to think of it at all.

She had her head down and was practically dragging her feet along, like a crestfallen child, but she didn't care about how she looked. She'd been through enough and was by then even more in need of a hearty meal and a good nap than before.

Constance and Officer Heath talked over the top of her head as they walked back into downtown. They spoke only of their own work: Constance was due back on duty at the department store, and Officer Heath was expected to return to his foot patrol of downtown immediately. They had jobs to do, lives to resume.

Fleurette thought she might just slip away from the two of them, but then Officer Heath said, "How much does Mr. Ward know about all of this?"

"Not a great deal," said Fleurette. "I went to him when it became clear that Alice had been swindled, but he wasn't interested. He said that no one was paying him to look into it, and that it was a matter for the police."

"He was right on both counts. If you haven't told him anything more, then it will come as a surprise to him when all of this appears in the papers. You're sure to be mentioned, as will the Martins."

Fleurette stopped and looked down Hamilton Street toward Mr. Ward's office. "I suppose I ought to tell him what's happened. Will he be kept out of it, him and Petey?"

"It all depends on how many victims are found," Officer Heath said. "The livelier the story, the less likely it is that the reporters would be interested in an attorney who didn't even take part in the investigation."

She was by then so tired that she could hardly put a coherent sentence together, but it seemed only fair to warn him. "I'll stop in. Are the two of you on your way?"

But of course they were not: it seemed that Fleurette was doomed to have Constance and Officer Heath following her around for the rest of her days. With her spirits sinking lower still, she dragged herself into the building, up the stairs, and down the hall to Mr. Ward's office. She loathed the idea of having to tell the story for the fourth time, again in the presence of her two overseers, and dreaded the inevitable clash between Constance and Mr. Ward.

She heard from some distance away a conversation within. She was about to call the visit off on the grounds that Mr. Ward was occupied with a client when she drew just a bit nearer and recognized the voice.

"What is Norma doing here?" she said, looking up at Constance.

Just then there was another voice. Constance stopped to listen. "I think Bessie's with her."

That was too much for Fleurette to bear. "I didn't come here for another lecture, if that was your plan."

"It's not," Constance insisted. "I told them everything this morning, before I came back to the jail. They know Mr. Ward had almost nothing to do with it."

They paused outside his door, but to what end? There was no turning back now. Fleurette pushed the door open, waving away the new girl sitting behind the receptionist's desk, and walked right into his office.

Mr. Ward didn't seem at all surprised to see them. "It's the rest of the clan, and a police officer to keep things on the level. Afternoon, Bob."

Officer Heath nodded. Bessie and Norma turned and rose from their chairs. Bessie rushed right over to Fleurette, smoothed her hair, kissed her cheek, looked her over, and whispered alluring promises of a roast for dinner, and creamed potatoes, and a particular ginger cake Fleurette was fond of.

Norma only stood with her arms crossed in front of her. "They released you from jail. I hope it didn't cost us a fortune."

"There was no bail. I wasn't arrested," Fleurette said. "I was a witness."

"You were arrested first, and then Constance came down and straightened everything out so they'd treat you as a witness." Norma, having had the least involvement in the matter, made it sound as though she knew the most about it.

"You ought to at least give Officer Heath the credit," Fleurette said. "Have you come down here to lecture Mr. Ward? Because Constance has already done that."

"That's not at all why she's here," put in Mr. Ward. "Your sister's quite the businesswoman. She tried to turn me upside-down and shake out my pockets."

"As I understand it," Norma said to Fleurette, walking up and down now as if giving a lecture, "from the little that you've told us, Mr. Ward was paying you twenty dollars per client, plus some rather generous gratuities, and now I've learned about the Martin case, for which you were paid one hundred dollars for a single night's work."

What, exactly, was Norma accusing her of now?

"And I put every penny toward Francis's debts," Fleurette said. "You don't have to approve of how I earned the money, but the charge accounts are open again and it's because I paid them. You're welcome."

"We're all grateful," said Bessie, "and I don't suppose Constance has had a chance to tell you, but the parcels of land are starting to sell. We'll have enough coming in to buy the Wilkinsons' house and pay off Francis's mortgage, or most of it."

"That's all fine," said Fleurette, "but I'm sure Mr. Ward has had enough of the Kopp family's affairs. I only stopped in to tell him about what happened last night, before you see it in the papers or find the police on your doorstep asking questions, but I can see Norma's told all."

"What I came to tell him was that he'd been cheating you, plain and simple, and it won't happen again," Norma said. "I know what lawyers charge for divorces. It's five hundred dollars if it's a penny. Twenty dollars for your part in it is robbery. From now on, we'll be paid professional rates, and if he doesn't like it, he can pass the bill on to the clients."

Now the room erupted in shouting.

"What do you mean 'we'?" said Constance. "I won't have anything to do with manufacturing phony evidence, and neither will anyone else in this family."

"And Mr. Ward won't hire me if I have you and Constance interfering," said Fleurette, "and I can't blame him. I won't argue over this any longer. I'm going back to Mrs. Doyle's."

And she did turn to leave — rattled, her every nerve raw, still famished, still weary — when Norma said, "Well, someone had to interfere. You were treating this like piecework, twenty dollars here and there, subject to Mr. Ward's whims."

"Which is exactly what it was," Fleurette said, "and I know you don't approve, so if you don't mind, I've had a long night, and —"

But Norma cut her off. "You're not going back to Mrs. Doyle's. We're here to form a detective agency. You'll be the one to run it, and you can't do that from a boarding-house in Rutherford."

Fleurette felt something ominous come over her, like a head cold. What had she just heard?

From behind her, she could hear Constance working herself up into a fury. "Fleurette can't run an agency. I'm obviously the eldest, and the only one with any experience. And when did you decide all this?"

"It was my idea," said Bessie placidly. "That lady — Alice Martin — talked to Fleurette even though she didn't want to talk to the police. That's how it was with your girls, too, at the jail. They confided in you. After you left this morning, I told Norma that I thought there must be any number of situations of this sort that ladies find themselves in. They might not tell the police, but they would go to a private detective — if the detective was a woman."

Now there was silence in the room. Fleurette couldn't help but ponder it. What if there was another Alice Martin out there, another swindler to capture, another parcel of jewels to recover?

Constance was thinking it over, too, and exchanging glances with Officer Heath. "It isn't just swindlers," she said, speaking quietly, as if only to him. "It's missing girls, too. Runaways."

"Family disputes," said Officer Heath. "Robberies and assaults, if the girl doesn't want her name in the paper."

"Anything with the threat of a scandal attached," said Constance. "Disappearing husbands."

"Wayward children," Officer Heath said.

"They want to know what the child's been doing, and why, but they don't want them put into a reformatory."

"You're forgetting about divorce," Mr. Ward put in. "Adultery's the most lucrative. Your sister Norma's going to bleed me dry, but I could use a lady photographer from time to time."

Constance seemed to be warming to the idea. "But of course I'll be the one to run it. Fleurette can't —"

Here Norma stepped in. "Fleurette doesn't like you telling her what to do. I don't suppose I'd like it, either. She's the youngest and the prettiest, and she's clever, too. We can't do it without her."

Fleurette squinted at her sister. It had been a miscalculation for Norma to admit how much she was needed: now Fleurette held all the cards. "Then I'd be the one to decide what cases we'd take."

"Not without —" injected Constance, but Fleurette waved her away.

"And there'd be no more lectures about Mr. Ward and his divorce work."

"Not a word," said Norma, shooting a stern glance at Constance.

"And I'd be the one telling you two what to do, and when to do it, and how."

Even Norma looked aghast at that, and

Bessie said gently, "You can trust your sisters to know what needs to be done."

Fleurette considered that. She could put Norma to work on the billing and accounts, and that wouldn't require any oversight. Constance could be sent out on the more unpleasant jobs: lurking all night in a doorway in the rain, for instance, or digging through a missing girl's garbage.

"I suppose," Fleurette said. "And they'd have to trust me to know what needs to be done, too."

"Precisely," said Bessie, already playing the indispensable role of peacemaker. "But why are we discussing this here? Couldn't we talk it over at home?"

Fleurette realized, with another thud in her heart, that by *home* Bessie meant the Wilkinsons', not Mrs. Doyle's. Was she really going back with them?

"Mr. Ward's going to draw up the papers for us, without charge, of course, considering how he took advantage of you," said Norma. "But we also came to ask him about our rights as it pertains to Francis's quarter interest."

"Oh, that horrible old basket company!" said Fleurette. "Why don't you forget about that? Francis made a terrible business deal and we're left owing the money. There's nothing to do but to pay it. Don't bother Mr. Ward with this."

"But he had the right idea," Bessie said. "As there's no paperwork that sets forth the terms of Francis's agreement with Mr. Griggs, we are free to interpret it as we like. Mr. Griggs could challenge us in court, but the business is nearly worthless as it is. We can do what we like with our share of the company."

Fleurette didn't like to imagine what that meant. Was it Bessie's idea that they'd form a detective agency with a sideline in imported baskets?

"Then what, exactly, do you intend to do with your share of the company?" Fleurette asked, quite fearful of the answer.

"We're going to seize the only piece of property that could do us any good," Norma said. "The automobile."

42

The automobile! Was Norma in her right mind? Norma, who had devoted considerable energy to detesting automobiles and criticizing their use even in war-time, even as ambulances? Norma, who despised all modern contrivances and didn't even like to pick up a telephone, and would've happily done without electrical lights at the Wilkinsons', had her sisters not bodily carried the old gas lanterns out to the shed in back and hidden them there?

Fleurette could see that her role in running the agency, if she truly was to run it, would consist largely in dealing with modern appurtenances that Norma loathed. She would answer the telephone and operate the typewriter. It was entirely likely that what Norma meant by "run" the agency actually meant running the machines Norma disliked.

But if one of those was to be an auto?

How perfect for Fleurette! She'd fallen in love with those gleaming, rumbling machines the first time she'd ever seen one, and she felt entirely at ease riding in one: a modern conveyance for a modern woman. Even Officer Heath's auto — back when he was Sheriff Heath — gave her a thrill, the few times she rode in it. It felt utterly effortless, to be carried along under the power of an enormous engine, so much more spirited and stylish than the plodding and wheezing of a horse.

How right Norma was to think that they would require an automobile, and to put Fleurette in charge of it. She could see herself behind the wheel already, in a smart hat, dressed in pinstripes or polka dots, or perhaps both. She'd go to work at once assembling the wardrobe of a modern lady detective, one with an automobile and a client list that included the wealthy and soon-to-be-divorced of Park Avenue. Mr. Packard and his glass emerald were nothing compared to the class of customer she could land if she were put in charge of it.

In the spirit of dashing around in automobiles, they rode over to see Mr. Griggs in a taxicab, the four of them (Officer Heath and John Ward having both returned to their own respective duties, and having no part to play in any further proceedings), and debated Norma's idea in high spirits and animated voices. Norma had worked it all out: their monthly expenses, the costs of running a business (stationery, advertisements in the local directories, an investigator's license, a camera and film), and the amount of time it would take to sell the remaining lots, purchase the Wilkinsons' house, and establish themselves fully as a business concern.

"You'll have to stay at Schoonmaker's until we have enough clients to keep us all busy, which is another reason why you can't run the agency," Norma told Constance. "And Fleurette won't ever be entirely out of the seamstressing business. We'll need disguises, from time to time and, besides, your ladies could become our clients."

"Do you expect me to take up hems and track down estranged husbands at the same time?" Fleurette said, intending it as sarcasm, but Norma only nodded vigorously. "Once you strip those ladies down to their bloomers, they'll tell you anything."

"Then I'll need a proper fitting room, with its own entrance," Fleurette said, already imagining quite an elegant ladies' lounge.

"And you'll have it."

"And we really should keep an office

downtown. Just something small and smart, with our name on the door."

"That will depend entirely upon revenue," said Norma, ever the comptroller. "For now we'll operate from the parlor. What we must have immediately is an auto, and it has to be something that won't arouse suspicion. That's when I thought of our quarter interest."

They arrived just then, and Norma added, "Don't any of you say a word to Mr. Griggs. I know exactly how to handle him."

At the front door, they were met by Mr. Griggs himself, on his way out. Fleurette had never been to Francis's place of work before and looked around the gravel lot eagerly for the automobile they'd be taking possession of. She expected an older model, something not particularly stylish and in need of a polish, but in fact saw no autos at all. Nonetheless, following Norma's instructions, she stayed quiet and went inside with the rest of them.

Mr. Griggs seemed excessively delighted to see them and said, when they were settled in his office, "I see you've reconsidered my proposal, and brought the entire family this time. That's just the way to do it. You must all think it over and be in agreement."

"We won't be making an investment," said

426

Norma — plainly, as she never knew how to say anything except in the most straightforward manner, "beyond our quarter interest."

"Oh," said Mr. Griggs, removing his spectacles and looking through them as if he'd misread her statement due to some blemish on the glass. "When I saw you, I thought, 'Here's Francis's family, come to save us.' We're due to close, you see, by the end of the week. We simply cannot go on as we have."

"That was apparent on our last visit," said Norma. "Why bother waiting until the end of the week? Sell everything off, and we'll take a quarter of the proceeds."

Mr. Griggs looked affronted at that. "If you think I'm withholding anything of value from you, you're mistaken. Nothing here is worth a dime. The building's leased, the furnishings are old, you've seen the baskets, the delivery truck is a heap . . ."

Norma stood up as if everything was settled and said, "Fine. We'll take the truck."

Fleurette flinched a little at the word *truck*. Surely Norma wasn't referring to the old delivery truck Francis used to drive? Mr. Griggs was right: it was a broken-down old heap, with an engine that only barely sputtered along, a high-sided wooden compartment in back that could haul baskets or donkeys equally, and room up front for only a driver and one uncomfortable passenger.

It was a horrible contraption, a real beast. Even Francis hated driving it.

Surely Norma couldn't be referring to *that* truck.

Mr. Griggs had nonetheless developed a sudden attachment to it. He said, "You can't go off in our vehicle! A quarter interest doesn't entitle you to take whatever you like."

"Unless you can produce a contract to the contrary," said Norma, "we shall decide for ourselves what our quarter interest represents and take possession of it at once. You just said yourself that the business is of no value. I don't see how you can object to us taking one worthless vehicle."

There was a bit more wrangling, but Fleurette paid it no attention. She wandered outside, around back this time, and stood looking at the old contraption. She had to admit that there was some sense to it. Nobody looks twice at a shabby delivery truck. A detective needed to go about undetected. Even she knew that.

Soon Bessie and her sisters joined her, followed by the erstwhile delivery driver, Thomas Wells, whom Norma had engaged to drive the truck back to Hawthorne. But before he could step aboard, Fleurette jumped into the driver's chair.

"It's absolutely enormous," she cried. "The pedals are miles away from my feet. I'll never be able to drive it."

"That's exactly the point," said Norma. "Constance will drive it, once Thomas shows her how."

What happened to her glamorous black machine, and her chic hat to match? How could she possibly motor into Manhattan in this contraption?

"Bessie will ride alongside Thomas," said Norma, "and the three of us can make do in the back."

What was there to do, but to scramble on board and to take a seat along a wooden crate in the back of the truck, wedged between Constance and Norma? As the beastly machine rumbled to life, it occurred to Fleurette that she hadn't felt the heft and warmth of her sisters alongside her since the funeral. Even in that moldy old truck, they smelled familiar, the fragrance of her childhood, the rice powder Norma patted around her neck and the coconut shampoo Constance smoothed through her hair.

Fleurette couldn't help but settle in against them, and to give in to the ease that she only ever felt when she was alongside her sisters, as disagreeable as they might be. The knot that had been tangled inside of her all these weeks began to unravel. None of them spoke: they just bounced along, their knees and elbows rubbing familiarly against each other.

The Kopp Sisters Detective Agency. Already the name had a certainty to it, as if she'd known it all along.

HISTORICAL NOTES

Like the other books in the Kopp Sisters series, this one is a blend of fact and fiction. The Kopps — all of them, Constance, Norma, Fleurette, Bessie, Frankie Jr., Lorraine, and the departed Francis — were real people whose lives played out more or less as described. Feel free to take a look at the historical notes in the back of the previous novels for more detail about all of them.

Francis didn't die in 1919. He died in 1923, at home, of a heart attack. It was around the time of his death that Constance, Norma, and Fleurette sold the farm and moved to Hawthorne. They actually lived two doors down from Bessie, not next door. The difficulties with his employer are all fictional, but he did work for a company that imported baskets from China.

Bessie didn't have a third child, but it was true that she had a very young child. In real life, Lorraine was born in 1918. In my novel

I've made her the eldest child, born in about 1907, because I wanted her to be around for the earlier events in the series. Frankie's age is accurate. He was born in 1909.

The Kopps did form a detective agency. In newspapers it is referred to as the Kopp Sisters Detective Agency, although I haven't found a directory or business listing with that name. (If anyone's holding on to some Kopp Sisters Detective Agency stationery, you know that belongs to me and you'd better send it to me!)

The agency specialized mostly in divorce cases, and they worked on many such cases with John Ward's law firm. Mr. Ward and his real-life partner, Mr. McGinnis, have been recurring characters in my novels, although their involvement has been, up to this point, mostly fictional. Now they assume their real role in the Kopps' lives. I should emphasize that while Mr. Ward was something of a playboy in real life, I know very little about Mr. McGinnis's real life at that age and have entirely invented his story.

The type of automobile the Kopps owned, and who would drive it, was a constant source of friction within the Kopp family. According to my conversations with relatives, and what I've found in newspaper coverage and other records, they employed a number of drivers over the years and got into their share of auto-related difficulties, all of which is still to come in future novels.

But there wasn't always a hired driver. According to one family member, "Fleurette drove the car, Constance took the pictures, and Norma sat in the back and remembered everything." So brace yourself — Fleurette will get behind the wheel eventually!

Another family member told me that Fleurette sometimes acted as "the bait" in divorce cases, which refers to her playing the part of the "professional co-respondent," the woman posing in an adulterous embrace with a man wishing to get out of his marriage. While I have no direct evidence of her doing this work, I do have wonderful historical records to work from, including lurid tabloid interviews with headlines like "I Was the Unnamed Blonde in a Hundred New York Divorces."

Other real-life details: I'm sorry to say that Fleurette really did lose her singing voice due to strep throat and gave up her theatrical career in her early twenties. Laura the parrot was real, but she'd actually been with the Kopp family since Fleurette was a little girl. She was a green Amazon parrot and quite a conversationalist. I'm collecting stories about clever things that these parrots can say and do, so if you have any experience with them, please get in touch!

Constance really did work at a department store at some point during this time, but it was Best & Co. in New York City, not Schoonmaker & Co. That was a real department store located in Paterson at 225 Main Street. All details about the store, its owner, and employees are fictional.

Robert Heath did not, unfortunately, ever serve in law enforcement or elected office again. He did run for sheriff one more time in 1919 and lost. He really did work for a company that sold pipe fittings and seemed to do similar such work for the rest of his life. I do know that he remained in the Kopps' lives, because his name pops up from time to time in my records, but as far as I know, he and Constance never worked together in a professional capacity again.

I do a lot of video chats with book clubs, and many of you have asked me if Heath would be coming back after the war. This question came up so much, and so many of you wanted to see more of him, that I decided to give him a fictional part to play in the Kopps' future — one that he might have enjoyed a great deal, had things worked out differently for him. As a police officer, he'll be very useful to the Kopps in their detective work. He might also be a thorn in their side from time to time. Stay tuned.

Alice Martin is fictional, but her case is a composite of similar cases from the era. All the other divorce cases are also fictional, but in every instance I draw upon real-life divorce stories from those days.

"You Made Me Love You" was written by James V. Monaco and Joseph McCarthy in 1913 and was performed at the time by Al Jolson.

I'm aware of dozens of real-life cases the Kopp Sisters Detective Agency worked on, which is enough to see me through the 1920s. I hope you'll want to come along. Stay tuned for the next installment, and please visit my website to see photographs, newspaper clippings, and more documentation about the real-life people and places behind these novels.

ABOUT THE AUTHOR

Amy Stewart is the *New York Times* best-selling author of the acclaimed Kopp Sisters series, which began with *Girl Waits with Gun.* Her seven nonfiction books include *The Drunken Botanist* and *Wicked Plants.* She lives in Portland, Oregon.